Resistance
and other short fiction

Oct 2002

Happy Birthday, Mrs. Yamashita!
Love,
Chris Japely

Resistance

and other short fiction

Christine Japely

AVOCET PRESS INC

Avocet Press Inc
19 Paul Court
Pearl River, NY 10965
http://www.avocetpress.com
books@avocetpress.com

Copyright ©2002 by Christine Japely

AVOCET PRESS

All rights reserved. No part of this book may be reproduced or transmitted in any form or by any means, electronic or mechanical, including photocopying, recording, or by any information storage and retrieval system, without written permission from the author, except for the inclusion of brief quotations in review.

This novel is a work of fiction and each character in it is fictional. No reference to any living person is intended or should be inferred.

Library of Congress Cataloging-in-Publication Data
Japely, Christine, 1954-
Resistance, and other short fiction / Christine Japely.
p. cm.
ISBN 0-9705049-8-5 (alk. paper)
I. Title.
PS3610.A64 R47 2002
813'.6—dc21
2002014067

The author would like to thank the editors of the following publications in which some of these stories first appeared in a slightly different version:
"Bashfulness is Required in the Kingdom," — *Tanzania On Tuesday*, *New Rivers Press*
"Call Up," — *Kinesis*
"Duty, Opportunity, Lost Cat," — *The Iowa Review*
"From Among the Ranks of the Amazons," — *Kinesis*
"The Grid, Escaping It," — *Fine Print*
"Ichthyosaurs," — *Global City Review*
"Resistance," — *The Florida Review*
"Teeth, Death, My Friend Louise," — *The Sun*

Front cover painting: *Fixing the Volatile*, Egg tempera and oil on wood
Copyright © 1996 Cynthia Large
Cynthia Large is an artist from the Santa Cruz Mountains who is living and working in New York City. Visit www.cynthialarge.com to see more work.

Printed in the USA
First Edition

For my uncle, Frank Huss.

As kingfishers catch fire, dragonflies draw flame;
As tumbled over rim in roundy wells
Stones ring; like each tucked string tells, each hung bell's
Bow swung finds tongue to fling out broad its name;
Each mortal thing does one thing and the same;
Deals out that being indoors each one dwells;
Selves—goes itself; *myself* it speaks and spells,
Crying *What I do is me; for that I came.*

— Gerard Manley Hopkins

Contents

The Present
Resistance 13
From Among the Ranks of the Amazons 30
Duty, Opportunity, Lost Cat 39
Abortion Before Menopause 57
In the Enthusiasm of My Confidence 73
Dissociate 83
Teeth, Death, My Friend Louise 91
How Do They Become Bag Ladies? 109
Suburban Living at Its Finest 129

The Future
Call Up 145
The Grid, Escaping It 154
Ichthyosaurs 165
Ben Croxton 174
Rauwolf 182

Arabesque
Saqqez 193
Bashfulness Is Required in the Kingdom 205

The Past
Escape 235
Bloop Bleep: We Posted It Everywhere 241

The Present

Resistance

Rachel ran up the walk and scrabbled at the front door and then reminded herself to slow down. Yes, the dentist's buzzing had ended and the filling was in, the workday was over, the weekend could begin now. Relax, she told herself. In just a few hours drive they'd be north and deep into the crimsons and golds of Vermont, all set to amble around in the woods. The dentist, he'd told funny stories about patients who wanted temporary fangs inserted for Halloween, and Rachel had fleetingly thought that *she* should have been a dentist; she too could have shared in the joys of intricate handling of gold, porcelain, saliva and gutta percha. As things were, there was a certain sterility to the books she designed, a certain lack of wet materials. She worked mainly at a computer terminal and her hands rarely got dirty, and lately her job seemed just a lot of meetings and rushing around. Her dentist, he'd seemed so pleased with himself, so king of his little turf. Oh, I don't know exactly what the problem is, Rachel thought. A dentist! How ridiculous. But still she wondered if there was much incidence of people at forty suddenly changing career and going into dentistry, finally developing an unrealized real bent. In the dentist's chair after the rushed workday she'd remembered Peptide, the tiny pet iguana that they'd forgotten to feed that week, and so Rachel had decided to go home after all, for she'd briefly fathomed the horrors of ending a weekend away on the note of a dead little lizard's body, and Yvonne getting all sad and teary although of course Yvonne no longer bothered to look at Peptide let alone feed it. That was fine because Yvonne was only seven, and Moms keep the pets alive; Rachel knew that.

Once inside she sank onto the couch and pushed off her shoes, lovely shoes, sleek and stylish, but not comfortable enough for the drive to Vermont and they'd been pinching since early afternoon. And she suddenly recalled that in the morning rush of searching for one of Yvonne's rubber boots Rachel had forgotten her own and had also neglected to check the thermostat. Good. More reasons to have come back to the house. She slid her tongue over the new filling; don't chew on it for three or four hours, the dentist had said. Great work, Rach, she told herself. You Fed-Exed the paste-ups to Dutton, you went to the dentist, and now you can enjoy Vermont. The foliage! Food, wine, a little country inn with a maple wood fire! Short hikes that even Yvonne would enjoy! And Dave had packed his guitar. Two days of bliss and indulgence. Her shoes were off; she started to relax, and yet something was dragging on her. Was there time for a quick nap? No, of course not, and besides, she'd slept quite well the previous night, so why did she suddenly feel so depleted? She didn't have to pick up Dave and Yvonne for another hour. All she had to do was go downstairs and throw two or three crickets into the iguana's terrarium.

Rachel pushed herself up and in her stockinged feet tiptoed down the basement steps and startled Peptide with a cascade of bugs.

"How're you doing, Peptide?" she said, staring in at him in a clinical manner. He looked healthy, green, wasn't shedding at the moment. "Eat," she said. "Eat those crickets." She stared for a moment or two longer as the iguana twisted its slim body this way and that, and then she went and found her boots. So now he won't starve, Rachel told herself. She climbed back up to the kitchen and thought of having a quick cup of tea, and in thinking this over she glanced at the phone machine, yes, it was flashing. Fine, she said to herself, another loose end I can tie up and then it'll be Sunday and we'll be back, almost as if we'd never left. And suddenly she realized she was out of sorts and weak because of the anesthetic the damned dentist had needled into her gum; of course, why hadn't she realized that immediately? But she'd pushed the phone button and a voice was breaking in on her thoughts. A stranger's voice: Dave, your father, heart attack, serious, please call, saint somebody hospital in Atlanta. And then the voice was rapping out a phone number but Rachel didn't have a pen and so she quickly pressed the button that would save the message. "Shit," said Rachel aloud. She sat down and felt herself caving in a bit more. Dave's father, yes, he was in his seventies now; it was the time frame for this type of call. Had he been out on a golf course or perhaps just reading the Wall Street Journal at great leisure, pretending he was still a man of affairs? Golf, business, a bore and a nuisance, Dave's father. She didn't want to deal with this now. "Shit," said Rachel with greater intensity. The weekend blown. The anesthetic, yes, that was what had weakened her. For something was slowing her down. She had to call Dave, and she reached for the phone. But maybe first she should listen to the message again and scribble down the number and yes, call it. And then call Dave. Her hand, she watched it hover above the phone but then she slowly drew it back. She thought for a moment. Disappointment, yes, but she also clearly recognized a definite element of delight jangling around in her brain. "Good, he's dead," she said. There was utter silence in the room and after a second she glanced at the phone machine to see if possibly it had recorded her three words.

No. Of course not. It was OK. It was fine that she knew what she really felt about this. The only slight wrinkle of course was whether in fact he really was dead or was merely resting comfortably now, hooked up no doubt to an array of devices and talking to the doctor, another bluff and hearty individual (no doubt), who would be assuring him that he'd be out in a day or less. Ben. Big Ben, Dave sometimes called him. A talker, a drinker, a man who'd spent his life at country clubs and in P.R. departments of various corporations. He'd laughed at Rachel once when she'd pushed aside the business section and reached for other parts of the New York Times. And there had been a multitude of similar incidents: that time for example at a family function; she'd overheard Ben telling a cousin of Dave's, yes, she worked, she designed coffee table books. His dismissive tone had shocked her as had his neglecting to mention that coffee table books were only a part of her workload, and she found she couldn't forgive and forget.

Rachel looked at her hands which now rested in her lap. Yes, she should be calling the hospital to ascertain Ben's status. Yes, she should be calling Dave. But the silence of the room didn't push her one way or the other, and she suddenly felt slovenly in not having asked the dentist the exact name of the anesthetic he'd used and the exact contents of the filling material. She could call and ask now. Just out of curiosity, she'd say.

So, I didn't get the message, she thought. "So, I didn't get the message," she said aloud, testing it out. Her tone, the echo of it: she noted a certain truculence. But that was a quality that could be blotted out with just a tad more practice. "The message, I didn't get it," she said again, pitching her voice a bit higher and brighter. She nodded to herself. No one would ever know.

And when she finally looked at her watch she realized she'd been sitting frozen by the phone for over twenty minutes. Dithering, she'd been sitting there dithering and time had melted away. No, it wasn't precisely dithering for she was completely sure of her immediate strategy. It was more a sort of pondering, a letting the situation sink in. So why did she want him dead anyway? No, no, it was just that she didn't all of a sudden want to be making rushed flight plans to Atlanta, not right now, not when they were practically in Vermont curled in front of a fire, holding glasses of wine, watching Yvonne sit and draw. Dave, yes, he'd want to fly right down there instantly. And she and Yvonne would have to follow. But maybe it was a slight heart attack. Maybe it meant nothing. The message. There had been no clue as to the time. So he's dying, so perhaps he's dead already. Or perhaps it's nothing, nothing, perhaps he's fine right now and laughing about it and relishing all the attention and *impending* attention, for he knows Dave, among others, will rush right to his side.

And the B & B in Vermont—a place recommended by a workmate—no one knew they were going there. It all fell together so beautifully; Rachel recognized this instantly. So I didn't get the message, Rachel thought to herself once more. She was standing now and she glanced again at the message machine. The numeral one glowed back at her: just a one, a virgin one. The button, she'd touched it initially and heard the message, but that left no hint; there was nothing, no, not even the clever vision of Sherlock Holmes would later be able to uncover any clue that she'd heard what the man had said.

So I won't ruin the weekend for Dave and Yvonne, Rachel decided. For me, well, it's clear the weekend is at least partially ruined for me, she thought. But she could see now that she'd been lifted out of that initial drop into misery. It's not ruined at all, she told herself, I've prevented that. It's just changed, the tenor of it has shifted. I'll have more on my mind now, it'll be more of a challenge, Rachel told herself. But no. That's a mistake, she thought. The best strategy is to forget I heard this message. It will be a Zen exercise in putting something away from me.

Yes, I haven't heard this message, she said to herself firmly, and that's the basis I'll operate on all weekend. Rachel looked around. The time. Oh, no time for tea now. Time to collect herself. The boots. They were there on the kitchen floor where she'd dropped them. Peptide. All fed. The thermostat. She'd adjusted it. Time to lock up and leave. She checked around her once again. Was there a clue? Was there anything that could reveal the truth? No. Of course she'd come back to the house; she'd admit that quite freely if the issue came up. But no, she'd say, she hadn't bothered to glance at the message machine because she'd been in a rush. Her bones told her no one would ever know. The ease of it was just the slightest bit demoralizing. But she shook her head. She wasn't to harp on it. The Zen thing. Nothing had happened, nothing was happening now. Rachel bent over and pulled on her boots and left the house. The air was glorious. The drive would be spectacular and unhurried, and they'd stop someplace for an early dinner; they'd even let Yvonne choose a Burger King if she wanted.

"When are we going to get there?" asked Yvonne an hour into the drive.

"Are you watching the scenery? Look at the fabulous colors," said Rachel.

"Yes, yes, I see the leaves," said Yvonne. "I know what they look like. I just want to know when we're going to get there."

"Where's *there*?" asked Dave. "How do you know there's a *there* there?" Dave was an interior designer. He'd opted out of architecture after the first year of graduate school, and he was an expert on fabric and tile now. His father, Big Ben, found it slightly embarrassing. Even after Dave had turned thirty his father had kept making remarks to him about going back to school, about finishing. Dave had laughed it off. "He's a jerk," Rachel had told him. "Oh come on," he'd replied. "Look at *your* mother. She gives all her money to the Catholic Church." Rachel had laughed a little. "At the moment we're talking about your father," she'd said. "We're concentrating on criticizing *him.*"

"We'll stop for dinner in a little while," Dave told Yvonne. "You watch for a place. And then after we eat we'll drive for another hour, and then we'll be there."

"I forgot to bring toys," Yvonne said.

"Toys? You won't need toys. Not out there in the wild woods," said Dave. "It'll keep you busy just staying alive."

"I brought some toys for you," Rachel said. "Oh look, look at the light on the leaves."

"Did you get your project off to Dutton?" Dave asked.

"Yes, yes, everything went fine," said Rachel. "How about you? How were things in the office?" she asked, and it occurred again to her how neatly she had saved the day for him, saved the evening and the weekend for him and Yvonne and herself. Dave was rambling on about a client who was a pain in the neck but a constant source of work.

"You're not listening," said Dave. "As usual."

Rachel looked at him and made an effort to collect herself. "If I seem a little weird tonight it's because I went to the dentist and he used an anesthetic," she said. Yes, there was still a deadened throb on that side of her face.

"Novocain?" asked Dave. "Since when is Novocain a big deal?"

"Oh come on. He was jackhammering at my head. I'm just *saying.* I may seem a little weird tonight," said Rachel.

"OK," Dave said. "Fine."

"There. There's the dinner place," called out Yvonne, and Dave pulled in to a roadside diner and they piled out of the car.

It started to rain just as they made the last turn onto the final two miles of country roads. They found the B & B quite easily and then they hopped over puddles on their run in from the car; it turned out to be a cozy old farmhouse with the aroma of burning wood. There were a few well-kept tanks of tropical fish, and Yvonne went up to one and began gazing but then the proprietor motioned her over to a TV which he clicked on to cartoons. Rachel looked at him in annoyance and then looked again more carefully. He had the same sort of withered and well-used Irish skin that Dave's father had; both men possessed that blush beyond ripeness, that perpetual need for a hat in the sun. Rachel found herself staring at him while Dave made the introductory chitchat. It was so easy to picture Big Ben and this stranger together: same age, same aura. But the proprietress was motioning for Rachel to follow her up the stairs, and Rachel turned away in relief.

The woman bustled about the room a bit and then left Rachel alone. She glanced around quickly. Fireplace, electric tea kettle, cot and double bed, big windows. She pulled the curtain aside but the rain was driving down now and anyway it was dark. She went into the bathroom and splashed water on her face and then went back downstairs. The man was there; he seemed to have handed Dave something golden to drink. Rachel went up to join them. He smiled at her but didn't let her entry dent the flow of his words.

"I didn't know anything then, yes, I thought boys who ran off to Canada should be shot. I didn't wish it in any hot-blooded way, I just thought it seemed the obvious response to treason. And Jack and Jackie, they were something. I hated Bobby, though.

It was clear he was one son of a bitch. But Jackie. I remember fervently wishing *please* let Jackie marry Lord Harlech, *please.* I was a royalist then I guess you might say. I'm different now. I read Chomsky."

Rachel found herself looking off halfway through this little speech, she found herself moving away, picking up a knickknack and staring at it. Dave would cover for her. He would respond to this fellow in an appropriate hail-fellow-well-met manner. The man was slightly rude, not having immediately broken off to offer her a drink. He'd given Dave one. It was rude, sexist. But she didn't have the energy to break into their talk and ask loudly and pleasantly for a glass of the same. Rachel mounted the stairs. Dave would know why she was leaving. He too would be bored with the man. *Lord Harlech!* Dave would blame her a bit for not sticking around, for not rescuing him.

Back up in the room Rachel opened a bottle of a good Bordeaux they'd brought along; yes, time to self-medicate, as the mental health industry so quaintly put it. I'm a good person and I know it, Rachel told herself. I do good things, on the whole. I started that mastectomy support group, I taught worm-composting at Yvonne's grade school. The books I design are lovely and a bit of the bulwark against the general anti-bookishness of the age. (So how's Rachel, Dave's father had asked him over the phone once. How's Rachel and the coffee table book business? Dave had passed the message on to her. How's he, Rachel had asked in reply. Tell him I asked how's he and the general geriatric retirement scene, she'd said to Dave.) There's no doubt; the bulk of what I do is good. So. So I'm not perfect. So. When an opportunity arises, I grab it, Rachel thought. The perfect murderess. The perfect accessory to a death, she thought. But now the door was opening. Dave came in and plopped down on the bed.

"So he reads Chomsky now. Has he also started listening to

Bob Dylan?" Rachel asked him.

"He shut up finally," said Dave. "Seems he went to Princeton too, so he sees us as bonded. The rain's stopped. Should we go outside and slop around a little before it's too late?" he asked.

"What's Yvonne doing?" Rachel asked. She waved the wine bottle at him but he flicked his hand no.

"She's boob-tubing it. It's Nick at Night or something. We'll have to turn it off on her sooner or later. That'll be your job. It's your turn to act civil down there."

"What are you talking about? They're used to guests. We don't have to pretend they're Mom and Dad."

Dave pulled his guitar out of its case. "Yeah, you're right. Christ, is that guy a bore."

"What guy?" asked Rachel.

Dave strummed once on the guitar. "That guy downstairs," he said. "Is something wrong with your short term memory?"

Rachel paused for a moment. "He's no more boring than your father," she said finally. "I mean, they're pretty much on the same plateau of inducing boredom."

Dave gave a small snort. "So we're back to heaping crap on my old man?"

"Oh, why not," said Rachel. "He can take it. It's just that you sometimes fail to put things in perspective. Yes, that guy downstairs is just as boring as your father. It's partly generational. You always give your father the benefit of the doubt, but you're not willing to extend that benefit to any other aging windbags."

"Rach, what's your problem? Are you drunk? Let's change the subject. I know you don't like my old man. That's fine. Let's just drop it. Let's go. Let's get out of here for half an hour so Yvonne isn't a little ape at bedtime." He put his guitar back in the case and snapped it shut. "Come on, come on. We're supposed to be having a good time."

"All right, all right," said Rachel.

It was dark out but the rain had stopped and there was the rich fragrance of wet leaves. Yvonne started running down the long drive, kicking at damp piles. Dave and Rachel trailed behind. "It's cleared up," Dave said. "Look up at the stars," he shouted to Yvonne. She stopped dead in her tracks and threw back her little head to peer upward.

OK, I'm rotten when push comes to shove, thought Rachel. Dave was holding her hand. I'm a mortal sinner through omission, she said to herself. Yes, yes, I hate Dave's father. But is this really an evil act, is this destructive? I'm not Attila the Hun; I'm just pushing the envelope of human experience. I'm just feeling how it is to be on tenterhooks, being alone with this burden, this wonderful horrible load. Was it delightful or monstrous? On the whole, she decided that she liked it. And besides, Dave's father had been around long enough. It wasn't like her own father, someone whose cancer death at barely forty had clearly been mistimed. Rachel remembered those last bits of his life; she recalled her mother sitting there in the hospital room and staring up at the TV as if in a trance. And there was her father in bed and dying, clad in a strange white gown and covered by a light sheet. The room was too hot and the air was thick with some impenetrable ether which somehow her mother was able to breathe through but only (evidently) by staring fixedly at the television. And one day her father asked her for a hug and a kiss, but Rachel turned away in horror yet not without noting the sad look her father gave her mother. He seemed to fail to understand that the room lacked oxygen for children perched tentatively on bed edges or even on chairs. Rachel found herself slipping from the room at every opportunity and getting lost and scared in the hospital halls, and besides, children weren't supposed to be wandering around there alone. And finally her mother gave up on taking her and left her at the home of an aunt. The envelope of *my* human experience, Rachel said to herself. Dave's hand, she was no longer holding it, but their arms were linked and they were sauntering peacefully in the dark. This is the right time for a father to die, thought Rachel. He isn't needed now. She still found it painful to recall denying her father that last living kiss. The pain was a pearlized thing, a growth from a tiny sharp irritation. It was something impossible to smooth out.

And then their walk was over, and back in the room Rachel made tea for Dave and herself and hot chocolate for Yvonne. It occurred to her that her period was soon due. Good. Tonight would be a safe night for sex with no encumbrances or equipment. Dave got out his guitar again and went through his repertoire of sleep inducers: Scarlet Ribbons, Puff the Magic Dragon. Rachel kissed Yvonne goodnight and tucked her into the little cot, and then got into bed herself.

"Daddy, you're singing those sad songs that make me cry," said Yvonne. "Stop it."

"I agree," said Rachel. "Something less mawkish, please."

Dave drifted into a slow rendition of Jimmy Crack Corn, and kept on strumming quietly.

"She's asleep," he said after a while. He put the guitar down, pushed off his pants, and got into bed with Rachel. She reached out for him. "Oh, good, you're in the mood," he said. "Or is it just the Novocain?"

"Shhh," said Rachel. She stroked his thighs.

"She's asleep," whispered Dave.

"Shhh," said Rachel again. It was wise of me to keep the secret, she was thinking. I'm a wise monster, she told herself. It felt to her slightly like Christmas eve; the surprises were all prepared and well hidden.

"Right there. Right THERE," Dave muttered fiercely into Yvonne's ear. He gripped her tiny shoulder, locking her in position to get a view of a downy woodpecker. Rachel noted that the rubber boots were getting full use; both she and Yvonne were muddy up to the ankles. She crossed her arms and tried to spot the noisy bird herself. I am luxuriating in stolen time and space, in a peaceful bubble all of my own creation, Rachel thought. But she suddenly felt a wave of dizziness. "Doesn't that pecking hurt the tree?" Yvonne was asking, and Dave launched into some sort of explanation. What would Dave do if he found out what she had done? That was the thought that had made her dizzy. But she was trackless, scott-free. Dave was tromping ahead now and Yvonne was skipping way up in front, almost out of sight. "Stay out of the puddles," Dave shouted at her. He turned back to Rachel. "We've got to get her some decent hiking boots, we can at least put her in correct footwear," he groused.

"Oh no, they're not at all necessary," said Rachel, not able to quell a sharp note of irritation. "She'll use them twice and grow out of them and she'll never break them in. It's not as if we're in the mountains every weekend." What was it? Why was she annoyed? The endless details, the child's shoes. "What she needs," said Rachel crisply, "is a new winter jacket. That's what she needs. Feel free to take her out one evening and get her one. And get her five or six new pairs of socks while you're at it." The crispness, Rachel worked to keep it in her tone throughout this brief speech, and she felt she mostly succeeded. She made a mental note not to carp; Dave would return home to a big packet of stress and she wanted him relaxed for it. The funeral, but no, she couldn't allow herself to think about it; it would be a strategic mistake to plan anything. Nothing had happened. No message had arrived. And yet a lightening in her heart told her that her father-in-law was most assuredly dead. She shook her head to dislodge all these thoughts. Machiavelli, the Nazis, Pol Pot. The banality of evil, Rachel thought. I'm it.

Yvonne was shrieking now; she'd immersed one leg in a deep puddle. Rachel strode up alongside Dave and the two of them stared down at Yvonne's sopping pants. "OK, we head back now," said Dave.

"We can finish that bottle of red wine," Rachel said, taking his arm. "And Yvonne's got a book to read. We can all read and nap," she said. But Yvonne had started crying and was sitting crumpled on a rock.

"Oh, forget it," said Dave. "We'll be able to dry those pants and warm you up. Don't you worry."

"It's Peptide. He's dead," wailed Yvonne. "He's dead because I forgot to feed him."

"I fed him," said Rachel. "He's fine. You'll see. We'll get home and he'll be just fine."

"We have to go to the pet shop. We have to get him more crickets," said Yvonne.

"Yes, we do," said Rachel, and she felt a surge of well-being. She wanted to patronize the shopkeeper, she wanted to nurture his little enterprise. It was a new little pet shop and at first the shopkeeper had been bluff and upbeat but as the weeks passed Rachel had noticed a change. He'd become nervous, preoccupied, probably too aware that all these small transactions (Rachel spent a dollar a week there, a dollar for a dozen crickets) would never, never keep his business afloat. The dentist, the fang-making dentist, in contrast was so plump and pleased and jovial, exuding confidence and goodwill and trust in an abundant cash flow. Things were out of kilter, Rachel thought, but she couldn't exactly start spending vast sums at the pet shop, could she? "Yes, we'll have to get more crickets," she said to Yvonne. She squatted down and took the girl's tiny hands and pulled her to her feet. "And do you want another iguana? Do you want to get a little friend for Peptide?"

Yvonne's brow furrowed up. "Maybe," she said. "Let me think about it for a while."

Dave and Rachel exchanged smiles. "Good, yes, think about it," Dave said.

And then it was Sunday and they'd left Vermont behind and made excellent time on the highway, and so it was just growing dark as they pulled into their driveway. Rachel found herself first at the door; she unlocked it and pushed it open. Dave and Yvonne trudged in and dropped things immediately on the foyer floor. Rachel found herself picking them up and feeling intensely nervous; it was the dentist there holding up the hypo and Rachel trying to keep her eyes averted and willing it to be done with. Dave, he was in the kitchen. "Want a drink?" he called to her.

"Uh huh. Sure," she called back, and made her way up the stairs with bags and guitar and assorted things to put away. Yvonne might be the one to notice the message machine. No, that was absurd; the little girl barely bothered to answer the phone. And after tossing dirty clothes into a hamper, Rachel descended the steps and picked up the scotch Dave had prepared for her, and yes, she was hearing that electronic buzz for there was Dave, having just pressed the button. She sipped her drink and watched him; yes, she'd better pretend to listen, she had to perform now, in fact she had to listen carefully and respond correctly, and besides, there might be messages for her.

And of course, yes, there was that message, that voice that she'd heard, and she watched as Dave gave a just perceptible start and then bent over and started quickly tapping out numbers but then he stopped instantly for a second message was blaring out now crystal clear: Dave, call immediately, we have urgent news about your father. "Oh my god," Rachel said, and she walked over to Dave and stood next to him while he quickly dialed Atlanta, and she knew Big Ben was dead, and she felt liberated and lightened. She knew enough then not to touch Dave, not to reach out for him, but she stood close by and worked to tamp down the thrill fluttering in her chest. Her face, was it contorting? But now the important thing was to make the arrangements to fly down there immediately, to contact both workplaces and inform them of a family death. Yvonne was in the kitchen and jumping up and down in glee at being home; she wasn't old enough to sense the sudden crisis in the air, and Dave covered the mouthpiece for a second and shouted at her to be quiet. She immediately started to cry, and Rachel squatted down and hugged the child and half-carried her into the dining room. There was so much to do all of a sudden; she had to quickly comfort Yvonne and then send her off to her room and next she must console Dave and help him with details. Dave was still standing with the phone in his hand. He had made contact with Atlanta now and he was nodding and making noises of assent; the stepmother-in-law must be explicating events for him. Rachel felt cool. Yvonne had wriggled out of her arms and slipped out of the room. Rachel put her hand up to her face; it was fine, a glacier. The funeral. They'd be going to Atlanta immediately; she had to gather correct clothing for all of them. She had a secret now and it was all enclosed. She would tend it inside its tiny room, and it would rest there forever like a covert love affair. And she went up to Dave and put her arms around him. He felt warm and solid and present but there was a stiffness, a steel rod quality somewhere between her arms and his body. She felt it. But she also clearly felt alongside them the life raft of formalities that would ride them through. That ride, she could take it. And she could treasure her knowledge, her collusion. Am I then partly a bad person, Rachel asked herself.

From Among the Ranks of the Amazons

My purpose here is to wax poetic about motherhood; right away let me say that the actual delivery was delightful, I still have happy-nostalgia fits when I drive past that hospital, I get slightly choked up when I think about the lovely little childless perhaps virgin blonde nurse (I went back a week after the birth and gave her Chanel No 5) and the elderly doctor (I took him Courvoisier). The delivery itself was splendid, kind of a cross between Alice's Wonderland (but I don't mean I used drugs, I didn't need any) and an inordinately satisfying bowel movement. ("Really?" asked Joan skeptically. "I dreamt I heard you crying all night.") I-was-Superwoman-I-didn't-need-anything, but I admit it was comforting to have the nurse and my husband there whispering to each other, solicitous. (There are a race of us Superwomen now, an elite breed really; I know it doesn't happen to everyone. But it happens often enough and so I strongly feel that this information I'm presenting should be disseminated to, among others, Girl Scout organizations everywhere.) There were dozens of squalling tiny infants in the neonatal wing that day but I got to take home *Mine*! *Mine*! (Joan's experience contrasted sharply; *Hers* came slowly. Joan needed drugs but the drugs didn't work. "Yes it was pain," said Joan, "it was terrible horrible pain and I'll never do that again never." And *Hers* cried without ceasing for the first seven days. "I'm about to impose some heavy discipline," Joan told me grimly, "such as throwing her out of the window.")

The extra weight you ask? Oh it just melted away before my eyes as I ate peanut butter sandwiches and drank chocolate milk at two a.m. and then again at four; this was in addition to my regular four diurnal meals. My god, the small creature *(Mine! Mine!)* was eating me alive! I was his supermarket, his snack bar, his night kitchen, which of course brings me to the issue of

Breasts!! Formerly useless objects and even kind of a bother (I used my legs to attract men), but now grandiose would not be an altogether inappropriate word choice as one stood in the bathroom gazing at one's mammaries a few days after the delivery. They'd become positively Himalayan, pure Italian mama (and this was true for all women—for slender women, for A cups, for women who'd worn out various pairs of Adidas, for woman who ran marathons, for triathloners). They'd taken on a life of their own. One day, for example, I was undressing, and I felt one of my milk-heavy breasts for lumps. *Mine* had begun preferring the right one and thus the left one was especially full. Odd—a thread had somehow gotten attached to the left nipple, a white thread that extended from my nipple to the top edge of my dresser. I tried to brush it away. It didn't. I tried again. It wouldn't. Infernal thread! And then to my amazement I realized it was a liquid thread, it was a stream of milk that my nipple was letting loose in a perfectly horizontal and powerful spray! I called my husband's name aloud and then remembered he was at work, I dialed his work number and said get over here quick you've got to see a strange phenomenon of nature perhaps never mentioned on *Nova*. I even thought of taking a few quick photos (one's camera is always at the ready when one's firstborn is in infancy).

(Males, your bodies can't do this!! Your bodies remain stable while ours are sometimes subject to a wild assortment of flux. Maybe my hormones were just happily out of whack; maybe a tiny pill could return me to bodily boredom. No!! No sabotage! I was having too much fun! *Mine* did such a marvelous job on my breasts.)

(Joan's experience was different. She wasn't Superwoman/ Magical Breasts like I was. She had multiple breast infections early on. "I don't know how to describe it," she said, "it's kind of like tiny pieces of glass ground into my nipples." She stopped breast-feeding *Hers* after six weeks and returned to the courthouse where she worked as an assistant district attorney. "Goddamn it," she said. "None of my old skirts fit." My skirts fit ME, I crowed inwardly. But it didn't really matter that much; I worked at home as a school textbook editor specializing in social studies — I mean I could slop around in warmups all day — skinny, fat, who cared. "I'm not an earth mama like you," said Joan. "I'm a disaster at this maternal animal stuff." Still, *Hers* developed quickly, able to hold her own bottle at four months.)

Postpartum depression takes many guises. ("There's no such thing as postpartum depression," Joan told me harshly over the phone, but she's wrong of course. "Of course the mind is affected when hormones are realigning themselves in such spectacular ways," I told her. "Oh? And are Jupiter and Mars part of the picture, too?" she asked snottily.) The guise it took for me was a sick fascination with sudden infant death syndrome. People talk about AIDS babies but there's also SIDS: the unwitting baby turns off for no apparent reason. I'd forgotten all about SIDS until after the birth; the pregnancy hormones short-circuited my brain's access to SIDS-related memory banks, but it all washed over me, it returned to me one day that winter when my sister, a nurse in Nova Scotia, called me and said, "By-the-by, make sure he sleeps on a slant, make sure he sleeps with his head higher than the rest of his body, and then you can rest peacefully. We recommend this to all new parents here and we've never lost a baby to SIDS." And then a couple came over to dinner, a childless couple, and the women had the lack of tact to discuss a friend of hers who'd lost a baby to SIDS and after these two conversations I became obsessed. ("People who discuss SIDS casually with new mothers should be shot," commented Joan.) I'd read somewhere that it happens mainly to male infants in winter, and this was winter and *Mine* was male, and so I was taking no chances, I was sleeping fitfully, jumping up every now and then to check that he was still breathing. It was easy to train myself to do this, especially since *Mine* himself woke up naturally every two hours for feeding. After a while my husband figured out what I was doing, he figured it out because I'd begun setting my Casio to buzz every half hour (I wasn't going to leave it to chance whether I woke up or not) and he asked why in god's name is that goddamned thing going off every few minutes and I told him about the statistical reports I'd read and he thought about it briefly and said I was getting really crazy but then he hugged me and said come on, please don't worry so much, he's a strong little guy, he's not just going to blink out. And then he went back to sleep and I stayed awake but I deprogrammed the Casio and I tried to tap into some psychic wave that would imbue me with awareness of the probability of *Mine*'s blinking out or not and then I fell asleep.

Winter passed, *Mine* and *Hers* fattened, SIDS was pushed into the background, fears of the P part of the DTP vaccination emerged (they don't use the same stuff in Japan, they use something safer, but here it's still a little like playing Russian roulette), and Joan jokingly suggested that we arrange a marriage NOW between *Hers* and *Mine* so that they don't contract AIDS (that was that short point in time when everyone believed they were safe from AIDS if they'd slept with one and only one person for the past eight years, and everyone began frantically counting backwards and then obsessing about one night stands six years ago or even occasions when they'd used their cousin's toothbrush, they'd been visiting their aunt and they'd forgotten their toiletry bag and the cousin—notorious playboy, former military, current drug dealer—had said use mine and they'd done so, strange how something like that sticks in the memory, could the memory in itself mean something, could the memory of such a nothing event actually be the virus inside one laughing and trying to terrorize. A New Age group had posited the possibility of just such virus behavior. No, the AIDS hotline said, no, it's not a likely way of contracting the virus, but we don't recommend it as a usual practice, that's for sure) and then I began to realize something.

SIDS, DTP, AIDS, there'd always be something. There'd be swallowing whole bottles of cleaner fluid and there'd be the nice kid down the block who accidentally opens another kid's skull with a swinging shovel. There'd be guns there'd be drugs there'd be football. ("And Jewish mothers," said Joan. "Let's not forget about Jewish mothers. I come from a long line, I am a continuation of that tradition.")

One's reading. Let's face it, one falls behind. By my bed I have a stack of unread *New York Reviews* dating from November of 1986. Sometimes I make inroads on a few copies but usually not, usually hamburger must be made for toddler, and the pile increases. I dust it semi-annually, nay, I vacuum it (quickly, averting my eyes so as to lessen guilt pangs.) I will not throw them out. (Similarly, Joan possesses twelve, fourteen yards of stacked *New York Times* of recent date.) Perhaps sometime in the dim future an excess of leisure will descend upon one, like manna from heaven.

Moral qualms reared their ugly heads. I heard myself telling *Mine* brilliant boy, excellent boy, you're such a big boy. Why am I sounding like a pet owner, I asked myself. But I couldn't quite pin down the real gripe. I thought about it off and on, and one night at about two a.m. I woke up in an angry sweat, I wanted to put my fist through a hollowcore door, I'd been saying good boy or variants thereof for nigh on two years and yet it had never occurred to me to say good white or good judeo-christian or good african american but always just good boy and I realized how very hazardous this parenting business is. Things can sneak up on one so quickly. I'd always thought I'd be the last person in the world to aid and abet the status quo of universal sexism. (Joan snickered when I mentioned this to her, she said her current problem was pink, pink dresses; *Hers* would wear nothing else, and fighting with a two-year-old was futile. "And so semantics doesn't interest me at the moment thank you very much," she said to me.)

Moral qualms continued: *Mine* contracted an ear infection but he refused to take the medicine and I couldn't really force it down his throat. I finally hit upon something that worked: he'd swallow it quite gleefully if I pretended I lusted after it myself. I'd put on a fake crying act while he drank it down, eyes sparkling, laughing at my assumed misery. "You be sad," he ordered me four times a day for almost two weeks, and then it became an ongoing ritual, a part of every single request I made of him: he'd quickly counter "you be sad." My husband was not amused, he muttered dark warnings to the effect that I'd planted the seeds of sadism and they'd taken root, they'd flowered. And yet, I think to myself, his hearing is intact. (Joan told me we were no longer in the same subgroup of parenthood; *Hers* had had seventeen or so ear infections, *Mine* had only the one. "Don't talk about his good ears," Joan advised darkly. "You'll lose all your friends.")

The play group (the coffee klatch of the eighties) involved certain inevitable norms of behavior, norms such as excruciatingly detailed discussions of baby's eating habits: oh you mean you actually give him hot dogs, raisins destroy the teeth, you can get baby-sized bagels in Chelsea it's a drive but worth it, he doesn't seem to like cheese, could peanut butter interfere with her breathing, the co-op has these really nice new sugarless fruit loops. I would feel the mask of my face cracking and I'd try to reply politely, "so Bartholomew prefers apricots, well, my dear I don't really give a fut," but I didn't say fut, I used a quainter variant thereof, and Joan gave me a warning look and then I guess the play group picked another place to meet because the next time I went no one was there, I guess they'd forgotten to call me, ho ho ho who am I trying to kid. Well, they had a legitimate gripe, I suppose it's true that nine-month olds shouldn't be subjected to blue language. These parents were Harvard intellectuals, people with long histories of saying bad things about Nixon, people well-aware that blue language in toddlers, if detected, precluded entry to top preschools. But what is life, anyway? (And later even my husband began resorting to excessive decibel use when he overheard me swearing within possible earshot of the toddler.) Joan told me there really wasn't any percentage in insulting people; "I'm giving you a little advice here," she said.

I am not a completely insensitive person. Joan was at my house and *Hers* and *Mine* were cavorting out in the yard. The radio was on: we were mightily dismayed to hear that Winnie the Pooh was owned by Disney World Enterprises and that Winnie's hometown of Winnipeg was not allowed to erect a statue of said bear without jumping through sundry hoops for the California-based multiglomerate. Joan started half laughing and half crying and I said *oh come on*, A. A. Milne and Ernest Shepard are *dead*, they'll never KNOW, but Joan said, oh it's not that, it's me—I'm pregnant again, pregnant, I can't wait to cuddle a tiny new little baby. I stared at her. Get a feather, I told her, you can knock me over.

Decision making takes on new dimensions. (So when are we going to have another one, my husband inquires. He's just gotten off the phone; an old college roommate has called to tell of the arrival of a second, nay, third son. We've got to keep up with the pack, my husband says to me now in that peculiarly male gotta-compete tone. I snicker inwardly, knowing about snowballs' chances in hell.) *Mine* was at a phase when he'd only eat popsicles. He'd had four in two hours and I was in a quandary when he screamed for another. I took the popsicles out of the fridge and then I put them back in. I took the popsicles out of the fridge and then I put them back in. I took the popsicles—this was an endless loop involving sugars and chemicals and ten percent fruit juice.

I never really had a body; I was always purely ether, but then small creature demanded out and the life of my body took off on its own.

Teeth!! Brush teeth!! Another parental challenge. He screams, he screams, and I feel I'm a Nazi. How can torturers not feel guilt? But lovely teeth are paramount and so I develop the habit of grabbing him, gripping his head vise-like, and scratching tartar from his teeth with my fingernails.

Our society today does offer some comforts. There are eight-oh-oh lines, for example, open at all hours. ("Call them up and ask for a new car seat insert," says Joan. "The ones we have they've found to be highly flammable.") At all hours one can dial eight-oh-oh numbers and discuss possible shards of glass in tiny containers of creamed corn or why the dinosaurs ordered from the juice company haven't yet arrived.

Duty, Opportunity, Lost Cat

> "Please Help Me!" -
> LOST CAT -
> Lost from Vet.
> Just declawed.
> Two year old black and
> white female— petite.
> Named Sutu.
> If sighted call 985-9485

I pick the photocopy off the front porch, glance at the cat's face staring out at me, and almost crumple the sheet immediately (in the interest of conserving energy for the real business of life). But I hesitate. "Please Help Me!" begs the cat, the cat named Sutu. And so I toss the flier near the jumble by the telephone. I've got to perform some social duties, after all. I can't persist in always being such a curmudgeon. Sutu. That's a splendid name for a cat. And the nine-year-old, my daughter, will be interested; she's more community-minded than I am. She writes letters to Bill Clinton and Hillary and she waits for the form letter replies. "I need a handsome dad like Bill Clinton," she mutters darkly in my direction. I am stunned at her perspicacity, for yes, she's right: he's attractive, every excessive ounce of him, every groomed and gleaming energetic iota. I remember myself at about my daughter's age, no, a bit younger, thinking Richard Nixon was good-looking and mentioning it to my mother. I can still see the appalled look she gave me. "No, no," she said, "*he*'s the handsome one, *that* one," she snapped, making stabbing jabs at the TV image of a debating Jack Kennedy. I hung around the living room through all those debates so I could steal glances now and then at Tricky Dicky. My mom was wrong. Tricky was far more attractive. I was five or six. Tricky was a dreamboat.

Maybe three days later I am in my yard cooing at all the pink buds on my carnation plant, the dozens of opening Shasta daisies, the upward-winding-but-not-yet-blossoming sweet peas. A major heat wave is on the way and so I'm watering with care and drinking gin, and as I finish I toss the hose back behind me and I startle a creature that bounds quickly away, a small black and white cat. Oh. It's that one. That cat with the pretty name. I watch it disappear off into a side corner of the yard. My hose throw spooked it. I put down my glass, run into the house, search for and find that notice, dial the number. An old lady answers. "Ah, the cat," she says. "Oh wonderful. Wait. Let me get my mother." And the phone is handed from a, say, sixty-year-old to a perhaps eighty-year-old. "The vet's office did it," she tells me. "Someone left a door open." I listen to her voice quaking in rage. "She was in to be declawed, and some foolish person didn't latch the office door." She pauses and there is a moment of allowing the angry waves to quell a bit. My heart has flown into my throat. But this is just a tiny disaster, a mere speck. I give my address. "The vet people will come," the old lady quavers. I hang up and go to peer out the window for the cat. Tuna. I'll put out a can of tuna. And go into the kitchen but all my tuna at the moment is the highest quality chunk white and so I hesitate but as luck has it there is a dusty old can of sardines which I open and run outside with. And place back in the corner to lure the little cat. I deadhead spent blossoms, diddle around pulling weeds, but mainly I am keeping an eye out for that cat; how can it resist the sardine scent? It can, however. It doesn't show.

But a real Girl Scout rampage has taken hold of my forty-year-old bones, and so I go on a bit of a search in the brush of the far backyard and even step over into the neighbor's. Yes, I am hearing a tiny crying, a tiny cat mewing. That is what's pulling me. I stop still. Nothing is darting toward the sardines.

And then a car pulls up in front and two blue-smocked women come out with boxes and a leash. I give them a big wave and put a silencing finger to my lips. They trudge down to me. Laborers. Un-enchanted with the task in front of them. "Shh, listen," I whisper. And we all stand frozen and straining to hear. "Oh look," I say, for I catch sight of it, there in the neighbor's yard, nestled amid shrubbery and weeds. Its eyes glimmer out at us. "Sutu," orders Blue Smock One, a bottle-blond of about fifty, and she stalks forward slowly yet firmly. "Here, Sutu," she calls, her voice all threat and steel. I watch and I smell failure. Sutu stares at the approaching woman and then turns and flees through a narrow-slatted fence. She slips off into nowhere. Evaporates. Blue Smock One and Two look at me, eyebrows perked up. Do they want me to join them in the chase? I beg off with a silent shrug which means look, look at my slim skirt, my wrong shoes to fence-climb, my lack of motivation cat-wise. The Blue Smocks, leave, rattled. They drive off around the block. I go inside but keep an eye out; through an upper window I see them pick futilely through the weeds in the yard back beyond.

It is…July now? I must quit frittering away time like this. I have senior theses to finish looking over, committee work to attend to. I must maintain my assistant professorship or the nine year old will be roof-less in addition to father-less. It's not funny but I still laugh to myself when I recall how my department head's gaze veered quickly off into the middle distance when I brought up the topic of tenure.

I prioritize my to-do list. At the top: conserve energy for the real business of life, to wit: Control my increasing bitchiness. Cut down on alcohol. Read at least one thesis, just to get started. *Find a Bill Clinton-type to be the nine-year-old's father!*

That evening and the next evening and the next, the owners and family and the vet's office people come by and occupy themselves in assorted searches for the cat. They bring Sutu's identical brother as a lure. Doesn't work. The little old lady owner, very D.A.R., totters down my backyard hill; I worry about the possible crack crack cracking of her porcelain bones. She stands on the grass and maintains a sort of vigil, a keeping-in-contact with the last bit of earth the cat trod upon before running off. Why did you take me to that place and why did they tear out my claws, asks cat at a distance, keeping an eye on old lady owner, all blue-haired, all aged elegance, but something frantic, crazed about the eyes. "Sutu, Sutu," I hear her call in a deep threnody. I'd love to go and comfort the old woman but she'd be sure to smell the evening liquor on my breath. I could I suppose invite her in for a gin and tonic. No. Must conserve energy. Won't go outside. Energy better spent in talking to nine-year-old daughter for five to ten minutes. If I go outside and small talk with stranger about cat, all energy spent, and only able to lie down, drink at elbow, book on one side, paperwork on the other, will only have energy NOT to scream at nine-year-old not to bother one. Must conserve energy. Won't go outside. Issue resolved. Five minutes pass. "Mother," says nine-year-old accusingly to me prone on sofa, "you're not helping catch that poor cat."

More calls about Sutu, more visits. I can read the signs; I can see that Blue Smock One, the vet's assistant, the peroxide user, is beside herself. She's told me her tale. Needs this job. Knows her days are numbered in the single digits if she doesn't get that cat back. How did it happen? Wasn't that damned woman, the Schnauzer's owner, partly to blame for leaving the front door unlatched? The vet doesn't see it that way. Wasn't there a clear sign on said door re carefully pulling it shut? Why had everything fallen on Blue Smock's head? The vet was so angry he wouldn't even look at her, and she knew he'd been in contact with his lawyer. Did she in fact need a lawyer here too? What would she do now— waitress again? How would she explain to her grandkids? She was fifty-two and had many years of work left in her, and to her grandkids she'd warbled about the wonders of tending animals, she'd made it sound as if she herself were the vet. Instead of merely a glorified pooper-scooper. Where was that goddamned cat? Why hadn't that stupid housewife grabbed it? Yes, yes, I can see Blue Smock One thinking this about me as she tosses the trap down, stomps into my backyard, and glares at the house. Little does she know that I am a professor; my annual contract so states. I could tell her and thus piss her off even more. But then I could explain tenure and the fact that I don't have it. I'm talking about the skin of my teeth, I could say, and the inexorable nature of monthly bills and the need to have milk in the fridge for the nine-year-old. That would mollify her.

We saw the cat again this morning and once more of course were unable to snag it. The heat has arrived and yes, it's hellish. It's so hot that a sparrow, heat-befuddled, hit my leg as I was walking down the street to get some milk and a bottle of wine; I was out to stretch a bit and escape my air conditioned box. The nine-year-old was next to me. And, yes, a sparrow bumped into my leg and then bobbled off. We watched the little thing. "See, not a sparrow, not an eyelash, not the least lash lost; every hair is, hair of the head, numbered," I said out loud. The nine-year-old gave me a sour look. "Shall I recite more poetry?" I asked her.

"Shut up, Mother," she said. "I hate you and you know it," she told me.

The nine-year-old is so heartbreakingly lovely now with her short black hair slicked down all over into a seal-sleekness, a Little Rascal-Alfalfa charm. "Please, Angel," I said. "It's so hot." Most of my better self has worn off but I still do mis-remember snippets of Hopkins. And I thought oh ho, this slow bird will be a delectable dish for that lost little Sutu.

The nine-year-old, fatherless and slightly bereft, is sick about the cat in the heat, sick about the so-close-but-so-far-away aspect of the whole thing, and she's been giving me dirty looks for not befriending the old woman, for not bringing the old woman inside for tea. "Didn't you see her crying?" she asked me severely. Yes, yes, I can see the little girl is watching with those fresh and all observant eyes of hers. She puts bowls of ice water out in the far reaches of the yard. She sits hidden in the brush and waits for the cat to reappear. She knows wild cats are dangerous; she knows feral cats are to be avoided. This cat, she notices, looks innocent enough but when she thinks about it she realizes that there will be a point where the cat shifts from tame to wild, and she believes that point has been crossed or that it is being crossed now in a slow-motion/frozen-time sort of way. Yes, she's heard the cat crying, and then she's heard it stop and slither off. That is a step toward wild. She can feel it. The cat will be out there and a part of nature now. Maybe it will make friends with the squirrels and root around with them. The squirrels can teach the cat to relish nuts. How do I know this is all going on in the nine year old's head? I know because she told me. I heard her sighing in her bed one night and I asked her. "The old lady should just go home and not do any more of that dangerous crying," the nine-year-old says to me. "The old lady should just accept that the cat is a part of nature now."

"Do you want a pet kitten?" I asked the nine-year-old.

"Oh, Mother," she replied, "you've missed the point. You've missed the point by a thousand miles," she said, loosely quoting Huck Finn, something I taught her to do. She's a well-informed child. She knows that Mark Twain is Samuel Clemens. She cries when she thinks about Injun Joe trapped in that cave.

Last night upon pulling into our drive after eating at a Chinese restaurant, the nine-year-old and I caught the cat in the glare of our headlights. Nine-year-old jumped out and hot-pursuited, but, alas, Sutu is fast. Nine-year-old ran back to me. "Next time I need a big net," she said. "I need like a big blanket to throw."

And the old lady: This will pass, she is thinking as she trespasses but yet again upon my property. It isn't trespassing. I've given her permission. But she's intruding on my envelope, on my Caucasian closedness. This will pass, she's thinking. I read it in the uprightness of her back, so admirably covered in a twinset dating from the fifties and imperceptibly moth-eaten. I think about her cedar closets. She's eighty-three. This will be a closed bubble in Sutu's life, she's thinking. Sutu is such a charming and lovely cat that she is sure to endear herself to some kindly humans; she will be taken in, she will be nurtured and comforted. The old lady knows this. And she knows that the pet shop in town carries a wide array of health food for cats, and Sutu is sure to share in that bounty. The only small concern she has is that perhaps a kernel of horror will be lodged permanently in Sutu's heart and she will be disfigured, unpleasant. But this will not happen; oh dear God, do your work here, prays the old lady, please, St. Francis, take care of your tiny creature. She's not Roman Catholic but she understands that St. Francis is not a subscriber to narrow tribalism.

Heat lightning and ninety-six degrees. A young man rings my doorbell and asks if I've seen a small black and white cat. He is dripping with sweat but his tone is slightly antiseptic and quite clearly lacking any hint of desperation. He is a hireling. That damned cat, I tell him. I've seen it and I've not seen it. I see it but I can't catch it, I say. Everyone knows it's hanging around here, I tell him. It's starting to bore me, I say. He gives me a puzzled and faintly frightened look, as if I've over-stepped some boundary.

It's so hot. "*Fuck*," I say when I cut myself as I slice a lemon.

"Don't say that word, Mother," the nine-year-old tells me. "It's not civilized."

"Not civilized?" I ask. "I don't agree. I think it's very civilized. I think it's ancient and estimable."

"Oh, Mother," the nine-year-old says, her voice heavy with disgust.

I smile at her person-hood, her separateness and completeness. "It's so fucking hot," I say. The cut is nothing. I continue making lemonade.

"Oh, Mother," the nine-year-old says. "It's going to rain. Have patience."

The heat has pushed me into a fantasy realm: I suddenly realize sex with Bill Clinton would be delightful, a novelty. Has this popped into my head because the nine-year-old professes to admire him? No, no—of course it has to do with these ongoing dog-days, this ceaseless astronomical humidity punctuated with occasional downpours but with no real cessation of the steambath soupiness of the atmosphere. Bill, Bill of the delectable excess lipids, Bill, a creature sure to see the pros of sex during a heat wave such as this, a creature sure to perform admirably and happily even in this hazy hell.

I must help find Sutu, I must put down my cool beverage and aid in rescuing her from the wilds. I see now that this will iron out a wrinkle in my past, for when I was tiny I lost a new kitten; it ran into the bushes and never came out. I sat and sat and waited. I kept returning to that small opening in the low shrubs, but no: no tiny cat appeared. I waited for days. Disappeared. Vaporized by something in the brush. But I knew her tiny soul had gone to heaven so I was partially comforted. Or she'd found a rear exit and was happy with a family down the block. So I told myself, all five-years-old of me. The truth is—and my mother said nothing at the time; my mother held back this information —the truth is, the dogs got her. "The dogs got her," my mother, the JFK enthusiast, told me darkly years later. What dogs? We hadn't had any. But yes: anonymous voracious dogs lurk everywhere, always. And my heart skipped a beat at the sad news, for it was as if a loose brick had finally fallen a notch into a more comfortable resting place, and the cracking of the wall was continuing. What wall? I don't know. All I know is there was a continuing cracking, and, yes, signs of structural weakness. JFK, for example. Bring up his name to a class of college freshmen, and there are blank stares, there is snickering, there is mention of Marilyn Monroe. They know that? I'm impressed. "Ah yes, Marilyn," I say to them, "the goddess." Those blank stares, that snickering: the name Richard Nixon evokes the same response. But in his case Marilyn is nowhere. I smile at the block of anomie there in the air of every classroom. But it's not funny. It's probably just another symptom that my professor days are surely numbered.

Another young man is making the rounds of the neighborhood. But instead of ringing doorbells he is stapling fliers to telephone poles. I watch him head off and then I send the nine-year-old out to explore. She returns with eyes lit up. "A reward," she says. "One hundred dollars for safe return of Sutu." I nod. She runs into the backyard and searches anew; she comes back in and gets a ball of crimson yarn and takes it out and webs it through low bushes. After a while she comes back in and gives me a hard look, a warning. I know I am not to make any comment. I go out and read the notice: REWARD $100.00 FOR SAFE RETURN. LOST CAT. Female black and white. Two yrs old and petite. Named "Sutu." Owner heartbroken. Call etc.

Blue Smock One comes by again on Sutu-search, and chats at me. Yes, the vet's given her notice. But she's got a new job lined up, she thinks, as a cashier in the supermarket—she'll get a discount on food, she'll be with an old chum of hers. She'll have to play it cool, she'll have to be frosty if certain bastards happen to use her line at the store; the vet, for example, shops there. A vet's assistant anyway is a disgusting and filthy job. She has to bathe carefully immediately after work each day; she can't lead a normal life. Not the right job for a grandmother, she tells me. I eye her narrowly. She is perhaps ten, twelve years my senior.

And then, miracle, I see the cat again, this time right next door, heading up the driveway. But I can't catch it, I am incapable, and so I quickly pick up the phone, I dial. But even as I'm hearing the ringing I sense something is slightly wrong and I realize it's the face, this strange cat in neighbor's yard has an all-white face. I pick up the flier. Sutu's face has a black blotch from the forehead down to the nose. No, this cat isn't Sutu. But now the sixty-year-old daughter is on the line and I'm describing this particular cat. No, that's not it, she says, and she pauses and so do I and I gather we're both thinking we may have been pursuing the wrong cat from the start. But no, that first cat we saw had the markings; that was Sutu. The pause lengthens. I see my drink making a large wet blotch on the nine-year-old's soccer application. I cluck into the phone. Well, I say, I'll still keep an eye out. Yes, do, says the sixty-year-old daughter, and we hang up. I try to blot dry the soccer application; I look at it to see if it's still legible. Damned cat. Odd how attached people grow to animals. My father never trusted cats, that I recall. I wonder why. I wonder what bad experience he had with them. The nine-year-old slips down the stairs and out of the house before I have a chance to stop her. Do you in fact really want to play soccer, I meant to ask. Will it be worth the expense of the cleats and the shin guards? And all those endless dreary practices?

The old woman is rooted in my backyard again and I can read her mind so clearly, it's the blue of a desert sky: I need my cat, I need my cat, I need my cat. I can't stand that little pool of sadness, I can't stand Sutu lost and confused and blaming me for this tragic chain of events, I can't stand it, oh Sutu, come back, I need you. Oh dear God, I've been a good woman for eighty-five years, I let you take little Benjamin, dear God, give me back Sutu. Sutu can't understand. God, God, dear Jesus can't you see it makes no sense, it only creates sadness that Sutu is out there and confused and probably a kernel of hate growing in her heart, hate for the terrible vet who did to it her. I need to comfort her, I need the opportunity. I need my cat, my kitten, she's just two, she's tiny still. Please dear God. Answer my prayers. There are so few things I've asked of you and this is purely right, this is purely goodness: that small creature should be comforted, and comfort is here; comfort is with me. Do it, God, do it. Damned useless incompetent St. Francis has done nothing, and so I turn to you, the all-powerful.

So the vet's office continues to put out traps. Blue Smock One has been replaced by a super-efficient lovely-young-thing. Athletic and capable looking. I watch her heft a trap into the back yard. Her lipids, they're all flowing smoothly and powerfully. That was me, me, not so very long ago. And I can feel the nine-year-old aimed that way, sure as an arrow.

I wake up early the next morning and think about the trap and so I go out to look at it. Yes, the two side panels are down, there's something caught. But I'm afraid to touch the thing. I find a stick in the yard and push the trap slightly to the side. I bend down and peer in. It's a furry young possum. Possum? What do *I* know of fauna? But possum, yes, the identification comes to me with great certainty. Poor thing. Its mouth is open and so are its eyes but it's immobilized in fear and panting quickly. What sharp perfect tiny teeth it has. I think briefly about letting it free but realize I can't, it would be foolhardy, the little thing would probably instantly sink those fangs into my ankle. That half-assed vet's office. They need a professional trapper. I go back into the house and start the coffee. The nine-year-old is up and about, I hear her moving around. She clatters down the stairs.

"Sweetie-pie," I say, "how about skipping soccer this year. Think of all the lovely fall weekends it eats up! How about going on a movie binge instead. We can do old B movies in Manhattan every Saturday afternoon and then have Indian food."

"Oh, Mother," the nine-year-old says, scowling. I stare at her and marvel at her beauty. I reach out to stroke her lovely head but she bats my hand away.

"Should I tell you why your father left us?" I ask her.

"No, no, no," she says. "You've already told me. I can't keep hearing that stupid story."

I nod and bite my tongue. "Oh," I say, remembering, "go see the possum in the trap." She flies out into the yard. I don't bother to call the vet's office; it's their job to monitor the damn thing.

It's so hot it's like we're walking around balancing atop metal grates over white-hot coals, we're on the grill of a huge barbecue and the fire of the barbecue is hell. This image comes to me in a dream, a sleeping dream. My heat-induced daydreams are far pleasanter and sometimes involve Bill Clinton. Yes, if stuck on an elevator with him, I'd have sex, yes, if I bumped into him on the beach in Tahiti, I'd have sex. We'd both be scantily clad; it'd be easy. Our lipids; they're well enough matched right now, age-wise. I'd go ahead and conceive a love-child but only of course as long as he's in office. It would be a novelty, a subversion of certain dominant paradigms. But the heat continues. There was the little confused sparrow that day, and today when I went to the campus to pick up mail I noticed a tiny mouse crouching on the sidewalk...not moving, just crouched and bent over, its dime-sized head hidden in its minute paws, crying for lack of water. I wanted to push at it gently with my toe so it would move over into the cool grass but I didn't in case it might turn suddenly and take a big bite out of my ankle.

Door bell ring. Annoying. I go answer. It's a man about fifty, handsome and outdoorsy looking. I catch him staring with bemusement at the picture of the Rajah prince that adorns my mailbox. "Yes, yes, it's a Rajah prince," I say. Because, fuck, I wasn't going to let that damn cliched eagle greet everyone who comes to my door. But here this person was, scowling at the Indian as if it were the anti-Christ. He transfers his wary look to me, the wariness drops, and he gives me the old once-over. Yes, I'm attractive, I know, I know.

"Hello," he says, "I'm here for Sutu, I'm a trapper," and he hands me a card. I look at it. There's a cartoon of a grinning forest ranger leading off a raccoon, a squirrel, and a skunk.

"Hmm," I say. "I was just telling my daughter, just yesterday, that a real hunter-trapper is the only one who'll get that cat, a true professional." He smiles and asks permission to set a bunch of traps in my backyard. I see his assistant already removing them from the back of a truck, four, five of them.

"Go ahead," I say, "go right ahead. Oh, we've seen her, yes, she looks good, healthy. We saw her, what was it, just Saturday night. She looks like she's doing fine." I notice a tiny shadow cross his face and I guess he might be more pleased if Sutu was slightly wounded at this point, slightly slowed down and ready to come in out of the metaphorical cold.

"Well," he says, "she won't stay alive very long, a big raccoon will get her. She's an indoor cat." I note that this fellow always makes determined eye contact with me. It must be a principle of hunting-trapping.

The assistant walks by with some of the cages. "Those look

just like what the vet used," I say.

"Well, those people don't know what they're doing," the hunter says. "They don't know anything about catching an animal and they've probably made things a lot worse. This family," he says, "this family is just sick about the loss of that cat."

I can hear in his tone the sudden shift into declamation, the affected bathos. And so of course I know who is paying the bill for this hunter-trapper who I'm sure is an expert on moose migration, who looks fat and glossy and is probably riding high on the current chic of fly fishing and probably has a wallet-full of catch and release instructor cards, too. I'm just fantasizing, of course. And he's not fat. He's compelling, actually. Older than Bill Clinton, but then this guy's lipids are more under control. There's a tautness here that I could tolerate. I catch hold of myself so that this hunter/trapper won't sniff out the chemicals I must now be emitting.

"Go ahead," I say. "Just come and go. It's fine with me. I hope you catch her."

"We'll be by three times a day to check the traps," he tells me. He smiles goodbye and walks toward his truck but turns at the last moment to call out, "you've got my card."

I half laugh. Yes, we've communicated.

Uh-oh. The old woman, her osteos depleted no doubt but still she's so very upright: look at her standing there with her hands on her hips, her feet growing roots into my soil as she sinks into some sort of Zen state in desiring her damned cat to return to her. Well! She has a purpose in life.

Why do I feel so good? It's still so diabolically hot. Maybe it feels so good because last night I had the most incredibly vivid dream of being an actress, elegant and accomplished. And I was cast opposite Jack Nicholson, and we engaged in something called "lap sex" in one particular scene. We were fully clad but he pulled me onto his lap and started discussing some murder plot we were involved in, and as he talked to me he kept pumping/bumping up and down and into me, and at first I thought he was just being friendly—this film was very Tarantino-esque and improvised—but then I realized his humping meant business and I was getting carried away and so was he, and finally he orgasmed on camera but inside his pants and I jumped off him and he got a kleenex and sopped up what was inside his pants, all on camera. The film was rated "R" and reviewers mentioned no nudity but, yes, lap sex.

Anyway, it was a good dream, and I awoke contented and happy. And then I remembered my hunter/trapper. Yes. Jack Nicholson can play him in the film version. That would be quite satisfying.

I have the hunter/trapper's phone number. I turn his funny little card over in my hand. I can call him whenever I like, at any hour. Rush over, rush over, I can say, the trap is full. And then when he gets here and finds nothing and looks at me sideways I can laugh at him and say, oh, I made a mistake.

That hunter-trapper. He left those traps on Thursday latish, it was Thursday afternoon. I've seen him running to and fro, to and fro. And here it is Saturday morning and sure as hell I'm staring into one of the traps and there is Sutu. Yes, it's she, the black blotch is dripping down between her eyes. I walk slowly into the house. Ooh, that hunter trapper. Does good work. Quick and to the point. I've left his card by the phone, and I start to dial his number. No. I'll call the owner. I have no real interest in telling the hunter-trapper he's nailed his prey. Let him learn about it second-hand. I'll call the old ladies.

"We're coming to get her," they say. "We're coming right now."

"Fine," I say. We stay on the line for a moment. "Take the trap in the car with you," I tell that sixty-ish woman. "Don't try to let her out in the backyard," I say. "Just to be on the safe side."

"Oh, yes," she says, "you're right."

I leave the house and lock it up before they come. I have no real interest in witnessing the reunion. Uh-oh. The nine-year-old. Off at the library. Will her heart be broken if she misses this? Should I rush over and collect her? I don't. Instead, I drop off the soccer application, just slightly late. I sigh deeply at the prospect of all those friendly parents on the sidelines, roaring out their children's names. And me among them, but mainly silent. Still, there is no point in cursing round inflatables.

I keep thinking about Bill Clinton and his delectable lipids. To think that during my lifetime there'd be so very sexually attractive a president and in my age category decade-wise. The beauty part is that I can oh so efficiently transfer this lust to the hunter trapper, a Perot-supporter, no doubt, maybe even a militia sympathizer. Certainly someone with a positive attitude toward the N.R.A., and quite possibly a soul who considers Newt Gingrich an eminent intellectual. Should I really fantasize sex with such a one? The dirty look he gave the Indian Rajah taped to my mailbox…it's not an Indian deity, it's not Blue Krishna. It's more an Indian soldier type, someone somewhat akin to this very hunter-trapper. I'm not fantasizing in any full-blown way, however; I'm not thinking about thrashing body parts or well-toned ripples agleam with sweat. I'm not thinking of basking in the afterglow.

No. I'm more just admiring upper body heft inside that red polo shirt of his, and his ability to pull that big trap out of the truck with one hand; I'm appreciating the lovely golden hair of his forearms. A hunter-trapper! How delightful to possess such a concrete identity, such a real need for a multi-pocketed khaki vest.

The fact is, the hunter-trapper called me and asked me to keep him in mind if I needed his services in the future. "Still have my card?" he queried.

"Yes, " I said slowly and carefully. "I think so," I was aware of the importance of keeping things at arm's length. "How did you get my number?" I asked him.

"Sutu's owner," he said briskly. "Part of the package." And then he asked me out to dinner, which stunned and pleased me, but I immediately begged off, of course.

"Rain check, then," he said, with his sportsman's upbeat certainty. "I'll call again."

So there's that. Dinner. It might be an amusing novelty.

Or else of course I can always maintain my monastic lifestyle. That's another pleasurable alternative here. Monasticism goes better with my bereft untenured professor persona. (My department chair told me I'm solid for one more year, but beyond that ...he shrugged his shoulders in beauteous world weariness.)

Sutu is at home again, caged snugly inside the old lady's house. Her wandering days are over. The nine-year-old. I'll ask her: should we go out to get you new soccer cleats? Should we go to the Humane Society and pick out a stray? Should we sit around the house and read, and feel like a pair of old shoes? What shall we do? You pick.

Abortion Before Menopause
(a cautionary tale)

The reality is, I enjoyed the abortion. Oh, I don't mean the two minute *procedure,* the actual little tugging feeling in my lower innards perpetrated by that robotic but reassuringly efficient technician in white. (Though even that, dear reader, was somewhat...memorable. The tug, the little tug, the repeated tiny tug, tugs which took all of twenty seconds. "Finished," chirped that robot then, and it sounded like clinking gold to me. Yes, I appreciated that, that and the crisp antiseptic smells.) But let me be clear here: what I enjoyed was the whole God damned eight-week experience, soup to nuts. *I celebrate myself, and sing myself,* as Walt Whitman said, *and what I assume you shall assume.* Let's face it: college was useful. I learned a little about Whitman, I read Dostoyevsky. I fell in love with that crazed father in *The Brothers Karamazov*—you know—the murder victim, the person who actually *deserved* death.

But soup to nuts: The soup here of course was the original sex act, the kick-off of the entire chain of events. The sex act, oh, the original sex act. It was in the afternoon. I used no protection for once, because what the hell, I was white-male-twenty-one, which is to say I was long-married, over forty, and financially comfortable enough for...oh, fuck, *eye tucks* and wasting time in Manhattan day spas if I wanted them, and definitely able to feed another gaping little mouth. I'd put in years at the office, and I'd also gotten in plenty of hours at soccer games and chauffeuring hollering middle-schoolers. That sex–it was hardy, wholesome–like honey sweetened bran muffins in the a.m. That sex–it was an isolated incident of afternoon opportunity my balding mate and I had snatched while the children were off at a *Star Wars* revival. And I was too lazy to search for the condoms. And my mate preferred Trojan-free sex. And I halfway thought my period was due in a day or two. And I relished the tiny illicit *frisson* of unprotected sex. And, and, and. I was just plain bored and so tempting the fates.

"That was...absolutely phenomenal," commented my husband as we lay in post-coital ennui. "That was better than...the sound of one hand clapping."

"Oh shut up," I said, already distracted by the need to get up and continue on with other mundane details of life.

When I consulted the calendar just hours later, I froze slightly when I realized, shit, my period *wasn't* due in a couple days–no, it was due in *ten*. I'd had embryo-creational sex at a, let's face it, fertile time. Christ, I thought, and I let the full impact wash over me. Should I phone my M.D. for a morning-after pill? I calmed myself and waited until the next day. When I called my, what is it they say so briskly, *health provider*, the girl at the desk said you have to wait for a missed period. What about RU 486, I said. RU what, she asked. You've got to be kidding, I said. It's not here yet, she said, the doctor won't prescribe it. OK, fine, I said.

And so I called Planned Parenthood. They had state-of-the-art information recordings, and the female speaker beautifully pronounced the word *mifepristone. Mifepristone, mifepristone*, I repeated to myself, and a live information source finally picked up. And they gave the same info, mainly. No easy-quick-legal *mifepristone* yet, they said, and besides, maybe the tiny very early surgery was better, safer, easier than hormonally nuking that tiny now attached egg-sperm stew, and besides, maybe you're not even pregnant. When your period's late, come in for a test. OK, I said. I hung up. It was actually all very reassuring.

And then one morning, reader, I vomited. It was exactly a week before my period was due, and I'd back-burnered all my minor anxiety. But early that day after two bowls of Kix and two cups of tea, I started feeling a little off. The second cuppa had tasted terrible, poisoned or something. I'd looked at it and stirred it again. Odd. But I'd gone ahead and finished it anyway.

Not much later, there I was at my job, me in my butter-leather pumps, me elegant in pencil-thin skirt, my stomach washboard-flat. Desiccated, you might even say, since I no longer had much youth dew coursing through my veins. Desiccated? Fuck no, I was burgeoning with incipient life. I was as alive and effervescently obnoxious as Fyodor Karamazov, that…paternal blemish, that brandy-swilling clown of dementia.

With a group of my colleagues I was hashing out the layout for a book on tobacco plantations. Tobacco plantations! This particular team included some of my more soulful and less ironic colleagues, and so everyone felt a little twisted and politically incorrect. And yes, we were all enjoying that particular hairshirt. An elderly male graphics designer cleared his throat and said, well, that morning he'd happened to open up Buddha's Tiny Book of Tips (I couldn't recall the damned exact title), and he proceeded to quote one of those zany little sayings meant to feed and challenge our souls. Everyone nodded and made oh-I'm-moved sounds and gestures. Weird, I thought, remembering my husband's Zen-ish joke. A young female production editor started to glow and gently vibrate. Oh, she said, just that morning, she too had opened Buddha's Bits of Advice. And teary-eyed, she shared with us her particular bauble. All of us were doing our damnedest to divert attention from the fact that this particular coffee table book would grace Jesse Helms and Arnold Swarzenegger-type coffee tables. We were all bookish sorts with socialist leanings, some of us even *Nation* subscribers.

And then amid the chatter about Buddha I felt bubble up that poison that had been in the tea, and so I excused myself and hurried to the nearest ladies room where I leant over the sink and stared at my ashen face. And I was suddenly beset with a wave of nausea, and then another, and I was so weak and woozy, I couldn't even lean over the toilet; all I could do was stay collapsed over that sink. I dryly heaved a few times but then I let loose with a lot of liquid. It was easy to wash it down the drain a moment or two later, after I blew my nose and rinsed out my mouth. And then it dawned on my feeble mind, dear reader. Morning sickness. Morning sickness. But I was far too old. It was aging I was really approaching and getting ready to fear. It was hen's feet around my eyes, it was eternity in hell or nowhere at all—that was the real dilemma looming ferociously ahead. Wasn't it?

That evening at home I rooted around my library for early pregnancy info. Nope. Not a whole lot. I could, however, re-read *The Brothers Karamazov*, I told myself, and I leafed through my well-thumbed college copy. That nutty Russian family, their Slavic hysteria. I thought of Dmitri leaping out in the dark at sweet young brother Alyosha. Wild Dmitri, the creature of no impulse control. Ralph Fiennes could play him. And Ralph Fiennes could play the insane father! And Ralph Fiennes could play Alyosha! And of course Ralph Fiennes could play the cold and calculated Ivan. Yes, there was something inordinately Dostoyevskian about Ralph Fiennes. He could even play Grushenka, the voluptuous; she possessed a Fiennian sort of melodrama. But on second thought, no, no—Fiennes doesn't deserve to play Alyosha. Dear Alyosha, reeling from crisis to crisis, but stouthearted. No. Alyosha is too good for Fiennes, who has too much of an asshole edge about him. He can be Ivan, Dmitri, Fyodor....

I felt just fine again, and I laughed to myself a little. Old? No, I was young and fertile. And then I remembered *Buddha's Little Book*—I'd get it as a holiday gift for my husband. I hadn't had a whisper of morning sickness during my other pregnancies. And before I knew it I was in a kind of euphoria of knowing I was *with child*, of knowing I'd have to spring into action; there was a clear excitement at the prospect of (for me) the new and uncharted territory of a perhaps heavy experience. An abortion! I'd never had one. Suffice it to say, I wasn't planning to delay and thus remain pregnant. No, I wouldn't shilly-shally my way into maternity.

I was forty-three, after all. I was used to a little personal luxury of time, of physical freedom from grasping tiny hands, from tiny feet waving feyly in the air during the diaper-changing process. That was all charming, yes. But I wasn't in the mood. Not this decade.

And so, the nausea: although this was strong evidence I was pregnant, I didn't yet have *concrete proof*. I stared carefully at the mirror image of my breasts, bra on, bra removed. Did they look suddenly hormone-enhanced? I couldn't tell. I thought not, not more than the monthly fluctuations. An abortion, I told myself. A worry-free wee procedure. A new experience that I'd somehow lucked into by the skin of my forty-three year old teeth! I'd treat myself to a state-of-the-art Rolls-Royce of abortions....

And then there was the issue of the husband, the other participant in that afternoon act, that meat and potatoes sort of coupling. Could I tell him? Tell him I was, methinks, a bit pregnant?

The idea of doing so flitted through my thought processes once or twice, but I somehow knew, no, I couldn't. He would be horrified, outraged, broken-hearted at the mention of abortion. He'd try to beg and bribe me into having the baby. No. I couldn't tell him. It would only result in an unseemly fight, and perhaps an ocean of atrociousness that would lead straight to divorce. No. No stormy seas for me. I'd keep mum. I'd let a woman friend know and act as a support person.

Which friend?

Actually, I had friends in Montreal. More enlightened Canada! I could whip up there in an afternoon, swallow those doses of mifepristone or variant thereof, and jet back home a day or two later. I'd tell my mate I needed to research museums or bilingualism or the national health plan. For coffee table books. The national health plan as a coffee table book? he'd ask me. I'd roll my eyes. It's not *my* idea, I could say.

I contemplated my little Montreal scenario while driving Henry, my fourteen-year-old, to a sporting goods store for a new hockey stick. The store was at one end of a shopping strip, and everything had that tatty glitter of approaching Christmas. "You're sure you need a new stick?" I asked. "I thought you were dumping hockey."

"No, no," he said. "I think you *wished* I was dumping hockey. Don't worry. After this year, I'm through," he said. "Come in with me," he said, as I pulled into a parking place.

"Nope. I'm too tired. You've got seven minutes," I said.

"No, Mom, really. Come in and pick a gift for me. I got Mr. Miller's name in the Secret Santa thing. Come and pick something out for him."

"Hey, you're old enough to figure it out yourself. What's Mr. Miller like?"

"Aw, he's just you know, he's weird."

"Well, does he like sports?"

The son stared at me a moment. "Nah, maybe not. He's like into New Age-y things, candles and bells."

"Just go," I said. "Focus on the stick. Just get it and hurry up."

Henry shambled off into the store and I picked irritatedly at some dry skin on my lip. I found myself gazing at the bookstore next door and I suddenly remembered the Buddha book.

Son re-appeared and hopped into his seat, carrying nothing. "Where's the stick?"

"Ah, I decided, screw it. I'm quitting hockey as of now. I got this," he said, pulling a hacky sack from his jacket pocket. It wasn't in any sort of store bag.

I controlled myself for a brief tic. "You didn't just *take* it, did you, Henry?"

Noise of huge disgust. "Christ, Mom. Are you calling me a thief?"

"It's just that...where's the bag?"

"Mom. Have you never heard of environmentalism? She was gonna put it in a huge bag for me, yes. I told her hold the bag. Mother, dear, I am not a shoplifter."

"Oh, all right, Henry. It's for Mr. Miller, right?"

Son gave me a slightly bewildered look. "No. It's for me. What? Oh, yeah. I'll run back in and get one for him," and he pushed open his door.

"Wait a second," I said. Should I probe gently re the instant decision to quit hockey or should I let well enough alone? And should I let him run off for a second hacky sack or ....

"No, how about a great little New Age-y book, perfect for Mr. Miller, *Buddha's Little Book*, *The Tiny Book of Buddha*—he'll love it. You can run into there," I said, pointing at the bookstore.

"*Buddha's Little Book*...is it more than four dollars?" Henry asked.

"Four dollars? Well, of course, I'm sure it's about ten," I said.

"But the hacky sack is only four bucks. I'd rather save the money."

"Well, how about I pay anything over the four," I said, digging into my handbag for a twenty. "Get two of them. I want one for a gift, too. *Buddha's Little Book of Advice.*"

Henry ran off and in a few second came back.

"*What's* the name of the book?" he asked.

"It's a smallish paperback and it's *Buddha's Hints* or the *Pocket Carry-Around Buddha*, or something. It's popular, they should know it." And he ran back and then a few minutes later came out of the bookshop shaking his head no and gesturing toward the sporting goods store. God bless the lad, he rushed out again two minutes later, and plunked himself back into the passenger seat. But then he hurled something at me, and it hit my gut hard.

"Shit, Henry, why are you throwing things?" I groped around to retrieve the object.

"Take it easy, Mom. It's a hacky sack. It's for Mr. Miller. Will you wrap it for me?"

"No," I snapped. I was thinking how he'd bonked his tiny little sibling. I was thinking how instantly protective I was. "You hurt me. You can't just fling things at people like that. I'm an old lady. And how do you know I'm not pregnant?"

"Oh, Mom, don't be such a wuss," said Henry. "Look on the bright side. I quit hockey and I'm taking up hacky. I'm gonna be a slacker," he told me. "Know what a slacker is?" he asked.

"Yes, dearest," I said. "I know what a slacker is." A slacker, I thought, is perhaps a person like me who throws away a perfectly good little embryo though I've got the money and I suppose the health, but as for the stamina.... I glanced over at Henry. He was so lusciously young and just on the near cusp of acne.

Walt Whitman would gaze on him with dewy-eyed enthusiasm; *field-sprouts* he'd be reminded of, yes and *winter-grain sprouts and those of the light-yellow corn, and the esculent roots of the garden....*

"Sorry, Mom," he said. He kicked his hacky sack from foot to foot the whole drive home. That Buddha book, I thought. I'll get a copy for *me*.

Thirsty before sleep. Craving orange juice, needing it, inhaling a large glassful and then immediately realizing it was that voracious fish inside me, that fish trying to embed itself ever deeper in my very bowels. Well, womb. OK, I'm pregnant. I'm nurturing another life. But I'm too old, too old for this crap.

And then one day when I was *sure*, I went to pick up my younger son, the ten-year-old, from school, and there was another woman driving up to collect a child. I knew of this woman. I'd been told the dollar amount she'd spent on facial surgery and chemical peels. She was Westchester-affluent in a spankingly late model Jeep, and I noticed her impeccably groomed blonde hair—it wasn't exactly *marcelled*, but it was processed in a 90's version of what *would* have been a marcel back in the 20's. And then I noted her bumper sticker—two, in fact, both saying *I love babies, born and pre-born!!* I chuckled to myself, all smug about being the *lectured to* and *not listening to the lecture*. I felt great.

And I guess I was also partly delighted that I'd proven still fruitful and yet could opt *not* to multiply.

But then one day while off at the library researching plantations, I happened to have fifteen extra minutes on my hands, and so I took it upon myself to do a little fertility research. I quickly came upon astounding statistics re the drop in fertility once you pass forty-three. Good lord. A few years back I was a friable field, and now I was on the edge of a lunar-like sterility. Blast. I began rethinking my options.

My options: Having a baby. Astounding my pubescent children. Possibly delighting my husband. Pissing off myself. That was one set of options. The other option: A tiny bit of surgery. And life going on as it had before.

The whole escapade was getting on my nerves, finally. And I was in a foul mood, foul, (pre-menstrually foul? hormonally foul? It was still too early for the damned pregnancy test!) and I was wretched to the ten-year-old, absolutely wretched, and I wanted to explain to him that my mood was subject to hormonal fluctuations, but I made a mental note to consider whether or not it was truly appropriate to pass along such information to a ten-year-old, to make a plea hormonally based—was it more ethically adult to just bite the bullet and shut up about it? And hadn't the 80's and 90's had a lot to say about this biting the bullet business? The wavy-gravy line of the "appropriate," the very term *appropriate* and its abduction by the moonies of the therapeutically correct, by which I mean the proponents of therapists and therapy, many of them self-proclaimed therapists themselves! (In many states they don't need a license!) (And some of them in fact hold master's degrees! In social work!) I loved scoffing at them, but then again, there was the whole other pool of psychiatrists, actual holders of M.D.'s: hadn't I read recently that they'd been so economically threatened by the non-medical therapists that they'd actually devised a plot to heavily re-introduce prescription medicine to the mental health-seeking public, so as to recapture that market portion lost to the non-licensed talk and touch therapists? *Mental health providers*—was that not their latest little user-friendly label? But let me not digress. The fact of the matter was that I screamed at the ten-year-old, and he only four percent deserved it. No, I didn't end up mentioning hormones to him.

"Sometimes people act like that, like assholes, for no apparent reason," I said.

He looked at me with his great and fresh young disgust, and I marveled at his still-budding curmudgeonliness. "Yeah, I know, Mom," he said. "I live with *you*, don't I?"

At this point, dear reader, it was indubitable that I was pregnant. And one night fear set in, but it was mostly due to a wee-hours spell of insomnia and the clock saying 3:37 a.m. Fuck. The valerian capsules hadn't worked, the hot mug of cocoa had been a spectacular failure. Pregnant. *Fuck*.

I was forty-three, I repeat. I had to go market-research my Mercedes Benz of procedures. And so the next day I forced myself into a Barnes and Noble to find out where in New York City a high-end abortion was available. There had to be a listing somewhere. But the NYC guidebooks were all about food, apartment hunting, hair cuts, workout joints. I picked up a few newcomer-to-NYC books and looked for abortion in the indices, but there was nothing. *Hell*. Wasn't there once a feminist Yellow Pages or some such thing? Boston-Cambridge had had one at one point, definitely throughout the seventies, if my memory served. What had happened in the interim? (I knew, I knew—Reagan had happened, corporate interest in finding slave labor markets had happened, health care as a commodity, the general devolution of public services, etc., etc.) I actually felt calm about the whole thing. I had no train to catch that day, no kids to pickup from basketball or chess-club; my husband had agreed to tend to all that. I trekked over to an info stand, and on the way there realized I also needed those copies of Buddha's Little Information Book, which I'd been in hunt of for weeks now. It would serve as a smokescreen.

"Yes, that Buddha book," the fetching young clerk said.

"Popular little bugger." And she tapped keys and stared into her monitor. "Yes. There are copies in Eastern Philosophy." She pointed a finger behind her.

"OK, and how about the *Women's Yellow Pages to New York*," I rapped out.

She tapped it in. "Hmm. Don't see it." And she looked up at me. "Haven't really noticed anything by that name."

"All right," I said, lowering my voice to down-and-dirty and moving slightly closer to her. "What I need is a woman's health-shopping book, a guide to abortions in New York City, quality reproductive clinics."

The clerk blinked at me; a sudden scrim of wariness blanketed her, and I realized she might be guessing I was some sort of bomb-carrying anti-abortionist, perhaps all wired up with a live grenade like the Professor in Conrad's *Secret Agent*. I thought about the energy it'd take to reassure her I was actually a respectable progressive.

"It's OK," I said to her. "Forget it." And I gave her a goofy little wave and walked off. I couldn't control myself from glancing back at her, but God be praised, she was busy with another customer, someone whose glorious tattoos and multiple face piercings had already driven me from her memory.

So I went to find the Buddha book. There was plenty to scan under Eastern philosophy, this being the Village and NYU all around us: Basho, Confucius, Lao Tzu, Rumi. There were plenty of *Jesus' Little Instruction Books* sticking out their tiny faces, right next door in Christianity. But the Buddha book — no, no, and no. As I looked and looked it dawned on me that here was Buddhism at its finest: me in book store, current shrine of the spiritual—me with neck cramped at a horrid angle, searching for a piece of inspirational crap a tic above a Hallmark card. And as this dawned on me, something else did, too: *fuck* — this perfection in searching would end, i.e. the perfection would end when

I found the damned book. I fleetingly realized I should stop searching immediately and thus conserve my Zen activity, but my general cussedness made me search on. And yes, of course, I found it. And so my Buddha-searching bubble was broken. I flipped through a few pages, reading the ancient sayings quickly. *Harm no other beings; they are your brothers and sister. Things to do today: exhale, inhale, exhale. Ahhhh.* I'd observe the correct method later: i.e., reading one and one only in early morning light, facing east, and then sitting down to eat a single clementine while trying not to sob quietly with joy. Or rather, *observe* that I was sobbing quietly with joy and then just letting it go.... Oh yes, I could Zen-fetish with the best of them.

So, reader, I bought the damned little book. The abortion. I'd just have it wherever in Westchester my middle-market HMO might send me. I'd go ahead and risk being fertilizer-bombed along with the innocent twenty-something receptionists; I'd chance that encounter with troubled malcontents bearing arms for a misbegotten cause.

None of this Buddha stuff is to imply, dear reader, that I would have a change of heart in a pro-maternal bent. Nope. It's possible to be concomitantly Eastern-spiritual and embryocidal. As old Walt Whitman put it: *Do I contradict myself? Very well then I contradict myself. (I am large, I contain multitudes.)*

Yes, I was pregnant, I was sure. And my mood was one of strange euphoria; I could hear it in the unusual animation of my voice as I spoke to my husband and sons. I felt, I felt, I felt...as if the Christmas presents were piled all around, ready to be opened in the next few hours. Husband, children—all suspected nothing.

Speaking to my HMO about where and when re the abortion. How exciting all this was! I jotted a few cryptic notes down on the phone pad. They could mean nothing to anyone but me, but later I removed the note and shredded it. I was so devious! The CIA: in a parallel life, that's where I belonged. If only there were two of me! Ralph Fiennes could play me in the film version, and play me beautifully. He could have some gray streaks, he could have a slightly creaky knee.

One bright morning, I opened the *Times*, and lo, I found it heartening to come upon a gossip item referring to the Japanese empress and her abortion of 1962. The Japanese empress. The Japanese empress and her abortion. Her abortion, a royal one. If an abortion was good enough for the Japanese empress, well then by God, an abortion was good enough for me. And if the Japanese empress was good enough for an abortion—oh, yes, this worked every whichiway. I clipped the little bit and stuck it on my pinboard. (A coffee table book. A coffee table book on reproductive anecdotes of far eastern royalty. Lavish illustrations. Rice paper.)

As it turned out, dear reader, as it turned out... I started menstruating. I hate to disappoint here. I stared at the deep red stain and pondered the fact that I was forty-three, niggardly of eggs perhaps but still abundantly producing menstrual blood. I'd read somewhere, hadn't I, of the precipitous drop in fertility of mid-40's women. I wasn't so very fruitful after all. I'd ripened and was aimed onward toward wizening. Ripening had been nice, yes, but wizening had its attractions too. *Wizening, wizening*—what a lovely word. A womb, yes, I still possessed one, but it was no longer an embeddable little mitosis haven. My womb was now a kind of dinosaur, a future dodo, a thing that might *drop*. Purveyors of hysterectomies would shortly be looking at me with glittering eyes.

That tug I described in my innards, that beloved robot technician. Not quite a pack of lies, dear reader. I had in fact had a breast biopsy at one point, and that's when I felt those tugs, those multiple tiny tugs. The technician had been plucking out a fibrous little lump. While doing so, he chattered at me about …the World Series. That's where I smelt that lovely antiseptic.

Has the life gone out of this story? I'm busy. I've got work. My son Henry, the fourteen-year-old, has a girlfriend, and I've discovered they engage in various forms of sex-play, which of course I will try not to imagine in any detail, and this is perhaps one area of many in which I differ from Walt Whitman. I think it is quite probable I will never be pregnant again, and I am on the brink of those estimable power charges. So…perhaps the life has gone out of this story. Well, then, *fine,* the life has gone out of this story. (*Is it not large,* old Walt might ask. *Does it not contain multitudes?*)

You thought I was gone, but here I am again, if I may loosely quote that twitteringly malevolent rogue, *pater* Karamazov. The fact of the matter is, I *did* have an abortion, but I feel compelled now to falsify the record, to cocktail-chitchat the whole thing. I did have an abortion, yes. It was a wee small procedure. It was only as blood-letting as a vigorous session with the dental hygienist on my oh-so-healthy-gums. God knows there is little blood *then*, though of course that lovely Latina wears one of those plexiface guards, and quite rightly, too. "You've got the dental bone structure of a twenty-year-old," my dentist tells me as he looks at the x-rays. He punches me playfully on the upper arm. And I laugh, even though I kind of hate him. There are a lot of things I truly love about the medical establishment: the gleaming chrome, the plastic masks, the sterilizing fluids. I keep the abortion a deep dark secret, dank even. Who am *I* to blurt it out to a blithely whistling world? Women drifting quickly from fertility —with whom can I discuss it? The Japanese empress. I picture her in green silk and tiny slippers, bending slightly over an elegant teapot. No. Chances are I will *not* have tea with her, but I don't care. Let her drink tea with whomever she chooses. I'm a little bit like Alyosha Karamazov, the blessed one: in spite of all these bumps, *joy, joy is glowing in my mind and in my heart.*

In the Enthusiasm
of My Confidence

...I myself, in the wild audacity of my perfect triumph, placed my own seat upon the very spot beneath which reposed the corpse of the victim.
  E. Poe, *The Tell-Tale Heart*

So Jing refuses to live with me beyond this term. I am out of my mind with horror and panic. I try to still my spirit: our suite has its winsome qualities, there's a certain charm in the lack of light. But it's cramped and covered with too many ugly items of Jing's: her filthy running shoes, her rain slicker, her candy snacks. I cringe at the phone calls she gets from her mother, sisters, friends; I detest her smug air of calm as she walks into and out of this, our joint territory. Won't she continue to share it? Will she collude in branding me an outcast, a girl no one can love? How will I keep this from being emblazoned onto my Harvard files?

Jing tells me I'm not a good friend to her, that I don't respect the fact of her separate personhood, and I know she is right. "Remember," she says, "you cried and made a scene when I went to the movies with other people. That was childish, Caresse. We're not married. And we're not little nine-year-olds." But why couldn't she have included me? Why? Now, however, I've stilled those questions forever. I'm sick of being subservient to her! I want to be the strong, valiant one, I want to *not need* the warmth and love that surround her and that she won't let me enter. I want her to look at me just once with the same hopeless, lost look that is my vision of everything, of everyone.

Time has passed and Jing wouldn't be convinced. She'll live elsewhere in the fall. Jing! I thought she was my best friend! How can the whole thing have escaped from me like water spilling though my hands? Now I realize there are no answers to these questions of mine; there's no balm to soothe my heart. And slowly I've felt my power returning and a calm descending. Art history—that class has helped remind me to maintain a frozen serenity. I'll just simply hate her. She murdered me with her rejection; I'll just simply hate her with a marble-like deadness. It's easy. It's inevitable. And yet I also know there must be some logical outcome to all this.

In the meantime, however, I am perfecting a kind of hard veneer, a steel-crystal sort of impermeable material around me. I'm proud of that; I can feel my chest swell just thinking of it. And Jing doesn't have this; she isn't capable of forming this rock-hard shell. I smile to think of it. I smile to realize it can lead me to accomplish everything, anything. *In the enthusiasm of my confidence*, as Poe said, I will finally vanquish all my demons, somehow, some way.

But Poe didn't say that. I'm always learning to be more precise, to cite correctly—that's one of the many fetishes at this most fetishistic seat of learning. It was a character that Poe created that said that: *in the enthusiasm of my confidence*. And still my rage at Jing is wide and in fact endless. She goes out with her friends, home to her family, off to the lab or library. It seems I mostly stay here in my room, mushroom-like. We no longer speak to each other but in the air there is this forced strain of polite veneer. Underneath which is a black hole sucking everything up.

Yes, that's when I'll do something. Not *some*thing, I'll do *it*, *it*. The last day. The last day of our togetherness. The last day before my ignominy begins, the ignominy of it being official and on record for all time that I have no friend who wants to live with me. I'll be able to live a decently cloaked life until then. The logical outcome—*I'll do it*. It'll be *my* act, *my* creativity.

Sometimes now in Jing's face I can see flashes of what I'd like to consider fear, fear of me, but it's also pretty clear there's disgust and even pity mixed in there. The pity sickens me and points out my failure. I have to train myself *not* to look at her face. It's the fear I want to see there, fear and fear only, like the purest, softest gold. This ludicrous United States with its cheap 14 karat stuff in all the shops. My mother laughed when I explained to her what passes for gold here. And American women think they're so elegant! How ignorant they are of the real elegance, the deeper beauty of purer gold such as 21 karat, such as my various necklaces and bracelets. (Sudden idea—yes, mail them back to Mother.) Soft, pure gold like soft, pure fear. Some day I'll see that fear in Jing, and my heart sings at the prospect. I'm a Picasso always working toward my goal here, always painting, painting,

painting. Just looking at the people a little bit now and then and making them sit frozen for long periods but it's my *own* canvas, my *own* work that's of real importance. Yes, if I concentrate hard enough I'll be great as Picasso and as respected. The masterpiece I am currently working on is the removal of the disgust from Jing's face when she looks at me. The masterpiece will be Jing's face trained on me and only full of a reverential fear, a trembling obeisance, and me not even looking at her.

Yes, I feel myself falling deeper and deeper into the joy of the project, deeper and deeper into the Picasso-side of me. He'd only look at his models a little bit, and now and then maybe he'd laugh but then he'd turn back to that immense canvas of his and he'd know, he'd know the genius was all there between him and his act, his own reaching out multiple times with that brush and never stopping until he was done. And I'm sure he got tired and his arm got sore but there was that joy gushing up in his heart. To research, if there's time: did he paint with both arms? Oh, and then with a shock I recall Rothko: did *he* paint with both arms? When Rothko died he slashed both arms at the elbow, no? Again, to research, if there's time.

There won't be time.

A young man was buying a fancy coffee maker— they sell those kinds of things in that hardware shop in the Square that I've learned isn't exactly typical of all American hardware shops; it's got that same old rarefied university air that I've grown so sick of. And yet I can use it for my own purposes now, and that melted my heart a little. The young man was a handsome student and he glanced at me but really just looked *through* me, and that's correct actually, because I was hardly there. That shop had suitable knives, and I stopped and looked at them for a few moments. But then I only picked out some rope, and that's all I bought there. It only took another few minutes to go to the sporting goods store and buy some camping knives. "So. Anything else?" the clerk asked me. "No," I said, "but these are a gift. If they're not right, can he exchange them?" The clerk noticed me then for just the briefest second but his eyes were only bored. "Of course," he said.

I took my magic parcels back to the suite and Jing wasn't there, thank god. I held them on my lap for a while and I could feel myself shaking a little, trembling with joy. Then I put the wrapped packages far under my bed, and I went about my usual anonymous business of life. Perhaps I might mention that there is a pleasant clerk at the post office, but I fully know that this isn't enough to build my life around, and after all, a postal clerk is really nothing. My mind, I have to control it more rigidly and subvert its tendency to stoop to these pathetic lows.

In the library I'm supposed to be studying and I *do* want to ace all my finals, but I can't focus and so I'll somehow get excused from these exams; I'll have them postponed, but how funny, for where do I assume I'll *be* later on? But of course I must not burn all bridges for life is big and who knows what may happen. Jing might look at me and say "Caresse, I was insane to want to room with anyone but you, I was insane, insane." But who knows what. And I certainly can't pin my hopes on such Disney cartoon dreams; I have a plan of action and I will fulfill it.

And in the library I had to control myself from laughing out loud; I wanted to chuckle at my strategy all concrete and solid and ready and waiting — the software all perfect inside my head and the hardware underneath my bed and perhaps covered with a fine layer of dust now, and in some ways I still feel I'm Picasso and I've painted a perfect Edgar Allan Poe. (To research: Did Picasso in fact read Poe? Did he even know of Poe? In many ways they seem contrasting personalities.)

When I was accepted to come to this place I was so sublimely happy! It was really an ultimate happiness but it ended; it was really only the acceptance and the pool of bliss associated with that—it was such a finite thing! And yet I can recall myself within that golden pool back then. And now I am in a magical pool *again* and it's so much better because it's a pool I've made *all myself*—I didn't have to fill in forms and excel on exams and expose myself to the demands of some ultimate authorities like the people *here*, people who are so cool and confident that they could happily have lunch with Queen Elizabeth at the drop of a hat, and their clothes would be perfect and their lunch chitchat would be absolutely stellar but relaxed. That's why I hate them all so much. And that's why I'm so powerful now: because of my plan—I created this pool of happiness all by myself just like Picasso making a really huge painting.

You know what annoys me? Sleeping with those knives under my bed. I dreamt about them last night, I dreamt the bed had half turned into a rocky boat full of sleeping people and the knives were under it, and I had to keep getting off the bed/boat to look beneath it and make sure the knives were still there safe and sound and that no one else knew of their existence.

Jing, she offered me some popcorn this afternoon and I forced myself to say no in a tiny, cold tone, but really I wanted to scream flames at her like a vicious dragon. I kept my wild anger tucked neatly in a steel case inside my chest. It's amazing how adept I am at sweeping and tidying this way.

All in all, I'm beginning to think I'm creating a Rothko here more than a Picasso. I'm beginning to laugh about those floating oblong panels. What a joke. What a joke that they're hanging there and all that reverence is paid. But it's a broad joke, a joke with depth, for I feel those floating panels weigh heavily in my own mind. I love it! I love his progress from bright colors to maroon to darker maroon to black, to deeper black, to nothingness, to infinity. No wonder he killed himself. I'm just like that; I'm Rothko, I'm Picasso.

There are all these fine points that I don't have time to research. If I were nine-years-old again or even twelve I'd go into art, I'd practice drawing five, six hours a day. I would be a truly great artist by now or at least assuredly hovering on the edge of greatness and international renown. There are so many avenues people can choose, and I could have chosen any one of them. But look, look! It's miraculous how things end.

I'm on fire now and this is the end of time, and I only have to glance at my calendar to know it, my calendar on which I've written nothing. I'm already burning in hell and I kind of love it for I control it now and I can make what happens happen.

But I had a yearning to let the wider world know a bit more of my real motives and so I bought a small packet of razors and then stopped for tea and an expensive chocolate biscuit and I, solitary, exulted in public at my plan. And then I went to the library and quite covertly cut slashes into as many books of Picasso's and Rothko's works as I could get my hands on. These were just small reproductions, of course, but I slashed hundreds of pictures, and people will see and get my point. My point, my point—to look, look, look—before it's too late. Can they see? It's too late already.

It was a delightful morning's outing for me, and I could feel my creative juices in full flow. The razors, I dropped them in the trash bin of the ladies restroom, and catching a look at my face in the mirror I noticed I looked flushed and lovely and satisfied.

A day or so has passed, and yes, I've gotten excused from my exams. It was a cinch. But now the book slashing has been nagging at me a little—I knew it wasn't a totally perfect act, I knew it was pretty stupid; I'm not completely insane. And yet it had vestiges, promises of the true and the beautiful—I was practicing, practicing, laying the groundwork. My real act of genius would come later. And so I was happy, cheetah-like, thrilled to be arrow-true directed toward my goal.

Yes, it's the day. Jing has actually been packing, and it tore at my heart a little bit— she's so close yet so far from a kind of smoothness, the smoothness of being away from me. Her packing made me want to laugh and to cry, and I so clearly saw she was like a tiny busy fly. A suitcase clasp of hers was broken, and she made an annoyed, impatient sound.

It's the last twenty-four hours, and I'm frozen all of a sudden and I can't get off my bed, and I realize that if I had *real* strength of will I'd be able to order my spirit out of my body right here, right now, me all curled up, and I note Jing coming and going and at one point asking me if I'm OK, a noise which I silently bat away like an annoying mosquito. I hate stupid, doomed Jing and her dull leaden lack of awareness. What is she, she's just *Pb* from the periodic table, lead; it's just something used for pipes, and in great contrast there's my exquisite gold jewelry tucked neatly away, all 21 karat. *Just go away forever*, I could have roused myself to scream at her but I didn't and she wouldn't anyway, and so she's doomed, and my plan looms near now and yet is heavy and forces me onto my bed. And probably again I'm only feeling sorry for myself, I'm only indulging the non-Rothko non-Picasso aspects of my stupid self. Up! You're as great as Picasso, you can produce as much. Up! Up! And so I'm up and out and walking in the May sunshine and I feel my energy returning and my Picasso self, and on my face I'm suddenly aware is a big smile, all for me, all for my own world that smiles back at me, and there is nothing but me anyway. And *Pb*, lead, is toxic, yes, I know.

She's asleep. I'm awake. It's already dawn. I hop up nimbly. I pull out the equipment and I go on automatic pilot. I will make this perfect. The rope—I set it up on the shower curtain rod, and the knot is just as I've researched it. It dangles in a virgin way. My whole body feels vibrant, my feet especially, my toes. I get the knives and I look at them for a moment, and a kind of instinct pulls my hand over to the one that will be most fitting for its task. My soft feet with their many nerves carry me silently into Jing's room where she's quiet and asleep on her side, her hands nestled up near her face. And I go instantly to work making jabbing motions *two three four* with the knife, jabs that connect with a firm but yielding texture that is cloth and flesh but then really just the flesh. I jab and jab at what is like a sleeping melon, *seven eight nine ten*. I jab and jab and Jing awakes and rises a little but I've already weakened her. She holds up her hands and it's a sign language to me and also an attempt to protect her head but I'm so efficient now that her motion is wasted, and she partly sinks back. *Sixteen seventeen eighteen nineteen*, and I lose count. These slow moments—there's something universal, something infinite here; these seconds are so slow, they're frozen, they become frozen the moment they occur and they move into the realm of the infinite, and I'm jabbing, jabbing, *twenty-nine thirty*

thirty-one thirty-two, lower on her and then higher and yes everywhere—and she tries to rise up a little but she's only like a capsized tiny boat on a huge swirling sea, and I'm jabbing, jabbing, *forty-three forty-four forty-five*, I've covered everything, I can stop now. And my arm feels a little tired like Picasso's. And time seems to have stopped and everything is so soft and frozen, and all here now is fixed in the endlessness of eternity, never to undo itself, never to rest again in the amorphous before. This is happening forever. And so I leave Jing there and go into the bathroom to enact act two of this performance, and I feel through my back that she's risen and is heading out the door but I don't let this worry me for the strange sudden acuity of my back tells me she's sunken down onto my carpet and fallen asleep again. And that's fine, and so I step up onto the tub edge and slip the rope over my head and adjust it and then I step off the edge and quickly see how beautifully all my plans have come to fruition.

Dissociate

Here was a woman who was half-way delighted to learn her grown daughter and grandson and son-in-law were coming to visit her from out of town for Easter. Here was a woman who warned her daughter that of course she couldn't house them for the weekend, but yes, she'd be happy to see them. Here was a woman who, when Easter in fact arrived, ushered her three kin quickly in and when they left ushered them out the back way— for fear of their bumping into anyone and gaining information and for fear of anyone bumping into *them* and gaining information. Information, information to the effect of nebulous and nefarious secrets that the IRS and the DMV among other government agencies had most certainly collected about the woman in all her years of ineffable suburban goings on, goings on amounting to such things as: (1) gazing out at the neighbors' peculiarly quiet driveway for hours on end, (2) wondering whether to put her mink jacket in cold storage for the summer or to go ahead and risk keeping it in an upstairs closet, (3) trying to convince one teenage son to begin multi-vitamin therapy for his ongoing depression, (4) ripping out another teenage son's flourishing marijuana plants almost lost in the profusion of green in the large back yard, (5) informing a teenage daughter that she (the daughter) looked terrible in a bikini because of the sad fact of saddlebags, as in fact all women looked terrible in bikinis, again due to saddlebags, (6) staring at a property tax bill and wondering how the town had the nerve to tax a widow whose house was owned free and clear, no hefty mortgage here, no, not like ninety-nine percent of the neighbors, (7) finding a plastic baggy of some herbal substance under one of the teenagers' beds, yes, contraband and evil but also of known monetary value, and so instead of flushing it down the toilet or grinding it up in the dispose-all she hid it in the bottom shelf of the liquor cabinet where of course the teenagers knew she hid things and in a day or so they repossessed it, and (8) giving most of her material wealth away in monthly contributions to a right-wing Catholic group with a Latin name and a penchant for patriarchy embodied in (among other things) their efforts to demonize birth control in all third world Catholic countries.

(Why hadn't she thrown out that baggy full of marijuana? Yes, that had been a lapse. But it didn't nag at her as sharply as her regret about uprooting her son's lovely green crop, oh how she regretted this subversion of her son's farmerly instincts! He'd become an optometrist and was miserable and overweight; she knew she was partly to blame that he wasn't a happy agriculturalist of some sort.)

Yes, yes, there were many things that the IRS and other agencies probably had multiple memos on, and it was too late in the day to risk neighbors in the apartment complex knowing, it was too late in the day for her grown children to twig on to the fact that dirty secrets were hidden, hidden ghost-like behind the smokescreen of the lack of vigilance re marijuana, the smokescreen of the moral posturing, but not hidden so irrecoverably that they couldn't be ferreted out if one had the will and the suspicion. And so this woman's mission in life was to remain ever vigilant and to keep those secrets clamped. What secrets? Some she herself had forgotten and this was proof of what an able secret-keeper she was. Here was a woman who was slightly pissed off about a lot of things, and things that had a history.

And so. She ushered her relatives in quickly. She actually met them at the front door of the lobby; she was half-pulling her coat on and carrying a shopping bag.

"Mom. Hi, Mom." Her daughter, the saddle-bagged one, gave her a quick hug and a kiss, and the woman felt the studied neutrality. "Why's your coat on?" the daughter was saying. "We want to see your place, have a cup of tea maybe. We've got time. Aunt Sara's not expecting us til two."

"Oh, all right," the woman said, and she led the three up to her apartment. It was sunny and bright and there were delicate lace curtains on the big living room window, but there was no furniture except a small desk and a chair, and the walls were lined neatly with a variety of boxes: department store boxes, white gift boxes, brown cardboard containers. Not an immense amount though, not enough to intimidate a mover with a small pickup and only two hours to do the clear-out. The woman kept half an eye on her daughter and noted the dismay that washed across her face. Yes, she'd been here a year and this is how she'd been living: poised to move out. Let her daughter be dismayed. There was no reason to be dismayed. Her capital had run out. And the woman dismissed the thought.

"Oh," said the woman, "I'm going to give you something nice," and she started fishing through the boxes. She handed something to the grandson, a nine-year-old. "It's a wooden puzzle. Do you want it?" she asked. The boy and his father got down on the floor and started working the puzzle. The woman's daughter walked around the room, peering at pictures on the window ledge, opening and closing some nearby boxes. One held a tiny painting of Mary holding a baby Jesus. One held various tracts put out by the right-wing Catholic group.

"Oh, those photos," said the woman. "Do you want them? Do you want some of them?"

"Hmmm," said the daughter, looking at a photo of her brother and his wife and their children, looking at a photo of her sister at high school graduation. "But don't you want these?"

"Not if you want them," said the woman.

"I don't really need them," said the daughter. "I've got lots of photos," she said. She moved into the kitchen and began opening and shutting cupboard doors. "Where's the tea? Or the coffee?" She asked her mother. She peered into the fridge but there was no milk.

"Tea, oh there's no tea. There's only the tea you sent me," the mother told the daughter.

The cupboards were not completely bare. There was a half bag of sugar, a half box of rice, a tin of paprika. The daughter had brought a bagfull of groceries; she laid the items neatly out on the counter. Canned soup, canned clam sauce, colored pasta, cookies, jam. She found the tea she'd sent and put on a pot of water to boil. "Who wants tea?" the daughter called out. No one answered. "I'm making tea for everyone," she said.

The daughter and the woman went back out to the living room. The son-in-law and grandson were half done with the puzzle. "He really knows the states now," the man said to his wife. It was a puzzle of the United States. The daughter picked up a piece and looked at it. To the woman it looked as if she were inspecting the quality of the wood.

"Look, look at this," the woman said to her daughter. "Would you like to take this home with you?" She stood in front of a ceramic bust of Christ, a bust with upraised hands and delicate fingers. It was the Christ of pastel tones and soft brown ringlets and elegant nose. The woman had owned and loved it for thirty years. It was in perfect condition, mint. Her daughter heaved a sigh.

"Oh, I don't know. Mom. I don't know where I'd put it."

"It's a treasure. It can be a family heirloom," said the woman.

"I don't know, Mom. Maybe, maybe a rectory might like it or a nunnery. I mean a convent. You could give it as a gift."

"It's a work of art. I thought you were interested in art," the woman said.

"I *am* interested in art," said the daughter. "But not exactly this kind."

"It's a work of *art*," repeated the woman.

"All right, all right, it's a work of art," said the daughter.

They were silent for a while and the woman worried a tiny bit about the strain in the air.

"Oh, look at this," the woman said, suddenly remembering something. She took a package from a drawer. "You can have this, too. This used to belong to you."

The daughter took the plastic bag being offered to her. A smile crept across her face. "Oh, my coin collection. This is my old coin collection, Patrick," she said to her son. "You know, I told you." And she took out a handful of coins and examined them, and the woman could see her daughter lost in the nostalgia of a certain third grade glory, a certain honor in the collection being placed in the glass hallway case of her Catholic grade school. There were also various pieces of paper money including one million deutschmark notes that one or another of the Slavic grandparents (the woman's parents and parents-in-law) had brought over on the boat at one of those points between wars when inflation zenithed. "Look, Patrick," the daughter said. "One million marks. Eine Million Mark. From the Reichsbank Direktorium," she said, peering at the note carefully, as if it were a bit of a strain, as if she'd just crossed that cusp of occasionally needing reading glasses. The woman frowned a little. Could her daughter be approaching menopause? The nine-year-old jumped up and took the note from his mother's hands.

"How much is this worth? How much is one mark worth?" he demanded.

The adults laughed. No one answered right away. "That's what we used to try to figure out, that's exactly what we used to say when we were your age. Aunt Patty, Uncle Paul, Uncle Frank — all of us," the daughter said to her son.

"So how much is it worth?" persisted the boy.

His mother had taken back the note. "Berlin, twentieth February, 1923," she read. She stopped for a moment. "1923. Mom, who was still over in Europe in 1923? Who brought this over?" she asked her mother.

The woman froze in what she was doing. She was taking bread out of a bag and putting slices into a toaster. The kitchen opened right onto the living room so there was no difficulty in everyone hearing each other. "What?" said the woman. "What are you asking?"

Her daughter sighed. "Where do you think these bills came from? That's what I'm asking."

"Are they worth anything now?" asked the nine-year-old. "Nobody's listening to me!"

"No, they're worthless now," his mother said to him quickly in an aside.

"Why do you think someone brought them over?" the woman was asking her daughter. "How do you know they weren't sent over in the mail? Look, your water's boiling."

"I don't know *anything*, I don't think *anything*," said the daughter. "I'm just *asking*. I'm just trying to figure out how they got here. Your and Dad's parents were here well before 1925, right?" she asked. She glanced again at the note. "1923. Way before 1923, right?" she said.

The woman was now rather determinedly buttering the toast, rye toast, toast that was emitting a delectable fragrance. "What difference does it make?" she asked her daughter. "Why do you want to know?" She bit into the toast. There was no place to sit and so she ate standing up.

The daughter put down the note and began pouring hot water over tea bags. "Oh forget it," she said. "It's not important." Her voice had that familiar tone of annoyed dismissal. Good, thought the mother. Case closed. But there was no reason for the daughter to be dismayed. It was merely that her capital had run out and she would no longer be able to contribute those large amounts to that Latin-named Catholic group. And thus her life was over, she realized.

The son-in-law was going for the bag of bread. "Oh, yes, this is good fresh rye," the woman said to him. "Please, help yourself."

She bethought herself: maybe the good rye bread would sort things out a bit. For the son-in-law seemed slightly pissed off but also hungry. The daughter of course seemed slightly pissed off, but she raised her cup of herbal tea to her nose and inhaled deeply. The nine-year-old seemed slightly pissed off and he kicked apart the just-completed puzzle. The woman too felt slightly pissed off and she silently berated herself for giving back to her daughter the coin collection that she herself had stood guard over all these years.

The daughter looked at the disarranged puzzle. "Did you think that was a cool thing to do?" she asked her son quietly but distractedly.

He looked at her in disgust. "It's cooler than half the things *you* do."

"Can I have the coin collection?" he asked his grandmother.

"Of course, of course, it's yours now," said the woman instantly, but it again nagged at her that yes, it'd been a tactical error to surrender this bit of evidence.

The son-in-law was raising his eyebrows at his wife and nodding toward the front door.

"Yes, we should go," said the daughter. "Mother, are you ready?" And they all left for Easter dinner at an aunt's house. Down the back entry. Quickly and quietly, as the woman had planned. No one was about. It was still early. The daughter and her husband were craning their necks this way and that to get a look at any neighbors, but they were stymied. There was no information floating around there in the crisp April sunshine. It was hidden, it was locked up and snarled away. The four got into the car. The woman's pissed-offness, it was dissipating. It was swirling off into the atmosphere. In fact it seemed that it no longer existed. She felt happy. It was good to get away from that apartment, if only for a few hours. She looked around at her kin. Everyone sat silently and stared off in different directions.

Teeth, Death,
My Friend Louise

Hmm. I'm forty-one but my nine-year-old son persists in thinking I'm only forty. He's at that phase when children obsess about their parents' mortality, and for him this takes the guise of frequent recitations of my age, my birthdate, and how old I'll be on my next birthday. I listen, holding my breath, biding my time: this will surely pass. And I find myself unable to clue him in that no, I'm not forty, I am in fact forty-one. (I know for a dead fact I can pass for thirty-eight.)

This is a lot of beating around the bush: the bush is Louise, my eighty-five year old Italian-born neighbor. "Get over here!" she screams over the phone to me at 7:30 one weekday morning. I'm in the midst of getting child ready for school, making breakfast, dressing for work. "Get over here and see how beautiful my hair turned out!" Louise shrieks. "I curled it, it turned out beautiful!" I count to three and beg off without screaming.

Louise is a woman who's lived in the suburbs of New York for over six decades but still refers to pasta sauce as "gravy," a woman who became my friend when she found I'd spend a few companionable minutes with her every now and then. She and her husband Ralph live two doors down. The Castinos, childless: he a retired cobbler and she a retired dressmaker. He'd been apprenticed out as a shoemaker at age ten back in Italy when his parents caught him too many times stealing plums from a neighbor's orchard. All right, they said, that's that. Off to work you go. Now all these many years later Louise and Ralph are tiny and shrunken but energetic in a doddery way. Louise is unsteady on her pins but she still makes fresh pasta. She has taken to coming over to my house to complain about property taxes and doctors and this and that, and then she drifts into Italian, but she'll always snap to and stare sharply at me. "Those teeth," she says one day, peering savagely at me. "Those aren't your real teeth."

I try to stifle a small snort. "Of course they are, Louise," I say, and I smile broadly at her so she can get a good view. She tilts her head sideways and a cunning look enters her eyes. "No, those aren't your real teeth," she tells me. The long and the short of it is that her disbelief will remain until I permit her to tap on my teeth, possibly to pull on them. Which I will never allow her to do. She comes over once a week or so to yell at me; I see her slowly tottering up my front walk. She shakes a finger an inch or so from my nose. You're lazy, she tells me, pointing at a bare spot in my front garden. Then she becomes distracted staring at me. Your hair is wrong, she tells me in her curmudgeonly way. Your flowers are no good, your teeth are probably false, your son is a-gonna-leave you....

Is this a pretty pass? I have independent, outside confirmation that in fact I am hardworking, my teeth are my own and quite sound (and yes, attractive), and when my son leaves me eventually to go off to college, well, that is exactly what I am planning for. But I find myself trying to decide to what extent this is actually a pretty pass, (oh what a pretty pass things have come to!), for now my bosom companion, my regular confidante is an eighty-five-year-old Italian immigrant woman, a person of slightly fascist bent: she hates the Pope and the Vatican but she keeps pinned to her kitchen wall a picture of Clinton and Gore snipped from the newspaper. It is an inaugural shot; both men exude that air of canary-filled cats. "Look," she says, leading me to it and caressing the picture with her fingers, "look at how handsome, how young." And she stands transfixed, gazing at the politicos.

"Mm-hmm," I say. "Yes, well, Louise, I suppose so. Yes, I do vote Democrat. But don't you think he's a little on the fat side?" I say, just to tease her, just to get her blood flowing. She and old Ralph and I are all so admirably gaunt, so admirably hovering just above a hundred pounds.

"Fat?" she asks, scowling at me horrifically. "What, fat?"

"Yes, fat. You know. He eats too much. And they both go to the hairdresser too often," I say, flinging my arm at the photo. I don't want to leave the air full of her bliss. She glares at me.

"Fat. Fat. You don't know anything about fat," Louise says. She waves her hand at me, shoving away an abomination. But then her scowl slowly fades and is replaced by a roguish smile. She turns away from me and is beaming again at Bill and Al. "Oh, they're handsome, they're very handsome," she says, "I don't care what you say."

And we amble away from the photo and sit down for some tea. I sneak a glance at my watch. Forty minutes? I've been here forty minutes? I have to get away.

"Lipton soup," she is screeching now, shaking the red box in my direction. "It's good. It's good," she sings out to me. "Just add a little more pastina. Give it for dinner for your husband and your son. It's good," she repeats. She is a true Lipton's lover. She can whip up a dinner for two for about thirty-seven cents.

She somehow reminds me of.... I don't know, Howard

Hughes and other story book eccentrics, people who daydream about aerodynamic brassieres and scream at naysayers. I've heard the Lipton soup litany before; she's blazed that recipe into my memory.

No, I'm not lazy. I'm a part-time accountant for a watch importer and I'm also starting my own small business from my house: a mail-order children's bookstore. And yet my laziness is one of Louise's constant motifs; in spite of this I am more and more attracted to her irascible charm, her glittery-eyed know-it-all-ness. Charm, no, not exactly, not to the world at large. My nine-year-old deplores her; "She's nuts, she says I'm a bad boy," he mutters to me. And it is true that both Louise and Ralph frown and shout at him for walking too slowly down the street, for squatting down to peer at an ant colony. They refer to him as the baby. "Oh, the baby," they say in front of him. I know they believe in hitting children with sticks to make them mind. And I know they believe I am a filthy sociopath for burying kitchen garbage in a mulch pile in my backyard. And though my son hates Louise, he rather admires Ralph, for one day he'd seen Ralph shaking a fist at some squirrels. "Damn bitches, damn bitches," Ralph had yelled at them. My son, starry-eyed in disbelief, tells me this tale a number of times. And then there is my husband: he makes brief slighting remarks about Louise, remarks at which I nurture secret grievance for quite a while. But eventually I begin challenging him outright. "Louise is my *friend*," I say. "I *love* Louise." I love seeing her enjoying being eighty-five and gleefully misanthropic, jabbing her finger at my nose, me as representative of all of recalcitrant humanity. Bossy Louise. For a few more bony years.

The Castino domicile is neat as a pin, no mess anywhere, no crucifixes, no books, no magazines. They are cleaning up their house bit by bit in an organized way so that when they die it will be completely empty. They seem to have a plan to leave this earth without a trace.

Louise calls me frequently to ask if I'd like an old single mattress, an aged set of Tupperware, a bit of unused carpet remnant. She mostly gets my machine and she doesn't leave a message but I always know she's called because she doesn't hang up until well after the beep. "Why you need that machine?" she asks me in person. "That's a stupid thing. I'm not going to talk on that."

"I'm tearing up all my old photos," Louise tells me darkly one visit. "Who am I going to give them to? Who is there to look at them? No one. I'm tearing them up," she says. "All I hope is I die before Ralph. What am I going to do without Ralph? Please, just let me die first," she tells me.

"Oh, come on, Louise," I say. "You could last another twenty years."

"Hah," she says. "You think I'm gonna live to be a hundred? No. I'm gonna die. Pretty soon I'm gonna call you up, I'm dead," she says, miming bringing a phone mouthpiece to her head.

Ralph laughs at me while I'm gardening. It's funny, yes, I know, for he's been doing it for sixty-five years while I'm a novice with a mere twelve, fifteen under my belt. Still, he eyes my grape hyacinth with great interest.

"What is that? Did you put that in there?" he asks.

"Yes. It's from a bulb. You plant it in the fall," I say.

"I need some of that," he says. "And you have to take it out?"

"Oh no," I say. "It's like the tulips." I wave toward them. "You just leave it in and it comes back every year."

"The tulips," says Ralph with derision. He doesn't say more. He knows I've already heard both Castinos denigrate tulips: their bloom time is pathetically short; only ninnies waste time and money on them.

In the summer Ralph always grows tomatoes, peppers, cucumbers, lettuce, basil and parsley. He never buys seeds; he harvests seeds year to year. He is proud of his tiny garden patch, and the bounty spills over to us for no way can Louise and Ralph make heavy inroads on all those vegetables. Louise brings the produce over in a brown paper bag. "Eat it. It's good," she scolds me. "Don't throw it out." I assure her we will happily consume it. "Please, please, don't tell anyone," Louise begs. She glances at my window in case neighbors are lurking about. "Don't tell anyone what I give to you." I assure her that her offering will remain cloaked in secrecy.

Our tomatoes are bigger and more advanced than Ralph's. My husband points this out with classic macho pride. "Better not tell him," says my beaming husband. "He'll have a heart attack."

"I have a jacket, beautiful, beautiful," Louise tells me one summer day. "A red jacket with long sleeves of course because you have to have long sleeves when they put you in that…box. It's beautiful, beautiful, it's all ready, it's hanging in my front closet. You can come and see it." She pauses, drifts off a bit. "The only thing I don't like is what they do, they put a hole in your foot and out comes all your blood, your liquid. I don't like that. I hate to think that. But what can you do. That's what they do."

I realize it is an official act of charity to visit the elderly, and so I ring Ralph and Louise's doorbell every so often and chat for a minute or two. I find myself sometimes begrudging them the time for I'm always behind on all the paperwork involved in my mail-order work. My house is a swamp of order forms, children's books, packing materials. My husband is starting to get quietly tense about this and secretly hopes I go back to my accounting job full-time. And so sometimes I'm annoyed at the time Louise eats up but other times I find comfort in her quavering vexations. And I don't want the Castinos to have a sense that they are always coming to me, always imposing. One day Louise pulls me aside in their living room. "Who did you come to see?" she whispers. "Did you come to see me or him?" she asks, indicating Ralph with a tiny jerk of her head. She is staring at me, trying to read the truth in my face. "Who do you come to see, Ralph or me?"

"I came to see both of you," I say slowly. Aha, so a tad of jealousy is at work here. But which way does it run? Damned diabolical Louise—depend on her to want to keep both me and Ralph all to herself but to keep us separate. That intersecting line between Ralph and me: no, Louise isn't interested.

The thing is, Ralph, the husband, is still incredibly sexy in his eighty-five-year-old way. It's in his wiry build, it's in the way he holds his arms, it's in the forward motion of his movement. He thrusts the space aside. "That Ralph," I say to my son one day right after Ralph leaves, having delivered a handful of fresh basil. "That Ralph is still a sexy guy."

My son looks up, disgusted. "You're nuts, Mom," he says. "He's old. He's an old shriveled tomato."

But I know I'm right.

On the other hand, both Ralph and Louise are so tiny and dry now that I have the sense I could pick them up and place them on a shelf with my Madame Alexander Dolls, and they would fit quite nicely.

I like them. I just plain like them. It doesn't matter that Louise is always belittling me for such things as not having adequate shades on the windows, not having a proper hairdo, not having purchased the right color of impatiens for my front yard. I just plain like them.

Louise, she comes one day unannounced and again interrupts me hard at work. My little business isn't working; it is failing rather inexorably in a steady downhill sort of way, and I will soon be forced to return full-time to the watch office. Damn, damn, damn, my sweet pipe dream is drifting off into vapor, and I am so heavily in the red I don't dare tell my husband. Louise butts into my depression.

"That doctor," she says, "I tell him if his wife had this pain he'd give her something, but me, no, me, does he care? No, he don't care."

And I suddenly burst into tears, and Louise pats me on the hand and says, "Oh don't be so upset, it's OK."

And so I tell her no, it's something else, it's my business, it's my small business failure. I point at the piles of paper all around me. Louise stares at me in sympathy. She sits quietly and appears to be thinking. "Maybe you better go back to school," she tells me finally. "You're a young," she said. "You're a young. Go back to school. Look at your face. You are so beautiful, your face looks so lovely and smooth and you have no wrinkles."

I smile at her and try to imagine myself in a zone where I can take a bit of comfort in the fact that I'm not yet a wrinkled old lady.

The lament of Louise continues: "I'm all wrinkles, I'm not like you. I'm-a-disgusting, my life. The medicine I have to take, too much medicine all the time and it doesn't fix me. I might as well die. I'm-a-disgusting, my life." She looks up at me. Her disgust with herself spills away as she stares at me. "Those teeth.

They're not really yours." She is again pointing a finger within scratching distance of my nose.

I heave a sigh. "Louise," I say.

"Are they yours? Are they yours? Are they yours?" she raps out at me.

Do I convince her that ninety-nine percent of people my age in the U.S. today have all their own teeth, thank you? I don't know. I almost open wide, I almost tug at them myself to show her, but I don't want her to see all the amalgam in my molars. She'll store it up in her heart as evidence against...something — my mother, my discipline in the face of sweets, the moral fiber of my forebears.

It's a hot day but I'm outside gardening, feeling the sun baking through my skin just like it does to the tomatoes. Louise is in her living room with her air-conditioner blasting, watching her 2:30 soap opera. She's in there: I feel her bony frame through the walls, I see her scowling at the screen, piecing together in her mind the nefarious goings on of Susan Lucci and assorted other daytime stars. Ralph. He walks four blocks to the grocery store every morning around eight, and then at 2:30 when her show is on he's off again, even when it's above ninety, down to the market and looking for a word or two with any old crony that might be about.

A few weeks later Louise again discusses her jacket. "I think I didn't say my sister made the red jacket. It's elegant, lovely, the sleeves and shoulders fit perfect," she says. "It'll keep me warm in the coffin. I'll have to show it to you, I'll have to show you where I keep it," she tells me, and I realize I'm becoming an instrumental part of Louise's death scenario.

We are having a small bath added to the attic of our house. Both Louise and Ralph think it's a big mistake. "You're crazy. Why you need that? You need a new car, you need a bigger television," Louise tells me.

I explain to her that it is for the comfort of guests, and besides, when our son gets a bit older he can move his bedroom up there if he wishes.

"You're crazy if you think your son stay with you! He'll find a woman, he'll leave you. He won't stay with you forever!" Louise hollers at me. "You in this house, you people don't use your brain!" she shouts as she turns away and heads back to her own home.

My husband helps Ralph get some manure for his garden; the two men pull it out of the trunk. Thinking the bags are too heavy for Ralph, I jump out of the car and try to help. He waves me away. "I can do it," he says brusquely. He and my husband drag the bags into Ralph's garage.

"You're in pretty good shape," my husband says to him.

"Hmmm?" asks Ralph.

"Good shape," my husband repeats, flexing his own muscles as a visual aid. "You're a strong guy."

Ralph nods. "I'm a hundred fifty pounds," Ralph says to us. My husband and I studiously avoid exchanging glances. "I'm a hundred fifty pounds and not any more. A hundred fifty. No more." He waves a stern finger at us.

"Yes, Ralph, I believe it," says my husband. "I believe you're not an ounce more than one fifty."

We walk home. We laugh. Ralph. He weighs one ten if he's lucky. I wouldn't be surprised to see him tip the scale at ninety-five.

"You're like a sister to me. I have no one left," Louise tells me. She hands me some lovely plum tomatoes, some fistfuls of that intoxicating-smelling basil. It is a late July evening and the air is heavy and sweet. "Don't tell anyone," she says, pointing to the produce. "Please. Don't tell anyone." She takes her leave.

It's Saturday chore time; I'm dusting pictures in the upstairs hall while my husband helps my son sort through the chaos in his bedroom. "You're five years older than Mom. You're an old man, five years older than Mom," I hear my son teasing.

"No, I'm not," I hear my husband reply in measured tones. "No, there's four years difference."

"Wrong, Dad. You're old. You're forty-five and Mom's forty. That's five years," says my son with dead and happy certainty.

I'd been enjoying the dusting, but my breathing changes; it isn't Zen-like now. I listen.

"Mom's not forty. She's forty-one," my husband says. "Mom's forty-one." Do I detect a note of malice? His voice is clear, ringing, definite. Do I detect betrayal? I wait for my son's response. There's nothing. A sea of silence. I'm not with them. I'm in another room. But what could I call out to them? Shit, it's true: I'm forty-one. Soon I'll be forty-two and then eighty.

Louise dislikes my long hair; every time she sees me she laments. "You look terrible. Your hair is terrible, old. Cut it, make yourself young. What's the matter, you can't spend a little money?" This goes on for months. Drip, drip, drip, I finally get worn down, and so I get a haircut. Louise runs over to my house three times before I return from an afternoon back at the watch company office. Ralph had seen me earlier and reported to her. She finally catches me at home. "Oh," she says. "You got your haircut. It's good." She stares at me, nodding. "But you didn't really get it short," she says, and her smile is fading. She tells me Ralph has lots of tomatoes, lots of cucumbers, too, if I want any. She tells me about her morning visit for a blood test. But then she breaks off and just stares at me silently. "I don't like what they did to your hair," she says finally. Her face has taken on that stricken look. "I don't like it. It's still too long. You need it shorter, shorter."

"That's OK, Louise," I tell her. "I like it. And if I don't like it after a while, I'll go back and get it cut again."

"Oh," says Louise. She nods to herself for awhile. Her face lights up then with understanding. "Oh, I see. Next month when you have more money you can go back and get it cut the right way," she says, and I realize she's cooked up a notion that I didn't have enough cash to get a decent haircut, that I'm working on some sort of cut-rate incremental system to improve my looks. I open my mouth to explain that it doesn't work that way; one haircut costs as much as another, more or less, but then I say nothing. Hell with it. Let her enjoy her own cockamamie theory.

Louise needs surgical support hose and is having trouble finding them, and so I volunteer to take her shopping. She happily accepts the offer and we plan to go. But she takes a second look at what I'm wearing—a tee shirt and denim shorts—and she says, Are you going like that? I never go out like that, she tells me.

My mother-in-law comes for a brief visit, and Louise is curious about some things. "Does she live in an apartment?" she asks me after the trip. I'm sitting in her living room drinking the small glass of ginger ale she's provided me. No, I say, she lives in a little house, a nice small house with two bedrooms and one bathroom and a nice yard. It's all on one floor so she doesn't have to deal with steps. And she has a nice dog, a golden retriever. Louise is starting to give me her classic horrified look again and so I pause.

"A dog?" she asks. "She has a dog? No dogs or cats!" she tells me. "Old people have to give away all dogs and cats because you will die in the middle of the night and no one will know and then your cat or dog will be left alone and start to starve and of course, they eat you. They eat your dead body in the middle of the night, they know when you stop breathing. So tell your mother-in-law. Tell her to get rid of the dog."

I nod at Louise and solemnly promise I'll pass on this invaluable information. We sit together quietly for a moment or two.

"Oh, my mother," Louise tells me. "My mother had one wish and that was to be put into a drawer. She didn't want to go into the cold earth. Put me in a drawer, she told us. She got her wish. Cost a lot of money too but that doesn't matter. She's in a drawer, nice and dry and high up off the ground." Louise gets up and takes something from her front closet: it's her red death jacket, her jacket that she wants to be buried in. She pulls it off its wooden hanger and tries it on for me.

"Oh, yes," I say, "it's a perfect fit." It's a rich crimson, soft and plush. She beams happily. "Do you wear it?" I ask her, "do you ever wear it?" Her face starts contorting into that terrified scowl of hers and I realize I've abominated myself again. "Oh, never mind," I say. But she's already turned away and begun pulling another jacket from the closet, a beige one.

"Here, my sister made this one too," she says. "This one is perfect, too. You try, you take. If it fits you, take."

"Um, all right," I say, not relishing the prospect of a mothball-scented antiquity just at that very moment. I can see it's too small, and when I put it on my arms hang down, wrists bare. "Oh, it's not big enough," I say. Louise tsks and tsks and examines the sleeve hems carefully.

"No," she says. "No. There isn't enough material. It can't fit you." She shakes her head wistfully as I put the jacket back on its hanger. "Look, look how lovely it is. No more. No more can you find this work this good." She returns the jacket to the closet, gives her own red jacket a few tender strokes, and shuts the door, sighing heavily.

I make my exit, and as I walk back to my house I turn and see her in her doorway, still shaking her head in slight dismay at the mismatch, the lost opportunity.

Louise comes and gives me a load of old lady doilies. Some are store-bought, some are handmade and of antique Italian origin. "You're a married woman, you should know how to iron these, you should know how to damp them and put in starch and leave them in the fridge for a while," she tells me. And I vaguely remember my mother doing something like this once or twice, just a vague gesture toward maintaining some sort of old fashioned upkeep, some sort of old-fangled elegant housewiving. It's not a method a modern slobby type like me would employ, to put it mildly.

"You do it," Louise tells me. "I'm going to come back and check," she says, shaking her finger at me. She looks at the long pieces of rectangular silk I've put atop a couple of my tables. Her face gets that horrified stricken look as if she'd stepped on a fresh turd. "Those are terrible," she says to me, "terrible. Get rid of those." Louise leaves, and I drop the doilies in a clump on a chair in a far corner of the room.

RESISTANCE

I take Louise a little basket of dried flowers. The flowers are from my own garden, and I've arranged the basket myself. It's tiny and charming, if I do say so myself. I'd love to keep it, but Louise gave me those damned doilies and so I want to give her something in return. I ring her doorbell. She's happy to see me. I hold the little basket out to her and explain its provenance. She glares at it horrifically for a moment. "I don't like that," she tells me. "Take it back home. I don't want that," she says. I laugh a little to myself. I'm kind of impressed with her ability to look a gift horse in the mouth. And I was so wimpy about letting her foist those doilies on me!! But she's eighty-five and I'm only forty-one. I've got forty years to perfect being querulous and assertive, forty years to learn how to scream and wave bony fingers and weigh one hundred and three pounds.

I'm back at the office full-time now, and so Louise takes to watching for my car in the drive; she then comes over and pounds on the front door with all the arrogance of a tiny woman in her mid-eighties who knows if she doesn't make demands on the world today, well, then, yes, there truly may be no tomorrow. I sigh. I get angry. But I always open the door when I recognize her little bird-claw pounding.

She comes in one day and reminds me of the time months and months ago when I burst into tears because my wee business venture had failed. "Remember? Remember when you cried?" she says, smiling at me. Yes, yes. Let's reminisce about the good old days. The watch importer loves me. I've got a secure office job. I can get fancy watches for a song.

Louise looks around at my furniture. She sees that I haven't put the doilies in their Louise-assigned places. "What about the cloths?" she demands. "Did you iron them?"

They are of course still in that clump in the corner. I imagine

I may have to kill Louise.

"You can give them back to me," she says.

"Well, maybe I'd better," I say.

" I don't understand this country," Louise says, "the customs are different."

"Yes," I say, "white doilies are not of such paramount importance now."

"What?" says Louise, giving me one of her nightmarish glares.

"Oh, I just don't really use these white things," I say to her.

"Ah," says Louise. "Ah." She pauses and is obviously thinking. "Oh, I see. You want to use those dark cloths so they hide the dirt," she says, pointing to my tablecloths.

"Yes," I say rather quickly. "That's it."

"Well, you can give me back those things. I won't be mad."

I put them neatly in a bag for her. She's not mad. I'm doily-free. We're both relatively happy. She starts to leave but turns back to scowl at me.

"That beautiful jacket. The beige one. Too bad you're too tall. Too bad it doesn't fit you."

Louise finally figures out how to leave messages on my message machine instead of just angry slamming hang-ups. Louise Castino!! She shouts on my tape. Get over here! You call me up! I want to see you! Now!! she screams angrily. I ignore the messages totally for a few hours and sometimes even for a day, but then I always do call her and of course she's quite pleasant. The thing is I love her and can ignore a lot of her cantankerous crap. And of course there's no issue anymore for we are friends; we have a history: if I come visit—fine, if not, not.

As it happens, Ralph is the first to die. A fast clean clap of pneumonia takes him off in a day and a half: the sniffles at home, a pain in the chest, an ambulance to the hospital, one final night. Poof. My husband and I make our way over to Louise's the morning of the funeral; we've offered to accompany her. As we walk up she's waving away a limo driver sent over by the undertaker. "Aaah," she comments in disgust. "They think I need that big black thing?" She turns and we follow her into her living room; I catch sight of her unzipped dress back, and I quickly zip it for her.

"Look," she says, pointing out some carefully packed bundles by the door. "Neat and clean," she says. "That's what he wanted." It seems that she's managed that very morning to bag a few loads of Ralph's clothes for Salvation Army pickup. She stops and looks at my husband in an appraising way, mouth pursed. "Nah," she says finally, shaking her head. "Too big."

"Come," she says to my husband, and she takes him into the kitchen. "Open this." She's pulled a bottle of Asti Spumante from the bottom of her fridge. "He got it for a Christmas gift," she tells us. My husband gives me a quizzical look, which Louise catches. "Open it," she repeats. "Can't you do?" And she makes a twisting motion with her hand and gets out some juice glasses. She leaves the room while my husband pours. I find myself reaching for a glass and taking a long swallow before Louise returns for a toast. She comes back wearing that crimson jacket. "Look," she says to me, and she smoothes her lapels. "Beautiful. Perfect," she says, and yes, I must admit, the structured shoulders hold their elegance.

The Asti is sweet and disgusting, but then again it does have a certain pre-funeral charm. Louise and my husband are quietly guzzling, and as my husband refills his own glass, I make a quick pointing jab at mine. I look at Louise and remember my grandmother's funeral: I was eight or so. "Pat Grandma good-bye," the undertaker had whispered to my younger brother and me, and in an instructive vein he'd thumped the corpse firmly on the folded hands. My brother and I responded by instantly bursting into sobs. A tear wells in my eye and I struggle to hide it, but Louise notices.

"Can't hold her drink, eh?" she says to my husband, smiling and glittery-eyed in her world-wisdom.

I'm a tad annoyed, but I just swallow a little more Asti. We get up and leave for the funeral home, all slightly polluted.

How Do They Become Bag Ladies?

It was the day she left the Pic'n'Pak with the aspirin bottle in her hand that Rose met Mrs. Harris. The good (meeting Mrs. Harris) canceled out the bad that day; being accused of shoplifting had been mortifying when all she'd really been doing was attempting to persuade the Tyson mother into sending her two little daughters to the Opus Dei summer camp, the camp that taught them to be dignified young ladies, to learn their place as good young Catholic women. Cathy Tyson had been in kind of a hurry, but she'd let Rose continue talking as they walked out of the store together, and that's when the store detective called out to them, yelled at them really, and Rose found herself back inside and faced with an angry manager and a stone-faced policeman. She looked at the bottle in her hand in disbelief; of course she'd been meaning to pay for it, she hadn't even started her shopping, she was a regular customer here and a daily communicant at Merciful Redeemer parish down the road; she'd merely walked out absent-mindedly because she'd been so deep in conversation with Mrs. Tyson. She'd never stolen anything in her life. And then Rose almost began to cry because the manager was still insisting that the policeman write out a report.

"This woman is a treasure," a strong voice proclaimed, and Rose and the manager and the policeman turned to see a slightly mustached old lady standing behind a cart full of cat-food tins. She walked over to the three. "You, I don't even want to talk to you, treating someone like this," the old woman said to the manager, flicking her hand out in a gesture of dismissal. She turned to the policeman. "He has to listen to me, I'm in here every Thursday spending my fifty-seven dollars worth. Sour milk. I've had to return sour milk on more than one occasion." She glanced balefully at the manager and then spoke again to the policeman. "This lady here is my friend from church, and I suggest you go out and make yourself useful somewhere else." The policeman was beginning to give the manager dirty looks, and other shoppers, older women mainly, were gawking and eavesdropping with obvious sympathy for their counterparts. "Aspirin," one of them said in an audible voice, "no one steals aspirin. Who does he think he is?" The manager sized this up quickly enough. He waved his arms. "All right, all right. Let's just forget it." He stalked off toward his manager's booth only turning around to blurt out "sorry" to the police officer. For appearance's sake, the cop stayed a few minutes to flirt with a blue- and orange-haired teenage cashier; he picked up a Snickers bar and half expected her to wave off his proffered two quarters, but she didn't.

The old woman took the aspirin bottle that Rose was still clutching and tossed it into her shopping cart. "We'll just leave this here and let them put it all away," she said. "Let's go." She took Rose's arm. "I'll do my shopping elsewhere from now on. Would you like coffee at my house? I've got a little project maybe you can help me with." And then Rose and the woman who'd introduced herself as Mrs. Harris were out in their cars, making a ramshackle little caravan of two service-weary, decrepit autos, heading toward Mrs. Harris' house which turned out to be large and in a good Cleveland neighborhood, but in disrepair equal to either woman's vehicle. They parked and Mrs. Harris waved Rose toward the house. On her way up the walk Rose noticed a neighbor holding a rake, staring at both of them intently. He was a youngish man, dressed in running shorts—courting influenza in the still brisk spring, Rose thought. She half met his eyes but he didn't smile or make any sort of friendly gesture.

Mrs. Harris ushered Rose into a dark house and down a hallway and into a huge kitchen. As soon as she entered, Rose was hit with a reek which she quickly identified as cats. There were cats, cats, cats everywhere, gently moving through the dimness of the hallways and rooms, giving the house a constant shifting quality. It smelled like a cat box testing facility. But the house was blessed; Rose noticed a nice wooden crucifix prominently displayed on one wall. It had dried palm leaves stuck behind it, and Rose could tell it was the kind of crucifix that had a little hidden compartment for holy water.

The kitchen was dark and cavernous and on the table were instant coffee and powdered creamer and a half empty packet of fig newtons. There were dozens of opened cans of cat food strewn everywhere on floor and counters. To Rose it seemed that cats of all ages, sizes, types, were gazing at her lazily, and one *jeté*-ed into her lap when she sat down, but then quickly hopped off again. Mrs. Harris rattled around with cups and saucers. She put them down on the table, shoving aside tiny brightly colored paper birds. Rose picked one up and examined it more closely.

"Know how to fold?" asked Mrs. Harris, taking a seat next to Rose. "I've got a court date in front of me, but the problem is that my lawyer is in the hospital with kidney stones. I'm working on origami cranes for him. If we make a thousand it's an aid in his recovery. Old Japanese custom." Mrs. Harris showed Rose how to fold the paper into the birds. Each one took a few minutes; Rose guesstimated that there were about fifty completed.

The cat reek was now just a warm essence in the background. A kitten had leaped to the table top and was batting around a paper bird; Mrs. Harris picked the cat up and dropped it to the floor, and the women continued working.

"My children want my money, so they've hired some lawyers. They think I'm criminally insane or some such thing because I don't keep a neat house," Mrs. Harris told Rose. She chuckled. "But I've been around a lot longer than they have, so I know what's what. What's what is that the money's mine, and there's no law against messy people having money. And the purse string holder holds the power. So let's just say the force is with us." She laughed again. "I don't mind going to court. It's a great way to get out of spending the holidays with those children for the rest of my life." She folded quietly for a few minutes. "I just wish I could figure out some way to rescind their college educations," she said. She looked up at Rose. "But I guess that gets us into the realm of magic."

Rose smiled. "Oh, there's a few things I'd like to rescind about *my* children, too," she said. "Paying for them to attend non-Catholic universities—well, that's at the top of my list." Oh, here's a new friend, Rose thought happily. How pleasant, happening into a soulmate so easily.

Rose finished her coffee and left after exchanging phone numbers with Mrs. Harris and agreeing on a coffee date for the next week. On her way down the driveway to her car, Rose was stopped by the neighbor, the young man from next door. He ran over and waved to her. His shorts again reminded Rose of the folly of youth—not knowing how to dress, taking parents to court, living thousands of miles from widowed mothers. She missed his introductory remarks, but then she tuned in: "… stinks, can't you smell it? She's got to clean that up, I've got children to worry about, if she wants to sell that house I'm in touch with someone who'll give her a very fair price. Her kids I know have tried but I realize family relations can get awkward, maybe you're a friend who can be more objective…" Rose noticed his eyes get a little less direct after a while; he was now examining her and the way she held her handbag and clutched the lapels of her overcoat. No, she thought to herself, no, I'm not going to respond to his secular humanism, I'm not going to listen when he gives me the name of a good realtor. She glanced toward the house, hoping Mrs. Harris wasn't watching this and reading it is treachery, but the house was closed, all curtains drawn. Rose looked back at the man and noticed his eyes dart toward her car, and when he finally made eye contact again she very clearly saw a tired, oh-no, here's-another-one look in his eyes. "OK, well, just try to help her clean up a little bit," he said, turning away, giving a shoulder shrug as a goodbye.

So that was how Rose and Mrs. Harris met, gravitated toward each other, two incipient bag ladies, parachuting gleefully out of middle class respectability. Mrs. Harris was actually quite well off and owned her home free and clear, but she ambled about the suburbs of Cleveland in moth-eaten clothes and carried an old May Company hat box with small holes punched in the sides. It worked perfectly as a cat carrier. She perused the classified ads and followed up free kitten announcements. She went to church, visited animal shelters and pet shops. She stood next to strangers and muttered things at them, and generally in all respects made her adult children cringe. Somehow she managed to keep a late 60's Buick running.

And Rose, well, all her life she'd been variously miscast: as a luscious teenager who'd inadvertently stolen her sisters' boyfriends, as a WAC in World War II, as a femme fatale through much of the fifties who'd lured and married an infertile woman's husband, then as a bridge-playing suburbanite and mother of four in the sixties who'd suddenly lost her looks, her interest in sex, and her husband's affection—these three things happening in such a jumble that she couldn't determine what precipitated what or how things were interconnected. And then the seventies and eighties brought the early death of her husband and her children's flight, and Rose metamorphosed into a member of a right wing religious cult, just barely drawing the line at becoming a full scale member of Operation Rescue. None of these roles had ever truly been home. Rose, a youngish sixty-five, continued the search.

Ted, Rose's brother and apartment mate, was rooting around between the chairback and the pillow, searching for the missing remote control. God, you got addicted to that thing. Ted's entire life these days was TV and print. He watched the tube till his eyes were bleary and read everything he could get his hands on, though his literary tastes ran to serious fiction, and he'd always thought that in another life he'd have been a Norman Mailer, a Philip Roth. Except of course that he wasn't Jewish. Now he was trying to think of a polite way to tell Rose to stop buying bargain candy and coffee cake, and to start bringing home fruit, vegetables and meat. Housebound since a serious stroke, Ted was dependent on Rose to help him meet life's necessities. She'd moved in a year and a half ago, and she still hadn't really settled into being a decent domestic partner. If only she'd cook a decent meal once in a while. He'd occasionally have the energy to do it, but with his weakened faculties it took days to write out the grocery list and to convince Rose to go out and actually buy the items instead of just coming home with Kentucky Fried or (on Fridays) Arthur Treacher's fish and chips. A life-long bachelor, he'd thought it would be nice living with a woman for once; women were supposedly good at cooking, cleaning, shopping.

But not this one. This one merely filled her bedroom with religious junk of every variety and tried to pull him out of his chair and into her car so she could get him to church on Sunday. Phooey. And she'd started putting religious pamphlets on top of his library books; she'd actually inserted a Virgin Mary holy card into his library copy of *The Vicar of Wakefield*. She'd have to move out if she pulled that sort of thing on a regular basis. He didn't want to be continually reminded of the existence of organized religion.

But Rose had her good points. She was company and she provided transportation and a weird sort of comic relief: she'd drive him around town in her wreck of a Datsun— the trunk wouldn't close; she kept it tied shut with a fluorescent orange laundry line. The car was crammed with half eaten bags of candy, prayer books, clothing, beaded items purportedly made by Native Americans. She'd get angry when Ted chuckled at her church-going ways; to fool him she'd put on tennis shoes and hide a hat in a big plastic bag, and then say something about bread and eggs and head off to the grocery store. But once she got there she'd stay in her car to change into dressier shoes and adjust her hat in the rear view mirror, and then she'd drive over to the nearby Catholic church for her daily Mass fix. The apartment manager had told Ted he'd seen Rose doing this. "God forbid she get primped up in the church parking lot," the manager had said, laughing. The manager's loyalties were all with Ted, who'd lived there seventeen years. But even the manager admitted Rose was strong and cheerful; the two men had seen her jumping rope with some of the small girls from the adjacent courtyard. That had been great—this old, muffin-shaped woman skipping rope amid elfin six-year-olds. The little girls even occasionally knocked on Ted's door to ask if Rose could come out and play. So it was kind of fun having Rose around.

But she wasn't really pulling her weight as far as food and

rent went; he'd have to talk to her about that. He suspected that her business-obsessed late husband had left a tidy sum of money, and he hoped sometime in the near future Rose herself would suggest paying half the rent. He didn't want to have to call her kids; Rose wouldn't appreciate that at all. They lived way off on the west coast, and her contact with them was minimal. She was kind of an abandoned mother, but maybe there were reasons for this. She seemed to have cut them out of her life; one daughter had sent Rose airfare to go out and visit recently, but Rose had sent it back. "Why don't you go on out there?" Ted had asked. "You don't have to feel I need constant help." Rose had shrugged him off; she was in the middle of a nine week novena or something, and the time wasn't right for visits to offspring. Ted noticed it never was.

Rose never discussed her finances with Ted, but he knew she let most of her money sit in a savings account. She'd left the statement open on the kitchen table one day, and he'd gotten a glance at it. He was reassured to see that she had a fairish-sized lump and that her social security was direct deposited. So she wasn't exactly destitute. And at one point she'd mentioned she had money in treasury bonds somewhere. Even though she apparently had enough ready cash to feed herself, she was cheap about groceries. She'd explained to Ted that it had been tedious shopping and cooking for four kids for well over twenty years, and that was why she wasn't much of a grocery shopper now. Ted knew she was very generous to her church, and he knew she sent money every month to feed and clothe Latin American foundlings: Rose made a point of mentioning these things to Ted in a big-sister-bossy sort of way. And then she would pause, as if to give Ted time to mention a few of his own favorite charities. Her personal expenses were absolutely minimal; she'd told Ted quite proudly that it hadn't occurred to her to buy herself a new dress in over seventeen years. But she admitted that every year or two she'd go out and splurge on herself; she'd spend one hundred dollars or so on two pairs of comfortable shoes.

Ted grasped his cane and forced himself out of his chair. He made his way to the kitchen. Perhaps Rose may have picked up a few items. He couldn't really tell. Oh well. Dinner would be a can of corned beef hash and a small jar of marinated artichoke hearts. Not so bad, really.

Rose and Mrs. Harris got into the habit of dropping in on each other for coffee, but one rainy Tuesday Mrs. Harris knocked on the door and found only Ted. He invited her in to wait out the storm. He'd been watching "Jeopardy", and she joined him. They sat and watched it quietly, neither one bothering to call out the correct questions before the contestants did. Ted felt vaguely annoyed about something, and when he stopped to analyze it he realized it was because Rose had promised to take him to the library that morning, but she was off god-knew-where, and so he was stuck entertaining the old lady. An idea popped into his head; well, what the heck, he thought. "Would it be out of your way for you to take me to the library and then back here again?" he asked Mrs. Harris during one of the commercials.

She smiled immediately and nodded her head. "Why, certainly. That sounds like fun. When were you thinking of going?"

"Oh, we can go when this is over if that's all right with you."

"Jeopardy" ended when no one could name the architect of the U.S. Capitol building. Mrs. Harris handed Ted his cane and helped him shuffle to her car. "Do you want to drive?" she asked him.

"No," he said, slightly taken aback.

"Oh, well," said Mrs. Harris. "I thought you might enjoy it. Dominant male and all that."

"I don't mind being chauffeured," said Ted.

At the library Mrs. Harris took a seat in the periodical section and peered at an old copy of *Field and Stream*. Ted made his way slowly over to the new fiction section, and was instantly pleased to find a copy of Salman Rushdie's *Satanic Verses*. He picked it up and checked it out, and he and Mrs. Harris got back in the car and drove to the apartment. Rose still wasn't around, so Ted and Mrs. Harris said good-bye, and Ted dropped into his chair and took a nap.

When Ted awoke, he actually smelled something cooking, and sure enough, there was Rose, bustling around in the kitchen. "Stuffed green pepper, coming right up," she announced when she noticed he was awake. "It's left over from the old folks' meal today. It was my turn to serve."

Ted flipped on McNeil-Lehrer, and the two of them watched it while the meal reheated. Rose made occasional snide remarks about the professors and other experts, but she had nothing negative to say about Judy Woodruff. "That woman is so exquisite-looking and gracious. She's perfection," said Rose.

"Where's that book?" Ted muttered, half to himself. It was nine o'clock-ish, his time to settle in for a few hours of reading, but he couldn't find the Rushdie book. He pushed aside an old newspaper and some of Rose's church bulletins. "Where'd I put that damn book?" he asked outloud.

Rose came in from the other room but then returned to her room immediately.

"You didn't see my new library book, red and black cover?" he called to her.

"No," called Rose from the other room.

I must have left it in Mrs. Harris' car, Ted thought, slumping back into his chair, disappointed, cheated out of a good read.

He picked up a *Sports Illustrated* but then let it drop. He clearly remembered carrying the book into the house and putting it right there, in the usual place for library books that he planned to read immediately. How had it vanished into thin air? This was a definite Alzheimer's symptom. He thought about his father's senility and how it had been the bane of everyone's existence for nearly seven years. That had been quite a while back, before Alzheimer's was a household word and universal fear. Oh well, thought Ted. Heredity will out. He fell asleep in his chair.

Ted opened his eyes to sunlight streaming in the window and birds chirping. He'd slept all night in his chair. *Where's that damn book* was the first thing that popped into his head. Then he laughed out loud; he'd just proved to himself that he wasn't senile after all. "Rose?" he called, just testing, really; he knew she was always out and about every morning, making her runs to church services. No answer. He was positive he hadn't left the book in Mrs. Harris' car, but just to be on the safe side he decided to give her a call. It took him a while to hunt up her phone number but he finally found it jotted on a Mass schedule in a pile of other stuff Rose kept by the phone. He'd learned to live with her disorganization, or at least to work around it. Considering Mrs. Harris' age, he let the phone ring about fifteen times, and sure enough she finally answered. Ted felt a little sheepish asking an eighty-year-old to trot out to her car and search for the book. But she was very pleasant. "Well why not. Of course. I need some fresh air anyway. I'll go out right now and look," she said, and then he heard the receiver banging, bouncing. He could hear her tromping down her hallway, and then there was no sound at all for the longest time, and he found himself reading the bishop's annual letter reminding all good Catholics of their duty to tithe. He shuffled through the pile, looking for something more entertaining but it was all just lunatic fringe stuff that Rose collected so avidly. "Hello?" he heard, and there was Mrs. Harris back on the line. "You're sure you checked it out?" she asked. "I couldn't feel all the way under the seats, but I don't think it's in there," she said.

"Well, thank you very much anyway," Ted told her. "Oh, and thanks again for taking me to the library yesterday." He hung up just as the door opened and in walked Rose with a large box of doughnuts.

"Are you sure you didn't see that book *Satanic Verses* around?" Ted asked her again. A suspicion was beginning to nag at him. She was futzing with the doughnuts and she didn't answer. He looked up at her and noticed her pursed lips.

"Rose? You didn't see my book, did you?" he repeated.

She looked agitated but refused to make eye contact. She sat down on the edge of a chair and folded her hands atop the box of doughnuts. "Listen, Ted. I want to talk about decency for a moment here."

"Decency?" asked Ted. "We can talk about decency later. I was asking you a very simple question about a book."

"I took it back," said Rose shortly. She shot him a severe look.

Ted wondered if he was hearing correctly. "You did what?"

"I took it back. I didn't want it in this residence," said Rose.

"What are you talking about? Are you talking about my library book, a red and black book called *Satanic Verses*?"

"Ted, I'm sorry, but I don't even want to go into this with you. I took it back. It's not something to keep lying around the house. It's not something that should be kept *anywhere*." Rose spoke fiercely, now glaring at Ted. He noticed that her lower lip was starting to quiver. "Standards must be upheld," she said. "Some people have a duty to set up and keep standards."

Ted sat and just absorbed this for a moment. It was hilarious, really. "You did what?" he asked finally. "You did what with my book?"

"I took it back. I told you. I took it back to the library," said Rose, now in an irritated voice. She opened the doughnut box and then closed it and put it down on the coffee table. She stood up.

"You took it back to the library," repeated Ted. He realized that something was happening to him, some unusual emotion was taking over. "And by what right, by what liberty did you take it back without consulting me?" he asked evenly. God, he thought to himself, I'm really angry. This woman has finally done it.

"By my right as a good Catholic woman," Rose said fiercely, riled up now, sniffing out the possibility of moral debate. She stood there, still in her coat, clutching her handbag, ready for combat. "I mean by my right as a Catholic. I'm trying to be a good one, but it's very difficult. It's a constant effort, we're all such sinners, and I know I'm one of the weakest. But that man is a troublemaker, a blasphemer, and I won't have his book in my house."

"Oh, for crying out loud," said Ted. "It was my book, and it's my apartment, and I'd ask you to have a little respect for me and my private property." This was getting tedious and bizarre; he didn't relish suddenly being on the receiving end of a harridan's frustrations. "All I can say is that I'd like that book back or else we're going to have to rethink this living situation."

Rose's face was a hard, angry scowl. She picked up the doughnut box but then put it back down. She gave Ted a glare and stalked out of the apartment.

She better come back with that book, Ted thought to himself, torn between anger and amusement. She was so goofy — who did she think she was? And her politics were all goofy, too; did she even realize that the Ayatollah had put out a contract on

Rushdie's life? But probably there was more to it, probably one of her priest friends had made some weird convoluted arguments about Rushdie tempting fate or something like that. Oh well. He picked up the clicker and watched the last half of "Yan Can Cook" on public television. He hoped Rose would come back with the book. He couldn't really imagine her returning it to the library so quickly; she just wasn't that efficient—she'd probably just thrown it into her car or something.

Rose walked in later that evening. She put some magazines down on the coffee table. She was so stone-faced and forbidding that at first Ted didn't dare say anything; he kind of assumed she'd silently hand him back the library book. But she didn't; she seemed to be pretending to ignore the whole issue, and he felt a flare of anger. He got up and went into the kitchen where he found Rose bustling around with a can of tomato sauce and some sort of meat chop, Betty Crocker all of a sudden.

"Well, where's my book?" he asked.

She looked up at him; a scared look flit across her face. "Ted, listen, I'm sorry, but I couldn't get it back because I don't have a library card." She paused and glanced at him. "I could return it without one but I certainly can't check it out without one. You're just going to have to get involved in something else." She walked out to the living room and returned with a magazine. *Scientific American*. She handed it to Ted. "I bought this for you."

Ted took the magazine from her but immediately threw it down on the counter. "All right. That's it. I think you'd better look for a new place to live as of the first of next month. Either that or get me a replacement copy of *Satanic Verses*. Get yourself a library card, for god's sake. Or just buy a copy. Either that or move out." He kept his voice even and not overly grouchy. He wished he could shout a little bit, but he just hadn't had enough practice.

Rose's face darkened into fire and brimstone. "All right. If that's the way you feel about it. I'm just trying to keep some Catholic sense of decency around here." She stopped talking and began cutting bits of fat off the meat, but then she put down the knife. She looked up at Ted. "You seem to have completely forgotten about Mother and her great devotion to the Church," she said. Tears were welling up.

Ted couldn't control himself; he let out a hoot. "Listen, Rose. I'm just asking for a little common courtesy around here. You're kind of my guest here, and I guess it's just not going to work out a lot longer."

Rose rinsed off her hands quickly, dried them, went into her bedroom and firmly shut the door. Ted suddenly felt exhausted. He found his eyes resting on the *Scientific American*. It looked fresh, inviting. He picked it up, took it into his bedroom and read himself to sleep.

Rose was up and out again early the next morning, and while Ted made his morning coffee he realized that something was still nagging at him. He thought about it for a moment and then realized that he didn't really trust Rose to actually have returned the library book. Eventually he'd probably be charged with losing the book. Knowing Rose, she probably just hid it somewhere in the hopes that it would vaporize. But he remembered her definitely saying that she'd returned it. Oh, god, this was becoming a depressing mess. He decided he'd search around the apartment a bit; it might be hidden under her bed or somewhere quite obvious. He stood on the threshold of her room and actually peered into it for a few moments but something kept him from advancing further. It was just too taboo for him to rifle through her room. Besides, it would inevitably be some sort of

Pandora's box. He suddenly had the brainstorm of calling the library. He wasn't at all surprised when they said no, the book hadn't been returned yet. Are you certain, he persisted. Of course we're certain; we're computerized, the librarian assured him a little frostily. He hung up the phone and briefly enjoyed his sense of oh-I-knew-it. But he also realized that Rose had crossed the last line. He wouldn't quite throw her things out the front door of the apartment, but this was it. She couldn't stay here another night. She had money; she could find a little furnished place easily enough.

"You set off a lot of ill when you bought that black devil statue for your brother Dan, you remember that summer he had those problems and then you just came along and on the surface appeared to help." Rose was writing a quick letter to her daughter out in California. She sat at a table in the library after searching around for that book. She'd finally asked the librarian and had been told it was out but she could sign a reserve slip. "But I just returned it," Rose had said. The librarian had responded that it was a vastly popular book, and had repeated the offer about reserving. Rose glared at her. "I'll think about it," she'd said shortly. Then she'd sat down and started the letter. She was writing it on the back of a library flier about a junior reading league. "And of course I'd love to come out to San Francisco to see that son of yours, but I have too many things to do here, and Ted needs me, and besides, I don't have that many trips left in me. I'm getting too old to travel—what would I want to do in San Francisco anyway? Why don't we meet in Mexico City and then we can all go visit our Lady of Guadalupe? You keep saying you have a nice big house, and I can tell you're very proud of it, but that house is for more children, it's not meant for guest visitors. You have to be careful, you'll be beyond the child-bearing years soon." Rose stopped writing and tried to collect her thoughts for a moment. She suspected that her daughter had called and that Ted had told her about the book incident. There was no real evidence for this, but Rose felt it in her bones. So she'd decided to take the bull by the horns and to respond to the situation as directly as possible. "I'll come out and visit when I find time in my schedule, but I'm warning you right now that my main object when I'm out there is to make sure you've set up some sort of Catholic training schedule for your son." She'd come to the end of the paper. Maybe she wouldn't continue. She felt a little better, after the initial defeat of having been forced to enter the library in search of that book. Well, it wasn't here. Ted would have to just forget about it. She got up to leave, and decided to drop the letter into the trash. But it was a shame to waste things, so she turned it over and put it back on the pile of library notices. She left the library lightheartedly, feeling that she'd accomplished something.

Mrs. Harris dropped in at Ted's to pick up Rose for a quick lunch out, but Ted informed her that Rose had moved out rather suddenly. He assured Mrs. Harris that he'd tell Rose to call her as soon as he saw her again. Mrs. Harris started to leave, but then turned around and very sweetly asked Ted if he'd like her to take him to the library. Ted was delighted with the offer; he'd been calling the library every three days to see if the book had been returned, and on the last call they'd said yes, it was in. So he got his cane and slowly followed her out to her car. At the library he found *Satanic Verses* and checked it out again.

"What book did you get?" asked Mrs. Harris on the way back out to the car. Ted held it up for her. She looked at the cover and then gave him a knowing look. "Oh, so that other time you hadn't quite checked it out after all."

Ted didn't have the heart to tell her what his sister had pulled on him. Mrs. Harris was a nice friend for Rose and it wasn't his part to trample on people's friendships. But thinking of Rose still annoyed him; she'd done him wrong.

One afternoon Rose sat in Mrs. Harris' kitchen giving her advice about what to wear to the court case. Rose also told her about the library book contretemps with Ted. Mrs. Harris gave her a startled look. "You took his library book?" She paused, ruminating a bit. "Isn't that a case of tampering with the public library system?" She looked slightly disturbed, but then her face smoothed out. "Oh, well, I suppose you're more of an expert on these sorts of moral questions than I am. I leave these issues to the people who really know about them." She put some opened cat food tins on the floor and then ambled to her chair. She sat down and then nodded her head for a while, deep in thought. "It reminds me of something. It reminds me a little bit of the time I was on vacation in Mexico and I visited a church where there was a pamphlet explaining all the positive aspects of the Spanish inquisition." Mrs. Harris stared out into space for a moment, thinking about the cool interior of that Mexican church. "I remember being kind of surprised, but I couldn't really follow all the logic because the pamphlet was in Spanish. But I was glad to find out that those inquisitors really *did* have some sound reasoning going on there, that it wasn't just a black piece of history like we're sometimes led to believe." Mrs. Harris nodded again, seeing the Mexican statue of the Madonna in her mind's eye. Rose nodded, too. She'd been sure Mrs. Harris would understand, and now she felt even more righteous, and part of a rich historical tradition.

Mrs. Harris appeared in court in her usual disrepair. Her lawyer was healthy again. Rose sat by her friend. The judge berated Mrs. Harris' children, threw out the case, and ordered them to pay all court costs. But he also pointed at Mrs. Harris and ordered her to have her house professionally cleaned within a month. Rose helped Mrs. Harris cost-compare various cleaning companies, but still the cleaning bill came to over a thousand dollars.

On the days of the cleaning, Rose picked up Mrs. Harris and the two women spent hours at church, malls with pet shops, and a local Denny's. When the job was complete, Rose dropped Mrs. Harris off to inspect her radically altered abode and Rose stood outside watching the cleaners leave with all their modern looking machines. They'd shooed all the cats out of the house for the cleaning, but even as they packed up their gear Rose could see cats stealthily creeping back in.

The neighbor, the jogger, was suddenly at Rose's elbow. "Well, I guess the problem is solved for a little while," he said. He and Rose stood together and watched as cat after cat slipped back into the house. "I wonder if the Humane Society would be interested in coming out here to see this," he said, half to himself.

Rose bristled. "The Humane Society? What are you talking about? These cats lead a wonderful life here. I don't think you understand the basic tenets of the Humane Society."

The man looked at her and shrugged. "OK, you're right. So I'm being kind of a creep. But everyone gets creepy when they begin worrying about property values. It's just one of the down aspects of home ownership and the American way." He smiled bleakly at her.

Rose felt a little softened toward him. She wondered what his name was. He seemed like a smart-enough fellow. She was thinking she'd maybe look at a few little houses, she was thinking she'd buy herself a small doll house to hang her hat for a while.

Or maybe a condo. All she needed was some sort of granny unit. She vaguely remembered this fellow talking about realtors. Maybe he'd be someone who could perhaps recommend a decent one. She'd have to concentrate a little; where exactly had those bonds gone?

At the moment Rose was without a closet, a phone number, a bed. It wasn't much of an inconvenience, it was only temporary. It was liberating, actually. She'd spent a few nights at an economy motel, but then she discovered she could park her car in the far corner of almost any large parking lot and catnap through the night. Her car was a nice domain. She knew she could probably move in with Mrs. Harris if she wanted to. And an elderly couple she saw every morning at church had noticed her changing shoes while she sat in her car in the church lot, and they'd come over and seen all the piles of clothes in Rose's back seat. The old woman of the couple had quavered that they had an extra room if that would be at all useful. Rose had smiled at them. "I'm between apartments," she'd said. She'd kind of liked the way it sounded. It made her sound gay-divorcee, merry widowesque. She was free, kind of like a hummingbird.

Suburban Living at Its Finest

So Matt, my husband, is gazing ahead laser-like, testosterone all involved in thoughts of gigantic rat traps, the snapping kind, the bloated big brothers of mouse-catching ones. (Mice are *fine* little creatures. Mice can be kept as *pets!* Not so those pestilential giants.) We're in bed, and I realize it's my male human against one lone rat, the two in mortal combat. It's a sunny Saturday morning in Westchester, home of the plush, the green.

"Hairspring, Jane. It's just a matter of making the trap more hairspring. I'm going to *get* that rat, Jane. I'm going to get him," says Matt. "He's come and eaten the peanut butter. I just haven't made it hairspring enough."

"All right, all right," I say, "Hairspring it up, then. And in the meantime, how about Charlie's trap?" I ask, referring to an elderly neighbor a few doors down, an avid foe of squirrel and opossum. "How about his little have-a-heart trap he's always using around his place? He'll lend it to us."

Matt looks at me. He breathes deeply in and out, a gladiator in training. "I'm going to get that rat. My trap is going to get him. It's just a matter of time."

The truth is, it's been over a week since said rat has been scuffling around below our bird feeders, near the small shed that holds our garbage bins. The rat has twice, thrice, gobbled the peanut butter from Matt's traps and gotten away. I fear the rat may have learned a thing or two in the last few days, may now be a creature of enhanced empiric knowledge.

"The thing I hate the most is how *comfortable* he looks, how *at home* he feels eating those seeds. He's like, wow, I've really hit pay dirt," says Matt.

I try to dispel from my mind's eye the sight of that long goddamned rat tail trailing calmly along the ground as its owner roots around down there in our garden. "I'm going to get Charlie's trap today," I say.

"Don't bother Charlie," Matt says. "He's an eighty-year-old man. *I'll* get that rat. It's my job. I'll get the fucker. I feel it in my bones."

"Oh, I see. You feel it in your bones. That's so comforting," I'm saying, but I'm interrupted, for my husband rolls over and grabs me.

"Let me feel it, let me feel it in *your* bones," he says, dragging me closer to him.

"Shhh. Alex will hear, and you're hurting me," I say.

"Let's fuck," Matt stage whispers.

"Oh no," I say quickly. "It's late. There's Alex. And we've got to get up."

"Alex is nine," Matt persists. "It's probably good for him to hear a little sex."

"No. I just...*no*. It's too late now."

"It's too late. It's too early. It's too dark It's too light. It's too... Christ, Jane," says Matt, turning away from me in disgust and getting up.

We're at the breakfast table and I've absentmindedly poured bowls of Cheerios for Alex and myself and forgotten about Matt, who's been briefly out in the yard checking for the hideous unmentionable, and now he's measuring out coffee.

"Doesn't Dad get any?" Alex asks. Yes, he's nine. He loves his father.

"Oh," I say. "I don't know. Matt? Cheerios?" I ask.

Matt looks at me and sighs dramatically. "It ate the peanut butter again."

I wave my arms wildly in shut-up gestures. Luckily, I'm neatly positioned behind Alex. Matt and I are keeping the rodent a dark secret from him. The knowledge of nearness of rats might erode his hearty sense of suburban...cleanliness and godliness. And besides, kids have a way of letting things slip out, and we don't want the neighbors to know.

"*What* ate the peanut butter again?" asks Alex.

"Alex," I say, "maybe you could go enjoy a few cartoons. Little treat for once." I smile at him. "Take your breakfast."

Alex looks at me and smells...a rat. But he takes his bowl and disappears up the stairs.

"Fuck," I say to Matt, sitting down to my cereal. "That goddamned thing." What if it bites Alex, bites *me!* Or Matt — but then Matt getting bitten would be more a line-of-duty type thing. That too of course would be awful.

"Maybe you should just sit out there with a shotgun or something," I say.

Matt gazes at me analytically for a moment, and a weird NRA glint comes into his eyes. "Don't think I haven't thought about it. I'd *like* to. It'd be easy. He'd come out and *pop,* that would be the end of it."

"Well, why don't you just call the Larchmont police and ask if you could borrow one of their guns for a night or two."

"Right, Jane, right. Blow it to bits with a *38*. Good plan. There'd be nothing left. You can't shoot around here anyway. It'd ricochet off. The police wouldn't let you."

"Oh, thank you for the info. I can't shoot around here. So I'll call Charlie and get his trap."

"No. I told you. We don't need it. My traps are going to work."

I pause a moment, feeling a certain reality is not quite sinking in. "You know what?" I say. "I'm getting the feeling you're losing sight of the bigger picture. The bigger picture is to eliminate Rat by any means necessary. The bigger picture is *not* a personal vendetta between you and Rat."

Matt turns his laser-like glare on me very briefly. "It *is* a vendetta. It's a struggle to the death." And he gets up to leave for the monthly meeting of his bonsai club. They'll stand around and gaze upon tiny tortured trees, and contemplate snipping bits here and there.

"Ask them for advice on catching a rat," I say.

Matt gives me a dirty look. "I *know* how to catch it. I'm *going* to catch it, Jane," he says with that hormone-laced certainty.

"Oh, come on, *try*. You could just ask someone there, someone knowledgeable. Just pull the most knowledgeable person aside and ask them *sotto voce*," I say. "Do you know what *sotto voce* means?" I ask.

"I know what *fuck you* means," he says. "Fuck you, Jane." And off Matt goes, whistling, no less.

As soon as he's out the door I pick up the phone and call Charlie, who's eighty-three and spry, spry as the devil.

"Your trap, Charlie. I'm calling about your trap. We have a small animal living in the shed, I think." I can't bring myself to say the R word, not in polite company. "Could we borrow your trap?"

"Yeah, yeah, my trap," says Charlie, and over the phone wires I feel him shift into alert. "You can use it. Whatcha got over there?"

"I don't know," I say, "maybe a possum or a sk...squirrel." I catch myself before saying skunk; I know Charlie will balk at possibly befouling his trap. Oh boy, how fibs lead us down the rosy path....

"Oh, you know, just a, you know, Small Bad Animal," I say, playing to Charlie's inordinate and long-lived hatred of all forms of non-human suburban life: insects, rabbits, birds, you name it. You should hear him on crows, benighted creatures who persist in rooting in his lawn for grubs. Over the wires I sense his alertness has shifted to super-alert. A noxious animal and a mystery, too!

"Yeah, I'll bring it over," he tells me, his voice all cagey and vibrant.

"I'll come and get it," I say.

"No, no, I'll bring it," he repeats firmly. Charlie is a virile eight-three. Matt, Matt is a virile forty-four. The rat, I guess wildly, is a virile one or two.

Ten minutes later the front door bell rings, and there's Charlie, holding a have-a-heart trap carefully at arm's length. It's all peanut butter-ed and ready to go.

"Where we gonna put it?" he asks, and I recognize the ether of super-alert upon which he is now floating.

"Hmmm," I say, wondering if old Charlie can make it all the way down the rocky path to the shed at the back of the house.

"I'll take it," I say, reaching out for the trap. "No, no," he says. "It'll snap. Let me put it. Where's your husband?" he asks.

"He's not here at the moment," I say. "I'll show you," And I lead Charlie down the proverbial garden path, but this one is in fact literal. He doesn't grill me again about what type animal, and I realize a kind of tact is at work here, for this is most certainly not the first time that rats have reared their ugly heads in well-mannered suburbia.

"So. Have you been thinking about the sex thing?" Matt asks me in bed that night.

"The sex thing? What sex thing?"

"Oh, come on Jane. Our *sex* thing. Our *lack thereof.* Our *I'm-about-to-find-a mistress* thing."

"Oh, that."

"Yeah, that. We've got to talk about it. We've got to do something. It's been, I don't know, since my last birthday that we had sex. And if I start judging the frequency *per annum,* I mean, it's clear we have a problem."

"Yes, yes, yes, we have a problem," I say, and I instruct myself to stay calm and think up a quick load of baloney. "But let's deal with a little reality here. We've been married sixteen years, together for eighteen. Sexlessness *sets in.* It *does.* In many cases. It's part of the human condition. It's a normal aspect of the ongoingness of life."

"Oh, thank you, thank you for that wisdom, Jane. So should I just *ongoing* to someone who's interested? Should I have affairs? I can't cope with the idea of a sexless future! I love sex!"

"Hmm. I don't know. I guess so. But then she'll fall in love with you and you'll have to leave me and then you're just in that vicious cycle, you know—new wife, new family." I'm making an effort to keep my voice hypnotic, narcotizing. "Really, face it, it's normal for a couple, for *one* of the couple to tire of sex."

"Good night, Jane. Thanks for caring," Matt says, and turns over.

"Hey, do you want to hear something funny?" I say. "I was in what's the name of that big bookstore, the one in Scarsdale across from Lord and Taylor."

"Oh yeah, I know. The big one with coffee."

"Yes, and there was this old man, he was definitely seventy-five and he was looking at a girlie magazine, a real nudie hardcore type, not just *Penthouse.*

"Well, good for him. I'm glad *someone* is having fun."

"And he was sitting in one of those big couches and everyone could see what he was looking at, the whole page, I mean he wasn't in the least embarrassed or covert."

"Good. Sounds great."

"But of course I didn't sit down next to him even though I was looking for a place to sit. I didn't want to...cramp his style."

"Well, blow me down, Jane. You actually did something to enhance someone's sex life. Blow me down."

"All right, all right. Good night," I say hastily. Matt is snoring gently in seconds.

The horrible secret Matt and I hold tightly in our chests is that this is rat number two. One night a few months back I opened the door to the basement and from the top of the forty pound bag of sunflower seeds slithered a shadow, a dark shadow which then spilled softly down the stairs. I slapped my hands to my cheeks as beautifully as that little *Home Alone* star, and I stood there paralyzed, shocked at that liquid furriness. It wasn't a mouse. What it *was* wasn't clear exactly, *not precisely,* but it wasn't a mouse. I informed Matt. The very next morning while quietly reading *The Times,* he heard a tiny rattling, a feeble scuffling, and he rushed to the basement door, pulled it open, and slam-crash closed the seed bag, trapping the interloper, whatever it was, inside. He didn't look into the bag at all, he reported to me later. He merely rushed it outside and clapped it quickly into the garbage can, and (conveniently!) the trash pickup was due in a few hours.

"Are you sure it was a rat?" I grilled him that morning. "How do you know if you didn't actually see it? Why didn't you look more carefully?"

Matt was perturbed, impatient. "I'm not going to open the trash bin and *dig* for it. It's a rat."

"But how do we really know? This isn't very scientific."

"It's a rat, it's a rat," Matt snapped as we heard the garbage truck rumble nearer and nearer. We watched each other and continued drinking our morning coffee. I thought about leaping up, running outside, and doing a little last-minute rodent research.

Or at least warning the garbageman. But I merely took my cup and went to the front window. I watched a heavily-gloved (thank god) G-man pick up the plastic bin and tilt it into the truck. He nonchalantly one-handed the bin back onto our front lawn, and he was gone.

"So," I said, returning to the kitchen. "You're sure it was a rat?"

Matt gave me his usual long suffering look. "I know what a rat looks like, Jane," and he headed out the door for work.

"But you didn't see it. How exactly do you know?" I called after him. "What close experience with *rodents* do you actually have?" He was on the sidewalk now so I had to hiss this so neighbors wouldn't hear. Rodents: that word I hissed particularly viciously. Matt gave a dismissive little wave and continued on his way to MetroNorth.

Phone rings. It's old Charlie chomping at the bit for a little news of the hunt; it's been a week. "Anything in that trap?" he asks. "Want me to come and take another look?"

"No, Charlie, there's nothing," I say. For some reason the rat hasn't been enticed into that metal box. This has its good points: it damages your heart a little to look at a caged wild rat close up. *My* heart, I mean. Charlie—he'd surely relish it. "No, Charlie, no, nothing in the trap. I'll clean it out and bring it back to you this afternoon," I say.

"Nah, nah, I'm coming over now," says Charlie. "I'll get it."

I rush outside in hopes of cleaning the trap before Charlie arrives, but he's there in a twinkling.

"So, no go," says Charlie, looking forlornly at the empty trap. I feel a little bad that this is turning out so anti-climactic for him, and I wish I could fluff him up somehow, but I can't think of anything.

"Well, wudda ya gonna do," he says. "Ya gotta do," he tells me philosophically. "Ya gotta do." A black squirrel corkscrews its way up a nearby tree, and Charlie catches sight of it. "Sons-a-bitches," he mutters half to himself. "Goddam sons-a-bitches." He shakes his head and slowly ambles home.

Have I mentioned the special agony of discussing rat problems in the local hardware store? It is a subtle thing; there is a certain quivering tension in the air when the wholesome suburbanite in fresh faded cottons must seek rat-relief advice so close to the Ralph Lauren paints and the glistening array of brass cabinet pulls. I stated my situation in what I thought was a down-to-earth and nuts-and-bolts sort of way.

"*What* sort of a problem?" the clerk shouted back at me.

"I think it might be a rat," I say, trying to keep my voice steady and respectably audible, trying not to let it dwindle to a covert and frantic whisper. "My *husband* says he thinks it's a rat," I say, for once thrilling to the existence of said excellent being, that great repository of blame, of accusation, the *husband*.

"*One* rat?" persists the clerk.

"One? Oh, yes, I'm sure. Oh, god, I hope so," I say. "Yes. One."

And he points me out the best trap, the surest poison. And finally he smiles. "Hey, people come in here all the time," he tells me. "Town's crawlin' with 'em." But I sense he's sized me up a tad differently from how he sizes up someone asking for a pint of spackling putty or a replacement fluorescent tube. I am somewhat sullied, I believe. My aura and the aura of my loved ones haven't quite kept rats off. How primeval of me to feel so. But I do. I suppose this is an issue of some sort, an issue I could work on. There are scores of persons in Westchester willing to welcome me into their home offices and listen to me most graciously on an hourly basis, willing to then send me bills on cream colored paper.

Alex comes in the house and drops his frisbee on the kitchen floor. He gets the milk out of the refrigerator. "Dad likes sex better than you do," he tells me.

I pause for a moment. "Hmmmm?" I say.

"Dad likes sex and you don't. He wants it and you don't."

"What makes you say that?" I ask, playing for time.

"Oh, come on, Mom. It's *obvious,*" says Alex, with the irrefutable logic of the prepubescent.

"Oh," I say, and I try to think fast. "Well, you might be right. I'm not saying you're right and I'm not saying you're wrong. But I *am* saying you might as well know that life is all about *some* people wanting sex and *other* people not wanting it. You're going to bump into this all your life."

Alex gives me an exceedingly disgusted look. He drinks his milk. I sit with him and try to convey peacefulness and hope, and yes, fecundity. His disgusted look fades into query. "Mom," he says, "is it true that some people have *everything,* I mean they're men and women at the same time?"

"What do you mean *everything?*"

"You know, *everything,*" he says, pointing downward toward his crotch.

"Uh, yeah," I say. "It's true. They're called hermaphrodites."

"What do you mean?" he asks incredulously, sitting up very straight in his chair. "You mean they have a penis *and* a vagina?"

"I don't know, Alex. Yes, I think so."

Alex splutters with laughter. "Oh, my god. Mom, so that means they can have sex with themselves?!"

I go ahead and nod in agreement, and I'm immediately beset with the vision of a poor soul trying to bend his erect male member backwards to insert into his own vagina. This can't be accurate. I open my mouth to inform Alex of a fallacy here, but he's already out of the kitchen and headed into the front yard, looking for peers with whom to share his new found pearl of information.

"Maybe a Chinese herb would work," I say to Matt, as we lounge in bed watching the eleven p.m. news. His birthday is approaching and it's making me nervous. "Maybe I'll go to Chinatown and hunt around."

"What are you talking about?" Matt asks.

"You know, a Spanish fly type thing, an aphrodisiac."

"Oh. Yes. By all means. Get something. Anything."

"Maybe marijuana. Maybe that's what we need."

"Fine, Jane. Go hang out in Washington Square Park for a while and then we'll see what we can do. I mean, what *you* can do."

"OK. I'll go ask around. A Chinese herbal aphrodisiac. Some specific root, expensive and possible putrid, but effective. I'm sure there's something."

"Go for it," says Matt. "Might as well experiment."

"Oh. And another thing," I say. "We could also try the reverse strategy. I could get an herb for you."

Pause. "What are you talking about?"

"Oh, you know, a tamping-down herb. A salt-peter sort of thing."

Long sigh, beautifully rendered sigh of high disgust. "Fuck you, Jane. Fuck you. The other herb. The aphrodisiac. Focus on that."

Weeks have passed. A rodent-free peace has slowly permeated the household. Rat seems to have ambled off to some other location. Haven't actually come upon a revolting little corpse, but clumps of poison from the hardware store seem to have done the trick. "Yes. *Yes,*" shouts Matt, shooting his fist up in perfect triumph. We are sharing our usual morning coffee. "Rat is gone. *Gone!*" he crows to me, and yes, I must admit: Matt was the one who set out those poison globs of whatever. He deserves his moment of jubilation.

In a month or so it will be high skunk season. Skunk: a word suburbanites can say aloud, heads held high, a topic to be discussed in hardware stores with nary a qualm. Rat is gone. The men have all calmed down a little. There's still an odd odor around that damned shed, the indefinable scent of squalor. Its lace-like tendrils extend everywhere. We suburbanites all tacitly agree to make every effort to beat it back with a stick.

The Future

Call Up

The military telephoned. Our records indicate you've never been in the service, they told Tom. Now's your opportunity. Their tone was broad and hearty, plum-rich with male camaraderie, and it tugged at Tom's heartstrings. Our sources indicate you're sound of body and mind and an eminently sportsmanlike person, the military said to him. It's true, thought Tom instantly, I am, I'm lucky, I was a successful gold arbitrageur but it bored me and so I made a go of trees, trees, I have such a magical touch with them...and in the midst of these ruminations Tom didn't hear some of the details, although his interest perked up when the recruiter mentioned a mutual friend, an old water polo teammate. The call from the military was a complete surprise, except that of course in the background was the recent buildup in that distant exotic corner of the world where people wore flowing garb and squatted for hours in pungent outdoor markets—a far, far corner, one of the many where U.S. forces had been sent for humanitarian reasons. The buildup was due to the natives' increasing restiveness; they'd killed some U.S. GI's and dragged their nude corpses through the streets. We need some of the best and the brightest, the military told Tom on the phone. It was evening time. Tom had just enjoyed an elegant eggplant-based dinner; he was still finishing a third glass of Merlot. Young Charles sat nearby drawing carefully with a blunt pencil. I'm needed, Tom thought to himself; yes, I'll go, he told the military there on the phone. We'll accept this as a verbal commission, they said, and they gave him a time, a day, a streetcorner. You'll see the military truck, they said. All you'll have to do is step aboard. And then click the transaction was finished.

The date, it was two weeks hence, Tom noted as he jotted it down on the calendar by the phone, and then he reminded himself to tell Angie, Angie off at work, off at her small bookstore, a bookstore that proudly flew the One-World flag which Tom had given her one Christmas. Angie late tonight due to a booksigning, and then wine and chatter. She was always at the shop it seemed. That was fine; they'd set up a kids' corner and a comic book stand so Charles could spend time there and not be deprived of his mother's company. Charles. They'd forgotten to start calling him Chuckie. Tom glanced at Charles's work. A lobsterman! A lobster superhero! How clear, how deftly he drew for a six-year-old! How quickly they grew. Something nagged at Tom. His commission. What length of time had been mentioned? Tom looked at the pad in front of him but he'd only doodled; he hadn't scribbled down any hard facts, and he hadn't gotten the recruiter's phone number, either. Had he enlisted or been drafted? Would it be two years or four? Charles—his childhood would flee by. But these thoughts were interrupted by Tom's glance at the clock; bath and bedtime, and he and Charles commenced the nightly bartering, threats, cajoling. After twenty minutes of superhero chitchat, Charles let go of Tom's shirt and Tom flicked off the light and returned to the living room. An eminently sportsmanlike person, he repeated to himself.

A key scratched and Angie came in the front door. Oh it was perfect, crowded, she said, lots of books sold, no one sloshed wine on the new stock, by the way, did I get a call from and then they were lost in the minutiae of day to day life and Tom had forgotten to tell her about the call from the military, and Angie had put on a kettle for tea and clicked on the TV to scenes of soldiers leaping from helicopters, oh god, said Angie. Oh, said Tom, this reminds me, but then the soldiers were talking and he paused, the soldiers were theorizing about where lost colleagues of theirs were being held. Coke commercial.

So did you get a gift for Charles to take to that party tomorrow, Angie was asking him, and he felt a jab of annoyance. Why didn't you just bring home a book, he asked, no she said, don't you remember Charles said he hates doing that all the time, he thinks people give him dirty looks. Tom had stopped listening and was nodding. OK, OK, tomorrow, he said, but Angie was already on her way up to bed. Tom followed her and then they were asleep, but something woke him in the middle of the night; a ping, a pebble flew from the floor for some reason and hit the ceiling. Angie, can you wake up, he said. Yes, yes, of course, I'm awake, said Angie in clear bell-like tones even though it was four a.m. and she had undoubtedly been sleeping. I joined the military today, said Tom. You what, asked Angie. I joined the military, he repeated. How can that be possible, asked Angie. They called up, they pointed out I'd never done it, they appealed to my manliness, they in fact really need me, he told her. That's insane, said Angie, you can't join the military over the phone. Oh yes, said Tom, it seems you can, they said it was a contract. I don't think so, said Angie, we can call them back tomorrow, and besides, who would tend the nursery, who knows trees, and she turned aside and fell back asleep.

Things were so busy the next day and the day after that, all the business of the bookstore and Charles getting to kindergarten and back and Tom keeping an eye on the lines of Japanese maples which all of a sudden looked as if they were toying with the notion of expiring. The military, it popped up in Tom's mind briefly as he washed dirt from his hands just before lunch. But they'd said nothing about preparing; they hadn't given him a list of things to pack, and so he didn't have to do much—the prospect of getting aboard that truck didn't engage his mind except at the very periphery. He ate lunch and went back to the problem of the maples. *Acer acer*, he kept looking it up in all his books about tree disease.

Angie too it seemed had only remembered about the military in a vague sort of way, for she didn't mention it at all, but then it was Saturday: Did you call them back, she asked Tom as they scraped bits of pancake from the breakfast dishes. No, said Tom, it slipped my mind. I'll call, said Angie, and she went for the phone and picked up the mouthpiece but then put it down again. It's Saturday, they won't be there, we'll call Monday, she said. I've noticed nothing has come in the mail from them, she said, I think we can just forget about the whole thing. I don't think so, said Tom, I think I've made a commitment, and he was about to mention water polo, but then crash Charles had accidentally pushed the glass pitcher of orange juice to the floor, and one of them went for rags and a mop while the other bent to quell Charles's wails. And they forgot to continue the discussion.

Well if I have to go, I'll just go ahead and go, thought Tom and then it dropped from his brain like sand slipping down an hourglass. Angie seemed to have forgotten about it too, but that afternoon at the bookstore as he helped her slit open boxes of new books, she went on the rampage: the military, how could he, what was it but barked orders, crewcuts, rope climbing at a furious pace. She shivered and that made Tom shiver, too. How could he cope, she continued, he was forty-two, he'd never been in uniform of any type, never, and in fact none of their friends, none of their immediate families of this generation had ever been in the military, it just wasn't the thing, they were uppermiddleclass, and besides, she bought calendars annually from the War Resisters League, what had Tom been thinking of? She went on and on, and Tom found that his nods of agreement had slowed down and then frozen, and besides, not slicing into dustjackets was taking all his concentration.

The maples stabilized for a few days, and Tom turned his attention to figuring out a list of desirable fairly rapid growers for Mrs. Hayes' backyard, for the privacy wall she wanted to create. Fragrant snowbell, Mrs. Hayes would like the sound of that, or perhaps Chinese zelkova, and amidst these thoughts he caught a glimpse of his reflection in the window of his office; he noted his rapidly receding hairline. The military. Could there have been a computer error as to his age? Forty-two was quite elderly in terms of new soldier material in peace time; Angie had a point there. Had martial law been imposed while he'd been napping, had the draft quietly been put back into effect? He'd have to get to the library, he'd have to research current issues of the *New York Times*. Damn. He'd faintly suspected there would be negative consequences to his immersing himself exclusively in the literature of flora, an ever abundant corpus of books, magazines, bulletins. Angie knew about current events, but she kept most of them to herself; she didn't intrude on his private interior obsession with plant life. What a mistake that had been.

The two weeks passed, the date arrived. Tom found himself grabbing the largest of the brown canvas L. L. Bean bags; he found himself stuffing it with his highest quality and most comfortable outdoor wear. What are you doing, Angie asked him suspiciously. I'm getting ready to get aboard that truck, that military truck, he told her steadily, only the faintest note of grimness in his voice. He wouldn't permit himself to feel afraid. You've got to be kidding, she said, and she stopped and stared at him as he stolidly continued packing. You've got to be kidding, she repeated, but this time her voice was laced with a growing edge of hysteria. You can't just leave like this, she said, you can't just, she threw her arms out, looking wildly around. Tom could feel she was considering the possibility of grabbing him bodily and tossing him down, and so he let out a brief laugh, for her weight was so minimal, so leaf-like. But the laugh caused her brow to darken further. You're forgetting about Charles, she said, you can't just desert Charles, he needs you, he'll forget you in two years, how can I cope as a single mother, we need you, he'll be a stranger to you if you leave now. Tom zipped shut his bag and then let himself drop briefly onto the bed. He ordered himself to stay calm and reasonable. I know that, he told Angie. I know all that. But the die has been cast. The whole thing is underway.

What die? screamed Angie. Yes, she was screaming, it hurt his ears. What whole thing? she shrieked. We can run away, we can change our names, she shouted. Tom looked at her and shook his head. Behind her he could see the digital clock, the green numbers glowing 3:37. I've got to be there by four, he told her and he picked up his bag and headed down the stairs. Angie grabbed her pocketbook and followed.

You haven't said good-bye to Charles, he's over at your mother's, you've got to say good-bye, she screamed as they rushed down the crowded city streets toward the department store the military had specified.

Angie, get control of yourself, this is temporary, this'll be over in a flash, cope, would you kindly be adult and cope for two years, he said to her, but to himself he thought dear lord I hope it's two, I hope it's not four. Angie kept tugging at his sleeve and his mind flashed briefly to water polo and guys grabbing him underwater but that had been nothing, nothing—the real thing had been the marvelous lusty fun, the shrieks, the whooping and blasting freely and ferociously about in the water. But Angie's little bird hands were still plucking at him; yes, he thought, I'd forgotten what a blow this will be to Charles, he can't possibly understand, Angie can, she's an adult, she's read Russian and

Slavic fiction, she knows the world, but Charles, Charles, he's all tiny glee and cheer. And as he thought these things he continued marching toward the appointed site with Angie scurrying along next to him, her hair uncombed, no earrings on; she must be quite beside herself for she was usually a paragon of good grooming. Not saying good-bye to Charles: he'd planned that, he'd planned that the whole thing pass quickly like a nightmare, something to get to the rear of you and then to forget. He'd send postcards, he could see the large block print now: DEAR CHUCK, HOW ARE THE TREES?

There was nothing military-appearing at the side entrance of the department store; Tom stopped and glanced about, he put down the heavy bag. What are you looking for, asked Angie. She was panting, her eyes were crazed. The truck, I'm searching for the military truck, he told her. Help me keep my commitment, he said. She looked about wildly and said nothing. He picked up the bag and headed into the department store, but then he realized it wasn't just a store, it was an immense mall. Angie still clung to his side; what are you doing in here, she asked. Can't you understand, he said, I'm looking for the military contact, please keep your eyes open for someone in fatigues, watch for camouflage, he told her.

Finally they found their way to a far end of the mall which opened out onto a huge transport area with a busy circular drive. Seen anything military around here, Tom called out to a passing security guard. Just open your eyes, the guard said derisively, and then yes, there was the lineup of transport buses, all drab green and blotched brown. Tom's heart partly sank and partly flew into his throat. Angie grabbed Tom's arm with both her hands, but she just wasn't physically strong enough to restrain him, to keep him from stepping onto the final bus. He was there, one foot on the bottom step. A soldier had immediately found his name on a list and ticked it off, quick as a flash. What's that, the soldier asked, voice dripping in sarcasm, boot kicking at Tom's bag. It's my stuff, my belongings. The soldier laughed but said nothing more so Tom clambered aboard.

Angie stood outside the bus screaming, Tom, Tom, come back, I have to tell you something, but from inside the bus Tom just raised a hand to her in resigned farewell. What a fool I've been, Angie screamed at the top of her lungs, what a fool I was not to take all this seriously and scotch it that very first night, that very first day. No one was listening to her except Tom. He noted that people gave her only the most cursory glances. She looked around desperately. And then Tom could tell that something had popped into her head; through the window he could see her running up to another bus, a different soldier. There's a man on that bus, he's too old, he's almost fifty, she shouted loudly, assertively, pointing toward Tom who heard every word for her roar was as fierce as a lion's. But the soldier barely looked at her; he waved his arm dismissively. Tom knew that he was already as good as gone, and he wished Angie could spare herself such grief. Step back civilian, he heard the soldier bark at Angie, and then there was a huge cloud of murk and grime as the buses were started up. Good, it's over, thought Tom, but then the bus door was being pushed open and there was Angie, pummeling her way aboard. I'm on the list, I'm on the list, she screamed at the soldier. He shrugged and the bus lurched into movement; it started to make its circuit around the rotary and suddenly Tom could see Angie's face gripped with a new terror as the two stared at each other. He could see with great clarity that she was facing the hard fact that it'd be impossible to free Tom from the inside; she'd have more resources if she stayed out, and besides, she had to tend to tiny Charles. Angie turned and pushed her way to the door and shoved it open and leaped out just as the bus speeded up. Tom watched through the window as she fell flying off into the road but she didn't seem harmed; she picked herself up, she stared at the departing bus, and Tom saw she was shaking with sobs and covered with grit; her skirt was torn but it wasn't a skirt, it was a nightgown, and now she started looking about in chagrin for passersby were giving her glances of great disgust. But Tom only noticed this fleetingly for the bus was picking up speed and the last thing he saw was Angie starting to run in the direction of their house.

He knew Angie, he knew she'd work to keep her energy up; she'd get frenetic and purposeful, she'd dress properly and fly to Washington and insist on meeting with the joint chiefs of staff. She'd be bathed, made-up, she'd have put on cologne. And she'd succeed in getting through to a U.S. Senator whose cousin patronized the bookstore; yes, these things happen, the senator would tell her, these things in their infinite wisdom. She and the senator would speak of this and that, and within half an hour they'd establish that Tom had played water polo with the senator's brother. At home, Charles, fatherless, would carefully examine new issues of comic books, not bothering to glance at postcards from abroad unless hounded to by his mother. Tom was gone. What a fool he'd been, what a fool, what a fool, what a lesson; obviously they had failed at learning to nip things in the bud. Charles, fatherless. Tom, gone. At what point had he and Angie failed at paying attention? But now the bus was bumping furiously down a potholed road, and Tom thought maybe he should turn and introduce himself to one of his neighbors.

The Grid, Escaping It

I've made wondrous transitions before. No one knows my special secret story and all my friends are too wise to enquire too closely for everyone has dark and treacherous pasts and secrets better left untold. Mine is somewhat pedestrian really, there are thousands of us hiding skulking inside this country and out of it although of course judicial rulings from Central Command cross all borders now. I'm a resister, a judicial expunction service resister. And so of course I've changed my name and left my old identity behind, and even my mother doesn't know where I am or if I'm alive but that's mainly because I truly feared she'd turn me in, she was crazed with religious zeal back then in my late adolescence, she was crazy in love with Our Lady of the Finger, figurehead of a weird and right-wing Tapist cult, a cult whose male leader encouraged its female members to sleep on thorns. Thorns? It can't be possible, but yes, it is. I still have a little pamphlet. I remember my older brother once shouted denigrating remarks about that group, I was cowering up in my bedroom, horrified at the shouting betwixt the two members of our little threesome, betwixt the two members that had real power. I'd heard my mother screaming in reply that she'd sew his lips together with a needle and thread. Sew his lips? It can't be possible. But yes, I heard it, it remains a jagged shard in my memory. The threat hung in the air for a while for my brother shouted nothing back. I was about ten at the time and sick in bed with flu. I heard my brother slam the front door and then my mother appeared in my room, her brow still darkened in anger but in her hand a box of chocolates, chocolate-covered raisins. She held the box out to me. I took it and hurriedly put it under my blanket but when my mother left the room I threw the box under my bed and never retrieved it. I knew there was a message in how sharply my brother had shut the front door, and I was right; he never returned. And so sudden disappearance had branded itself into my mind as an effective and obvious way of leaving home.

And of course a little later it was the Tapists who were charged back then with the job of initiating the citizenry into the duty of judicial expunction service, the Tapists were given this particular division of the Central Command, and I remember the inklings of alarms from the left, no they were more than inklings, there was a general huge hullabaloo, libertarians put up quite a cry about this violation of the separation of church and state, and the reigning Tapel then was particularly right wing and bloodthirsty and so even moderate types were very worried. People who strenuously objected to some of the C. C.'s rulings did something called falling off the grid, god knew what that really meant. For I was just seventeen or so and had no real political awareness. I just had inklings of impressions of what was going on. But prisons then of course were filled to bursting and new ones were planned for every corner of every town, new prisons could be seen from the air creating fresh rectangles in the landscape what with their immensity and special electronic capabilities. Grids, grids, off the grid, on it. Busy chockfull prisons, there just couldn't be enough of them. And then all of a sudden the construction stopped, and all schools were required to teach a new athletics curriculum including fencing, swimming, and sharp shooting. I hated them all and dragged through the courses wearily, doing the bare minimum just so as not to fail. The coaches were Tapist nuns and monks, and the one who taught me fencing was particularly harsh and jeering. Josemaria was her name. I wasn't the target of her cruelest taunts but I kept an eye on her as she tormented others. I remember how delighted my mother was. "How marvelous that those good people are teaching you," she said to me. "What wonderful skills for them to be passing on to you." I'd ask her what was so damn great about foils and guns, and she'd say something like your body is the temple of god, and then she'd run off to one of her cult meetings to iron gold-threaded vestments for the various officers of Our Lady of the Finger. I'd examined them curiously on one occasion, awed by their opulence. My mother had suddenly appeared at my side. "You could wear one of those one day," she said, "if you join the girls' group and they find that you're qualified to continue The Work."

"The work?" I'd asked. "What work?"

"The Work of promulgating the ideas of his holiness the Father who was the first graced with the knowledge of Our Lady of the Finger."

I didn't reply. I remember tossing the garment onto the sofa and escaping from the house for the evening. Still, my mother tried to lasso me into joining a preparatory class to become one of those student Tapists, but I'd made myself scarce. I was inexperienced, but I was sentient enough to realize that swearing off sex for life at age eighteen was probably not the wisest alternative.

And then the phrase judicial expunction service entered the lingo, and all able-bodied people between the ages of eighteen and twenty-four had to register and be available at all times if called up. So I got my first call-up just a month or so after my eighteenth birthday. I was still living at home and had privately decided to become a sculptor. Clay, I loved working with clay, I loved the way it outlined every tiny indentation of my fingerprints. I'd seen and fallen in love with Degas' ballerina figurines, and when I learned that he'd been blind something clicked in my brain: I can do that. I can do that. I can do at least that. It was a gauntlet I picked up. I smile now at my young arrogance. But then, back then in those dark ages I knew I'd have to run away, for my mother who scoffed at art of any sort had been hounding me for months to go into pharmacy, even going so far as getting application forms to pharmacy colleges and demanding that I sit down and fill them out. My mother was a person who reserved all her respect for those in churchly professions or in middle-brow technical jobs; there was nothing else that she could actually envision.

One of my friends had gone through with a judicial expunction service task and survived all right. "I closed my eyes," she told me. "I just closed my eyes and shot. And when I opened my eyes the guy was gone, there's a kind of trap door and it opens after the firing and the body just drops out of sight. It was nothing to get too upset about. You're standing there with twelve other people, it's not as creepy as it would be all alone. I mean, it's awful and everything, but it's the law." She lowered her voice. "Besides, they say there's going to be a lottery so that ten percent of evaders will be judicially expunged themselves."

"What did the guy do?" I asked her.

"What guy?" she asked.

"The guy, the guy you…judicially expunged," I said, feeling uncomfortable about something and not being able to identify until much later that it was my slipping for cover behind euphemism. "What was the charge against him?"

"The charge? I don't know. They don't tell you. They only tell you the name. Who knows. He might have actually deserved it."

I was only vaguely comforted by her words. Ninety percent of me felt sick and out of focus. It wasn't that I had any strongly formulated opinion on capital punishment. I was still at that young blooming age when self-absorption blots out almost everything else. I had a sense that my service requirements, a tedious necessity, would be over soon, just as would my formal education, another tedious necessity, and then I could go on with my life.

The day of my first judicial expunction service arrived, and my mother woke me at six-thirty so I could have breakfast before I left. She stood in the doorway holding the orange directives card.

"It says to have eaten over an hour before. It says wear casual clothes and soft, low-heeled shoes. Why don't you have something now before hopping into the shower?"

"I'm skipping the shower," I said, turning over in bed and pulling the covers over my head. I was angry at my mother for treating me like a child, for I was perfectly capable of getting up, following the directives, arriving on time. But I'd be damned if I'd primp for whatever I was going to be forced to do. I'd go there all smelly and disheveled.

Two minutes early I pulled open one of the glass doors at the address I'd been directed to. A uniformed guard took my card and motioned me toward a brushed steel elevator door. "Down," he said. "You'll be directed once you get there." A few other people of varied aspect but all roughly my age had come in, and we went down together, studiously avoiding each other's eyes and feigning expressions of long-suffering boredom. I snickered—we reminded me of tedious old farts ambling toward office jobs. The snicker prompted glares and also grins of amusement betraying the true age of all present. But no one said anything. And then the elevator door opened, and who was standing there to meet us but that old battle-ax Josemaria, that fencing hag without sympathy for those who couldn't thrust and parry. Well bless my soul. I instantly decided I'd pretend not to know her, but I felt the little click in the airwaves that meant she'd recognized me.

"We're waiting for just three more and then we'll go down," she said to us briskly, throwing back her long black sleeve to glance at a watch.

"Down? We already are down," muttered an Asian-looking young man in black leather and chains. He was tiny and dark, fierce-looking and handsome. I looked at him and thought, oh. Maybe we can go for coffee afterwards.

Josemaria flicked a glance at him but didn't reply. She stood like a statue, her arms folded and hands hidden inside her sleeves. The elevator door opened and the rest of the crew arrived. "Your cards," said Josemaria. "Everyone's to register them now." She indicated a gray box behind her.

We crowded round and one by one stuck our cards in, watched the laser and listened to the tiny beep. The black-leathered boy's card didn't beep.

"Pass it through again," Josemaria said.

He did so and again it didn't beep. It made me feel a little heartsick. Something was amiss.

"Let me see your card," she said, and then she moved to a computer terminal and inserted the card. "This isn't your card." She glanced up at him and then back to her screen. "It's your brother's card. He's now in contempt of C. C. You will be credited with fulfilling a point of your J.E.S. duty."

"Hey, I'm trying to do him a favor," said the boy. He now had a scared look on his face. "He had to work today, I didn't want to come but he couldn't get off work. I'm done with my J.E.S. I'm just trying to help him out. What difference does it make?" His pitch got progressively higher and angrier.

"It's not accurate that he had to work," said Josemaria in a coolly neutral voice. "He neglected to fill out the forms for precedential activity work release."

The Asian boy was now crumpling and on the verge of tears. I felt a lump in my throat. "Then let me out of here," he said. "I've done my service. If it can't be credited to him, then I'm leaving." He started for the elevator.

"That's not the exit," said Josemaria. She glanced at her watch. "We're almost a minute behind schedule." She pointed to a stairway. "Down the stairs. Everyone."

I sensed her awareness flick toward me, but I was watching the Asian who had found no button, no laser eye to open the elevator. He slouched over and followed us down the stairs. Josemaria brought up the rear. I could feel the vibrations of the boy's sobs though they made no sound. I was on the verge of crying myself, troubled by the dissolution of the Asian's facade. How dreary this was. How horrible life was when these things happened. Why couldn't his brother be credited? Why couldn't respect be paid to someone trying to do a simple favor? I willed time to speed up, for this to be an event in my past. The staircase was surprisingly long. Our disorderly trudging down it slowly and mysteriously evolved into a lockstep pounding, hammering, and I realized we were all now marching in step. How funny. The ants go marching one by one hoorah, hoorah, the ants go marching one by one hoorah, hoorah, and they all go marching down—into the earth—to get out of the rain, boom, boom, boom. I listened to our drum-like beat, but then someone hopped on a downbeat, skipping a step and breaking the rhythm. Someone else followed suit and soon we were back to the comforting chaos of distinct footfalls. So that handsome boy had done his service already; he didn't need to be here at all. There was a superfluity, legally speaking, a superfluity. Hmm, I thought. A superfluity. I loved the liquid sound of the word. And then I felt some sort of gathering of strength and the fog in my mind cleared instantly. A snap decision descended upon me. I wouldn't take part. I would take advantage of the superfluity. And if the Asian did the same, fine, then there would be a super-superfluity. But at least the chief superfluity would be honored, accounted for. It would be like acting out a law of physics. I instantly felt strong, happy even. Judicial expunction—a given? No, no, for here a loophole had leaped into my lap; I didn't have to take part. Life was good, life could be fine. Maybe I was human but I was also a tiny white free-flying wren, a ladybug in summertime eating aphids off rosebuds. A super-superfluity. Einstein would clap in approbation.

And then we were at the bottom of the stairs, in a small and dark, oddly shaped corridor. I cocked my head but from where I thought the Asian was I picked up no vibrations. There was a humming noise of a fan or something; it muffled any possible whispers. The dark was deep enough so that the entire crew of twelve, thirteen counting Josemaria, appeared only as amorphous lumps. Josemaria suddenly was in front of me with a rush and a bustle. She was pressing something black and glinting into my hands. "You get the first issue but all issues hold ammunition," she breathed at me, and I noticed the odd energetic animus that she suddenly possessed. I instinctively knew it was directed at me; she'd chosen me to have the first gun. Why?

"No," I whispered back to her. "I've decided not." I curled my hands into tight fists and crossed them over my chest.

She ignored me and quickly passed out guns to everyone present, quietly, covertly—everything was shadowy and indistinct. One couldn't make out faces or identities other than Josemaria's. Then she came back to me and again tried to press the gun upon me. "Take it and perform your duty like everyone else," she hissed, steely snakelike, but I just shook my head and inched backwards, bent on resistance but also loath to cause a general commotion. Like everyone else, she'd said, but I vaguely suspected that the Asian hadn't taken a gun either, for Josemaria was still clutching a brace of firearms. Let her struggle with them, I thought. They didn't need me to do this. There were plenty of shooters, plenty of the twelve had taken guns, I said to myself. Damn Josemaria herself could shoot. She kept pressing into me with that gun.

"Cut it out," I finally snapped at her. I no longer cared if I disrupted the entire proceeding. "You shoot. You shoot, if you're so anxious. Or go ahead, you can shoot me. I'm just not going to." I didn't bother to mention my superfluity theory. Josemaria was only into received texts, that I knew.

From Josemaria I felt waves of anger and tension, she glanced at her watch again; it had one of those faces that glow in the dark. "Stand on one of the luminous marks and fire at the target after the third beep," she called out to everyone. "The beeps will start in about thirty seconds. The convicted is William Walters Jackson."

There was a bustle of following her orders. I leaned back against the wall. The luminous marks all seemed shrouded now by readying shooters, except for a mark right in front of me, mine. And then a light went on over by the far wall and we saw the back of a man, a man in a white tee shirt and white pants, an African man, he stood there and held a guitar which he appeared to be playing but we heard nothing at all; there must have been a sound suction device in operation. He was slight and waves in the air told me he wasn't yet aware of our presence there behind him, but then something told him and his shoulders shifted and he turned toward us and looked out at us, but his eyes didn't stop anywhere, they just kept scanning, trying to pierce deeper, and I realized that there must be some sort of one way visibility barrier hovering in the air there. But he kept peering in our direction and scanning for something, I tried to divine what he was looking for by the slight squint in his eyes, and then his lips dropped open and then closed. Home. No, not home. Mom. He was asking for his mom. And I at once began furiously wondering why his mother couldn't have been present—the legal system, it must be the fault of the legal system, while at the same time I was remembering I'd read that it was better to be shot than to be electrocuted because electrocution wasn't instant, it caused the skin to cook and stick to the restraints on the electric chair.

"Five seconds," said Josemaria, and I suddenly realized I should run up, run to the side of the African man and shout I love you, I love you, some people love you, and so I ran up there but I found myself shouting your mother loves you, she's here and she loves you, she'll hold you in her arms, don't worry, she loves you—and then there were the three beeps and my heart froze because I couldn't recall his first name, my mind was frozen and my throat suddenly hurt from my loud screaming and I fell backward, I slumped against that rear wall. In fact I found myself slipping down to the floor under an avalanche of sudden whispery whishing noises. And then the man disappeared and we were all just there in the dark again, but a pinkish light started coming up. I straightened up. My throat ached.

"File out," directed Josemaria. "You'll register your cards again in the next corridor, and then you'll follow the black lines to an escalator which will take you out of the building. Good day."

I filed out along with everyone, the machine in the next room beeped over everyone's cards and returned them, and then it was my turn and just as I was putting mine in I heard the Asian behind me whisper don't, but it was too late, the machine vacuumed up and kept my card and I glanced back at Josemaria who was trying not to look at me and trying to conceal the flash of triumph that suddenly illuminated her face, and I quickly stuck my hand in my pocket, it felt burned, and then I tried to run up the escalator but I couldn't trample over the people in front of me. The Asian rode up behind me, there was a crashing jarring weird music all the way up so as to discourage conversation, it was also the type of noise that made people slightly nauseated at the sight of each other and so at the top of the escalator we all found ourselves compelled to run to the exit and then disperse along very separate pathways, but the Asian stuck with me long enough to mutter, "congratulations, you're off the grid now," and I found myself on a busy sunlit city street in front of a Greek diner, staring at the lithograph of a gyro lunch plate special and suddenly remembering that the name was Jackson.

Off the grid. OK. I could figure that out. So I'd have to hit the road, strike out on my own. I went home that day expecting to find my mother and rehearsing in my mind a little story of having to go to a local C.C. gym for some C.C.-ordered fencing practice, but my mother wasn't home, so it was quite easy for me to grab a small gym bag, stuff it with clothes and a few gold chains that I owned, lock the front door and skip from the house forever, dropping the front door key into the grate-covered manhole at the end of the street.

That was how I lost my first identity.

Ichthyosaurs

We are on a boat, a huge ship. It is completely made of wood, it has lavishly high masts, it is one of the tall ships. The boat is populated with women, only women. Where are the men and children? That is unclear. We are sailing westward toward the lands known as the Americas, but we do not use this name at the moment. We are closer to the western shore now than to the continent of Europe far behind, lost in the wake.

We face westwards, and some of us can imagine that we smell land. But then our peripheral vision catches a streak of light, our attention is arrested and we swivel our heads back, we peer behind us far to the east and slightly south. We turn completely and stare intently rearward, trying to keep our vision up and away from the hypnotic swirl of parted water in our ship's wake. We make out mushroom clouds and flashes of red and purple and gold, and soon we can discern rivulets of lava which seem to be descending from the heavens. Our on-board geographer tells us that it is the lands of the eastern Mediterranean going up in flames. Our on-board physicist posits the opinion that there will be a ripple effect, an actualization of the domino theory. Our on-board chemist hazards the notion that something noxious is raining down on us, right here, right now in a fine, barely observable mist.

In horror we watch the sky surrounding us turn slowly from crystal blue to a hazy green and then gray. Our vessel lurches. We peer aft; we can no longer see any light at all much less the cloud play and metallic-seeming rain over Europe. We turn and try to peer westward, onward. A fear has long gripped everyone and now some of us become panic stricken while others are overcome with the debilitating weariness of despair. It is clear that devastation is nigh.

One of our stalwart leaders makes bold forays back and forth on the now sickeningly listing ship; she pairs howling, shrieking women with mute women who have turned inward. "Adrenaline will save us," shouts our leader. "One adrenaline flow per couple. Despair will give way to action: remember this." She makes a mistake when she gets to me, for I am standing catatonic while inside I'm a pent-up typhoon of emotion. (I want to live through this! I want to live!) She only sees the immobility and thus pairs me with a middle-aged blonde woman, a beauty, slight and delicate and screaming with horror into the wind.

The choppy sea has grown even more frenetically angry. The stalwart leader pushes the slight blonde into my arms; we collide and grip each other in the chest-to-chest life-hold that we have practiced so often. Then we peer into each other's face. We recognize one other; it is a miracle! We worked together in the distant past, teaching weaving in a Spanish shore town. We smile at each other and tighten our grip as the rocking of the ship worsens.

"Swordfish," calls the deep voice of another of our leaders. "Swordfish." It becomes a chant. "Swordfish. The swordfish have begun. All eyes open, all arms ready." We peer upward and through the gray we can decipher immense sea creatures with glimmering lancet noses diving completely over our ship, squinting down at us briefly with dead plunderous eyes. We have been lectured on the possibility of such an attack but in the terror of the moment and the sheer brilliance of the leaping huge fish we are frozen. The fish seem to communicate by sonar, by radar, for suddenly they begin diving suicidally into our ship, spearing it with their sharp proboscides, increasing the listing and tearing open gaping holes. We are sinking apace.

I cannot remember the name of my comrade, my fellow weaver, but my arms are clamped around her neck. "No, no, arms around the back," she calls into my ear, and we grasp each other in the survival hold that will keep us together and afloat.

Our ship is going down, down. Women all around us are wailing and screaming and being ripped apart by the sea's demolition of the ship and by the action of the swordfish. I have forgotten if we are supposed to close our eyes or keep them open. I am relieved that we cannot see blood; the gray storm swirl makes visibility nil.

"Pray," my partner shouts to me, "pray that the wood doesn't hit and kill us." An immense eddy sweeps us up from the boat for a moment and then tosses us downward. We crash into part of the deck but before we can feel the full thrust of the fall we are swept upward and away again in a soft but icy pillow of water and we are thrown into the sea. We keep our arms around each other; our intense training has paid off.

The swordfish are everywhere now spearing and swallowing women. I shut my eyes, blocking out the assault of saline and broken body parts. We ride the waves, the crashing forces; we try to become indistinguishable from the foam. We keep only one thing in mind and that is maintaining our grip on each other. In my partner's grip I feel a positive force, an optimistic communication, and I realize that she is pleased that we are being pushed west, shoreward. There is the glimmering of hope; this will keep us alive for a while longer at least. We try to will ourselves westward. Sometimes the water pushes us down into the depths and we open our eyes for brief seconds to take in some of the phosphorescent sub-reality studded with peculiar sea creatures. At other times the water pushes us back up into the air and we splutter for breath. There are assorted other women floating and bobbing around us, but finally we see fewer and fewer as we are all dissipated, diluted out into the ocean.

For escape I try to remember my partner's name, I bask in the delight of the coincidence. I try to feel happy because happiness is a seemly way to meet death, but then I reproach myself for this momentary resignation, and I again concentrate on fighting the sea.

Time passes, the light changes. It seems that my comrade and I are in the water for weeks. Oddly, we do not feel cold, but if we were alone we would have frozen long ago. We squeeze each other and send mind messages. By certain squeezes we can even sleep in turns, brief three minute naps or perhaps three hours. Revivifying. We develop a language of pressures: YES, we're being pushed westward, YES, the smell of land is clear even in the water, and YES the sea creatures are smaller here and some of them seem to possess rudimentary legs.

Slowly my mind opens out and becomes used to our plight. I remember my comrade's name. Donna. I remember that she was a painter from Japan, a person unable to find work in Spain except as a weaver. I remember that I had to teach her weaving quickly and under cover of darkness so that the Spanish authorities wouldn't pick up on her lack of qualifications. I remember that her weaving ability soon surpassed mine, and that I became her assistant. I was happy in this role until I grew weary of weaving, and I tried to talk her into opening a small art cinema. We make an excellent team, I told her then, oh so many years back. She was older than I was, she had a calm wisdom, a gentle acceptance of things while I had passed my first youth but was still embroiled in childish angst. When we were denied further allotments of a crimson fiber that I had grown to cherish, I was dejected for weeks. World capitalism reigned but still there were so many shortages! Still there were so many regulations and rationing was universal. Donna didn't let any of this bother her. She laughed and said, we'll use pink, we'll simply use pink. Grievances grew on me, stuck to my heart like barnacles. Not to hers. She was carefree, chipper, blazingly optimistic always. I loved her and wanted to be her, but because I knew that was impossible I tried to steel-hoop her to me. We can build some sort of small empire, I told her. She smiled at me fondly but gave me a dismissive wave. She was still enthralled with weaving. Even a few men, young and progressive types, would come to her classes occasionally. I wanted to continue on as her assistant but in another field, anything unrelated to fabrics. But she got another job, a better position in one of the Scandinavian countries. She was invited there to be the royal weaver, the creator of soft pastel blankets and shawls for the royal infants and ladies. "You know, you could think about heading north, too," she said to me as she boarded a trans-continental express, and I lost track of her.

I remember all this at a snail's pace and in bits and pieces as we swirl together in the sea. It doesn't sound likely, it seems more probable that one would remember in a rush, but surviving in the ocean means conserving every tiny atom of energy, and that includes mental energy such as scanning the contents of memory banks. Still, we have grown used to riding the water together and we have perfected our language of presses. We communicate to each other our shared sense of luck at being thrown together.

The sea grows especially turgid and *terra firma* is nigh. We brace for new dangers. We try to remember why we have been heading westward. Sadly, any conception of the reason has been obliterated from our understanding or perhaps we have never known. We can't even recall if we were prisoners on that ship or refugees or explorers or ambassadorial artisans.

And then we are thrown upon land.

I wake up in a cornfield; my mouth is full of pebbles and for some reason they nudge me into consciousness. I open my mouth and let the pebbles drop onto the soil next to me. They're not pebbles at all, they're glistening pearls, broken bits of my teeth. I sit up, palpate my arms and legs for injury and then look around me. I am alone. The final thrust of the ocean divided us. My intuition tells me I will find Donna again, but I immediately suspect that my mind is playing a survival game, feeding me on hope. I stare at the tall corn. Corn, just corn. Where am I?

It is a dusky time of day, but I can't quite ascertain if it is morning or evening. The sun doesn't seem to be coming from any clear direction. There is something askew about the sky, and staring upwards disorients me; I almost fall over. I grab a stalk of corn and quickly shuck it and eat it; my remaining teeth are jagged and make quick work of it. Then I get up and begin to walk. The air is warm; I am still clad in the leather dress I put on so many millennia ago. I walk and walk. Finally in the distance I see the red glow of a fire. I walk toward it but am kept back by a fence, a running structure of slim reeds. I stop at the edge of the fence and peer toward the flames.

There is a group of people, strangely foreign-looking creatures clad in leather. With a shock I gaze at the men of the group. I have almost forgotten the existence of men. Both sexes are dressed alike and both seem to be engaged in preparing a meal. The food smells don't tempt me; my shrunken stomach has been well-filled by the corn. I stand and watch the very domestic appearing scene for quite a while, trying to catch snippets of the language. All I can hear are occasional high notes and then once or twice a baritone throb.

At last I turn away, anxiety in my heart. Will I find Donna? I plod onward. Will I have to communicate with these foreign people, these unknown members of what appears to be my species? I walk and walk and try to gather courage. The work in front of me, the building of a new life, seems daunting and perhaps impossible. I walk and try to find again that cornfield, but everything around me looks new and untouched.

I continue walking and try to proceed in a very straight line. The light is fading and I begin to grow tired. A rest place for the night must be found. Why didn't I grab more corn when I had the chance? The shadows are growing longer, and so I stop between two trees. There is a soft, protected area just underneath them, I drop down and hug myself. I scratch my upper arm and notice the sleeve of my dress. It no longer merely loosely covers my arm; it is affixed to it. I look down at my chest, my thighs. Somehow the thrashing ocean caused the dress to meld upon my skin.

Light wakes me and I sit up. The glow in the sky is seamless; again I can't determine east from west. There is no moss here, and I can't remember other compass substitutes. I curse my lack of practical knowledge. However, I maintain my faith in intuition; I get up and continue walking. Motion will engender progress. I wonder about the fate of the other women. I went to find Donna, we can keep each other alive, she can tell me of her adventures in the royal court amid the icy blondes. Something makes me halt suddenly. Something in my mind. I stand and pay attention to the thought. That fence. The way the reeds were woven. It didn't make sense. It wasn't strong, it wasn't lasting. This is something, I think to myself. This is something I can offer. I turn and head back. I pray briefly. Our leaders taught us that prayer is useful. I pray that I will be able to find that fence, that fire.

I become dizzy with deja vu near one particular stand of trees and so I stop and try to clear my head. Have I been walking in circles? And then I notice that the grass is matted down here, the low-growing shrubs have been recently disturbed. Oh, yes, I've been here, there's the corn. I rush toward the six foot stalks but to my great disappointment the ears are all gone; someone has been here and harvested them. I sit down and weep, my face in my hands, saltwater dripping through my fingers and onto the ground. Perhaps I am not welcome in this strange western land. This is the spot where the ocean tossed me, and I suddenly remember that this is where I spit out my broken teeth. I go and search for them. They are gone too, but in the spot I dropped them a small bush has sprung up, a bush with star-shaped fuchsia blossoms with tiny aqua pods in the middle. The blossoms are so very lovely that I stare at them, drink them in; they have befriended me. I sleep briefly next to my flowers and then I wake up with a start and continue walking, not giving the blossoms a backward glance, for I know something of the tricks of the gods.

Hours pass. I walk and walk. And then I think I begin to recognize various bushes and meadows and then, yes, I come upon the fence. There is no one here now, no group of people around the fire. I curse myself, I curse my timidity in not approaching those beings the day before. I had been too fearful to wager, to risk, and now I may have lost everything. But there's the fence. I look at it closely. Yes, very poorly constructed, yes, an incompetent manipulation of that particular type of reed. I drop to my knees and find loose reed ends; I pull them and begin a new weaving process. I open my eyes more and notice that the material is all around me, I rest back on my heels and work quickly, rocking a little, over and under, in and out. The work is smooth and satisfying and restful and unending. I weave and weave and find that it helps dissipate my anxiety, it gives me respite from what I assume is my near future death of starvation or attack by wild beast or sudden cataclysmic weather change. I even find myself chuckling, chuckling at some old joke lodged deep in my memory banks, some joke that Donna and I shared about circumventing the weaving regulations.

I continue working and my emotions flow smoothly between peaks and valleys. Too soon I will have to stop this and journey onward seeking other possible survivors and vestiges of my old life. In the meantime I just weave. If Donna chances to see this she will recognize the pattern. After a while I find that hunger is disturbing my smooth productive flow. I look up to find that the light has changed again, pinkish shafts cut through the blue. The sky is lovely but meaningless. Food. I am timid about actually climbing over the fence and inspecting the fire site, I fear being nabbed as an intruder. But I overcome these thoughts and hop the fence and make my way to the scorched spot. I root around like a dazed squirrel. There is nothing. There are only the remains of burnt wood. There are foot prints in the dry earth. I squat down and peer at the prints and trace them with my finger. I inhale deeply and then stand and shout out: "Anybody! Anybody!"

The echo of my voice returns to me, the screech of a macaw. There is a small bitter kernel in my heart. I will have to control its growth. I remind myself of the existence of the star-shaped fuchsia blossoms, and I return to my weaving task. I smile at how little I've done and at how vastly the fence stretches northward. Northward? How do I know that? There are no known indicators. But it is northward. That is the direction in which I am working. I sit back on my ankles and continue.

Ben Croxton

Croxton, Croxton, Ben Croxton. I smile as I repeat his lovely name. A prince of the leftist activist community, a superb speaker, quite often the orator at large rallies. He was a thin and bearded redhead, a biologist. I hated him a little bit because...I don't know why but I think it was because he couldn't see me. He'd look my way and I could tell he was seeing only a filament in the air. He was an acknowledged leader, a mantle he'd inherited from his father, a doctor who'd achieved sainthood by having been machinegunned by Marines while on a medicine delivery mission to Haiti. Ben Croxton. It was in his genes.

And there was something else in his genes, something else straight from his father, a quality upright and American narrow and professionally trained and puritan to the marrow. It was simply that he knew everything about everything just as his father had done; the two of them, neither could be informed by others, both had a grasp of all, all knowledge, all areas of endeavor. What's the deepest ocean, I'd ask Ben, and his face would go blank and fathomless for the briefest second but then he'd instantly recover. Indian, he'd reply. The Indian Ocean.

Yes, his heritage from his father was this vast all-knowingness. The subtleties in the relationship between Malcolm X and Martin Luther King—they knew. The location of the nearest genuine flying buttress—they knew. The exact percentage of nutrition in potato skin as compared to the white interior—they knew. I recall Croxton Senior berating me for not being able to make clever conversation after viewing a film about the Rosenberg couple, but then he softened into happy tranquility when I asked him questions and stood nodding and listening. And the mass of his happiness broadened and deepened the more I queried and nodded and listened. Croxton Junior and Senior—they were sweet people who would give you the shirts off their backs but they wouldn't accept from you a kernel, not a crumb of information or knowledge. What bird is that twittering so angelically you might ask all innocence, oh what is that divine creature. Neither one could share your air of wonder, no, they would have a response, they would know and be iron sure of their knowledge of tufted titmice and boreal chickadees. Nothing, nothing could they be told, there wasn't an iota of information that could be presented to them that would make them cock their head and eye you quizzically and query you. No. They always knew. It was staggering after a while. They were supersaturated sponges, no absorbent ability left.

And so how could I love the junior so dearly? How could I pine for closeness to such a formidable ego passed father to son like a family bible? That is why when I met Phillip my soul after a while whispered…Phillip! That is why I slowly gravitated toward him. But the body thing strapped me to Croxton who was always uncannily canny re my real intent. "Aramaic. Is that a dead language," I remember asking him, testing him, and he glanced up at me with his fathomless depths of nothingness, and, having sniffed out the test, said nothing. Damn steel plates that he and his father possessed!

Now the father was dead, a martyr/hero, so ill shouldn't be spoken. I wasn't speaking ill. I adored Croxton. I adored his dead father for sharing his genes.

Ben Croxton. I hated him a little because I knew how his mind worked, I knew how he'd categorized me as comrade, colleague. But never as friend, never as a pal. We'd all been stunned by his father's death and then I'd foolishly hoped that it might open Ben a bit to the possibility of facts and fantasies beyond him. But no. He calcified into more his father than ever before. We'd known each other off and on since childhood but Croxton was eminently trustworthy and never betrayed that he'd known me by my earlier name, known the location of my childhood house.

And we'd worked together. The wars in the Slavic lands, we'd researched how they'd coped with the deaths of children. Our interest had been the nitty gritty details about dead bodies and burials. We wanted to shove these specifics in the faces of the fat and happy at home within Central Command. And so together we went to the war areas, found a translator and traveled around as best we could through the sniper-controlled lands. We wore tattered, loose clothing that concealed small cameras within the folds. Both of us were young enough to blithely risk getting killed.

How are the children buried, we asked each other as we prepared our points of research. We knew of course that none of these peoples practiced cremation. What are the specifics on the caskets and the graves? Are there tiny white wicker boxes? When did that supply run out? Are there smooth and pristine childsized pine boxes? When did that supply run out and what did parents use then? Are the caskets lined with pastel satin? When did that supply run out and what did parents use in its place? What do parents use now? And what do they put in the grave with their child, what do they wrap around their child's shoulders and place in their child's hands? Who digs the grave and how deep do they dig it? How do they mark it? All these questions were in our minds like blocks of concrete. We've got to keep to a narrow and specific line, Croxton told me in his strict tones. We can't get sidetracked. Just remember, get the details about the tiny victims. Take the photos. That's what we're after.

Our translator first took us to orphanages, large holding centers for children whose parents were lost or killed in battle. The children were scrawny and hollow-eyed and poorly dressed, and they kept chanting something at us, what are they saying I asked the translator, food, he said, they're hungry, they think maybe you have food. I felt horrible that my pockets were empty, that I didn't have loaves and fishes that would magically multiply. I took a shadow of comfort in the fact that both Croxton and I were on the thin side; I glanced sidelong at our plumpish translator and couldn't control the small trill of fake virtue in my soul. But I had nothing to offer the hungry children, nothing. I searched in my bag and found small pencils, a lip salve, coins. I covertly gave one item to each child pressed up against me and all of a sudden I found myself in a sea of scores of children pressing into me, plucking at me gently but insistently. Good god. Would I have to call out to the translator for assistance? No. He turned back at the commotion, his face calm and conveying gentle forbearance. He pushed through the children and took me by the elbow and wordlessly led me from the room. Croxton was down the hall, communicating in sign language with the resident medic.

Later that day I said to Croxton maybe our mission was misbegotten, maybe we should be organizing food delivery to children, to pregnant and nursing women. He cut me off harshly and said no. Control yourself. There are a thousand desperate needs. Don't think about them now or you'll lose your mind. Keep focus. The photos of the dying children. The facts about the wooden boxes. Focus, focus. I listened to him. But I noticed he never ate, he found some way to save his food and then it magically appeared again when we came upon a half-starved waif, alone and shivering in an alley, or a woman and a small child struggling down the street with loads of scavenged wood. And I remember one day we happened to come upon a small group of people huddled together; we went up to them and found them gnawing on the picked over bones of a dead horse. Those people, something spear-like shot out of their eyes at us, a warning not to come too close. Croxton and I backed up a little and took another route. We were thin, thin. Our ribs poked out along our backs, but in comparison to those people grasping those large bones our flesh was ample and robust.

But the orphanages were nothing. We were taken to a morgue. We used our gas masks. We saw a young girl who'd been raped and murdered. She was so young that her breasts were as flat and childlike as a ten-year-old boy's. Her murderers had slit her body open from abdomen to neck. Someone had sewn it closed, perhaps someone trying to save her parents extra grief, trying to give her parents a somewhat intact body to bury. So conjectured our translator who couldn't fully understand the morguekeeper's dialect. I'd stared at the girl's body for a while and suddenly I had the urge to crumple into a corner and take a nap, and so to force myself awake I'd returned robotlike to our main line of questioning. But where do they bury them and what sort of boxes do they use, I found myself repeating and repeating.

Croxton was squatting on the floor flatfooted Arab style, his head in his hands. The morguekeeper and our translator talked for a long time in their tortured way. The translator finally turned to us and told us the morguekeeper would greatly appreciate it if we buried the girl, her kin were unknown, a shovel could be lent to us if we left a suitable deposit in hard currency. Those were the days before the monetary system was internationalized. Croxton gave the morguekeeper his wristwatch. The translator let us know that we would have to carry the body in our arms but the morguekeeper interrupted him and after a long period of haggling it became clear that we could borrow a small wagon, again if we would leave an acceptable deposit. We left Central Command money, and the translator and Croxton lifted the girl's body onto the wagon. The morguekeeper covered her with a dark cloth, he tucked it gently around her. But then he straightened up and starting gesturing at the body and giving our translator instructions again, and it was clear he wanted that cloth back along with the shovel and wagon. OK, OK, said Croxton. The morguekeeper looked over at him and laughed. OK, OK, he repeated. It was dark by then. The translator took us to a burial ground and left us after telling us to be calm about our task; no one would bother us. We didn't ask him how he knew this but a theory sprang into my mind that it was because Croxton and I still had fresh stores of vitamins within our bodies while the rest of the residents of these lands were in advanced stages of night blindness; all the carrots had long been plucked from the earth.

Croxton set to work right away with the shovel but all it did was make ping noises on the rocky surface. Ping, ping in the blackness. I took the tool from him and tried for a few minutes as Croxton clawed at the rocks with his hands. Put it down before you break it, he finally said to me, and we both worked on our knees, scrabbling at the rocks. It took hours and the hole we made was oddly shaped and not deep. No, this hole isn't right, I said, but Croxton didn't reply. We could barely see in the clouded moonlight. I recall Croxton fitting the girl into the hole, curving her at the waist. I recall asking is that correct to bury her that way. I recall no reply from Croxton who was busily covering the girl with the stones and the rubble. Come on, he finally whispered fiercely to me, help me, help me. We finished at last. How are we going to mark the grave, I asked. We stood silently for a while. Let's go, said Croxton. I looked around in the dimness for some beautiful object but there was nothing. Let's go, said Croxton again, picking up the shovel. I didn't have anything, not an earring, not a ribbon. I thought furiously and then I tore at the collar of my shirt, the label I recalled was a bright red, I ripped out the whole collar and I started burying it atop the girl's grave. What are you doing, Croxton asked. I buried the collar part but the red label I made stick up and out of the earth, a tiny red marker. All right, come on, said Croxton. He handed me the shovel and cloth and he carried the cart back in his arms so as to minimize the noise.

We returned the items to the morguekeeper the next day. He wouldn't take the shovel from Croxton's hand, and he waved us into the morgue. I started following him but Croxton caught me quickly by the arm and then I understood. Are there more children, I asked Croxton. How do I know what there is, he said. We stood frozen there as the morguekeeper kept waving at us to come in and cajoled us in his incomprehensible language. I can't recall what happened next but we only buried that one child and we never got the watch or the cash back, but we hadn't really expected to.

We only buried that one child. Perhaps that is why Croxton can't abide me. Our project—when we got back within Central Command and publicized it, the only people who were interested were the peacenik old ladies. They opened their bags, pulled out tissues, wept. Otherwise people pretty much ignored it. "Perhaps the photos just aren't good enough," I said to Croxton. He looked at me angrily and shook his head. "No no. They're good enough, they're good enough." The problem was out there; that was very clearly in his mind. The problem wasn't us.

And so Ben Croxton was one of those heartrending men who awakened my sex-addiction, my need to tease and tantalize. Sex unleashed self-destructiveness in me. It wasn't a matter of just wanting to embrace particularly lovely male flesh, no, it was wanting that person to become my slave in body and soul, and in the process becoming his slave. I wanted to nurture and caress and hover near the love object, whoever he was at the time, I wanted to talk to him on the phone and gaze at his handwriting. Croxton. He was it. It was something I couldn't really control and for years hadn't seen the need to until I realized that it was eating up ungodly amounts of time and energy and creativity and overall making me feel miserable and wildly out of control in that I couldn't work, I couldn't concentrate, all I could do was stalk the love object like a starving jaguar. So I forced myself to stop it, but it came out in other ways. What else could I do? I couldn't sleep with him or else I'd find myself in that maelstrom once more. It was so much better to calmly produce something rather than to skulk around spending enormous chunks of time and energy devising love potions of one sort or another. And I could see through myself; in the midst of all the potion plotting I frequently told myself to tell the love object, hey, I've got this thing about you, can you help me shatter it. But I couldn't do it, I couldn't break through to just grabbing the love object by the elbow and saying let's make love or could you move to a different coast perhaps. I'd done all this potion stuff on Croxton; it was a conditioned reflex of mine by then. But as I analyze this I realize that of course it didn't matter that the potions didn't work really quickly; in fact the delay was quite good for it prevented me getting into the actual affair and then the prolonged lovenest scenes which would only again eat up my time and energy and distort my life. So I'd trained myself to steer pretty much clear of people I found sexually enticing. If I were going to have sex I'd have it with someone calming, someone like Phillip. Or maybe I'd just have to sublimate completely like St. Paul, like Buddha, like Andy Warhol. Fine. There were many pathways.

Rauwolf

(Rauwolf, a world potentate, talks to a psychiatrist who among other things is trying to determine if there is any psychogenic angle to Rauwolf's recurring problem with infestations of intestinal worms:)

"Yes, I've been thinking about it, I've been thinking about it. I think about it every day. I like thinking about it, it's a pleasure I allow myself, it's an indulgence, one of my few. Now get this straight, all I do is think about it. So that effectively scotches any real worry, any real concern that I actually might do something. But thinking about it, well, that's relatively harmless. How do I envision it? Oh, I envision it a variety of ways. It seems there are endless easy ways to do it, dumb accident type things. I've got this fantasy of being out on the New Golden Gate Bridge walking along with Patsy, gazing down at the blue. Photo op after some big natural crisis or other. And there I am with Patsy arm in arm. And then I let her arm go, all very natural, very calm, and then a moment later I step off into the blue. And I'm gone. Released. And Patsy stands there, her skirt fluttering a bit in the breeze, her mouth agape, her eyes staring out after me. Maybe she then jumps in too, a bit of classical Japanese drama come to life. Whatever. That was one of my early scenarios, but I've refined it a little. I realize that there are barriers to just falling off the bridge, or at least I think there are. Should be. Anyway, for a while it preyed on my mind, how exactly to get over the barrier without some of my guys rushing up and hustling me down, saving me type thing. But one day walking along one of the upper hallways in the Manor it occurred to me that with just one semi-hop onto the bottom of the railing I could vault over any structure that was in the range of three or four feet. And that calmed me, really gave me kind of a boost. So now when I fantasize about this—and you see, I freely admit that I do fantasize, and I think it's a darn healthy outlet—what I picture is strolling along with Patsy, just like in the earlier version but then I step away to the edge and then hop up and gently throw myself over. I'm gone before anyone can really react, and in fact it happens so smoothly that everyone thinks it was quite natural, scripted, part of the agenda. So, yes, in answer to your question, I've got it pretty well scoped out, on a fantasy level.

But my real complaint, yes, yes, my intestines—I'm being blinded again, I'm seeing goddamned protoplasm floating around in front of my eyes, pink, blue, every color of the rainbow. At first I think it's just a slight tension headache, affairs of state crashing in on me from all directions, but then the goofy loops get so mesmerizing and just so dang pretty that I feel my eyes going crosswise, and then my hands fall asleep and so does my face, and even my lips I swear to God. And then a sudden craving for junk food sets in, and I've discussed all this with the doc and he said knock off the salt and the white sugar, George. But he's a good forty pounds overweight himself so he's not exactly the last word. Potato chips these days, they're healthy, good for you. Too bad the media boys couldn't have fixed me up with those. Those other stinking things, I hate them of course. I mean, in actuality I'd probably never even seen one let alone eaten one.

They were things that belonged tossed into a shopping cart along with orange fanta, white wonderbread, a few pounds of plastic wrapped chicken legs, oh and argo starch. And a big bag of fresh shrimp. All paid for by food stamps and then thrown into the back seat of a dented and dated boat of a Cadillac. By a huge overweight person teetering on broken bright aqua plastic high heels and clad in a polyester dress coming loose at the seams. But I'm letting my imagination run away with me. (And people say I have none!) No, I'd never even seen a pork rind close up, but the notion came up during one of Trep's and my gab sessions, and we chortled for a while and then he circled it on his yellow pad and drew arrows toward it and it became solid, an entity, just as the damn tootsie rolls had been for Trep. The difference of course being that Treponeem actually ate the plastic sugary things, fistful after fistful. I'm not saying that it was in fact a real weakness of his with a history. No. It was just another tiny p.r. ploy, but the difference in this case being that Trep took it on and made it real and forever after had to have on hand tootsie rolls in all sizes. I'd watch him eat them sometimes; that guy was blessed with his own sterling quality chompers, no getting around that. Then I got stuck with pork rinds.

It's ironic because Trep actually originally had a yen for salty junk food while I am more partial to junk sugar and have always been so. I still clearly remember the thrill of Halloween, dressing up like a little spook and collecting bags and bags of plunder. More than I could ever eat, but I tried, oh I tried and I had the cavities and the bellyaches to prove it. I always had this thing for those penny candy things and nickel chocolate bars and anything, anything with sugar. I'd keep a supply at school under my pillow, and as for sharing, no, I guarded the stuff jealously. I'd hear a kid crying at night and one time Whitley, the smaller one, suggested that if I gave the crybaby a half a Baby Ruth then perhaps he'd stop crying and we'd all be able to sleep. I got out all my Baby Ruths and quickly ate them myself just in case Whitley's real motivation was getting the bars for himself.

Yes, I've always loved the stuff. It wasn't much of a problem in school except for a few recurring bouts with those little ah that intestinal thing that sometimes happens to kids from eating candy that's a tad too old or has been on a shelf too low to the ground, but that's probably just something I imagined when I was small. I mean how else can those things actually get into the packaging? Sometimes I vaguely suspect that someone in the household, whoever it was who did the shopping and sent the treat packages off to us was actually buying things at cut rate, at a fire sale of some sort. Which wouldn't be a bad thing in all cases, but in this particular case I do have this horrifying memory of the recurrence of those little things, I can't say the word, those little creeping intestinal things. The doctor was always so snidely pleased, feigning shock and disgust. I'll never forget.

But now and for a long time I've been quite powerful and it's been quite easy to get hold of very fresh sweets and I have almost completely forgotten about my early health misfortune. And yet now that I am at shall we say the pinnacle, now that I am Prime Minister, well, it's hard to find the privacy. I've been skulking around, trying to find a quiet place to suck on a jawbreaker and then chew it right when it gets to that tempting point and Patsy's judgment on the matter be damned. God damn it, I'm calling the shots. If I can't enjoy the very small vice of refined white sugar, a proud Federal product, let me say, then what's the point. Oh I grant, it's painful to sit in the back of the limo and try to throw m & m's into my mouth during the all-too-brief seconds when I know there's no danger of the driver glancing at me in the rear view mirror, but I'm used to doing this. What is worse is that too often I must take another passenger along with me in that damn car, and then I rarely find that I can munch on anything. I'd like to, I'd really like to, but I realize full well that it doesn't convey the right image, it's just not done, and it scared the bejesus out of me when I read about that pinhead Karl Kude, and his breakfast of a Snickers Bar and a Pepsi. Consumed at an early morning meeting with his opponent. That's what lost him the governorship. The opponent, clever bastard, played it to the hilt for the press. Kude, no, not a real grasp there on keeping couth in the public eye, not a contender. But, yes, that shook me up a bit. Because I've secreted candy in the bathroom of First Mach in Flight, and there's lots of it stuffed in the backs of the drawers of my desk in Crimson Room Hexagonal. But even getting hold of it in the first place was difficult until I hit upon the idea of ordering large amounts of it for visiting school children. I think I overheard two staffers joking about this one day, I think I overheard giggles. But it may have just been something that hit my ear. I shut it out of my consciousness until I noticed chickles wrappers crumpled in one of their ash trays, and yes, my largest supply at that point was in chickles. Excessive use of the executive tennis courts was a charge that I could squarely level at both those dinks, and I had my chief of staff fire them no questions asked. It went well with my integrity in office thing. Rooting through my trash bins. I wanted to have those guys shot.

Do you see the tribulations of high office? And some joker on the Hierarchical Judgment Commission actually gave me a bag of pork rinds once as a gag, and I had to pretend to enjoy them. No. I didn't like them. It's just another one of the sacrifices of public life. I could have been a painter. I could have been someone who just sits at home all day long and eats into the capital his forebears worked so hard and long to pile up. But no, I've always had a sense of bigger, better ways to control things. And I am an artist of minutiae, of the tiny but telling detail. Old allegations creep up every so often that my power base came from my early years as a government censor, a reader of official and unofficial letters, a checker for information or exchanges that betrayed the public trust. I was a freshly minted Marine on a battleship in the South Pacific, an information specialist of the highest category, and it was my choice to work as a censor. Yes, this lowly-seeming but very necessary task was mine, and it was a thankless one, a godly one, but not so very cleanly, no. After learning the tricks of the trade on that battle ship I moved on to land assignments, I spent years in dusty back offices in storerooms, but by God I got the dirt, yes, it was a real eye-opener, an education for me. I learned things that no one can even begin to guess...I've forgotten some of the things, but none of the important ones, no, I'm not one to lose things though it's been known as a family failing, generation after generation of Rauwolfs losing things so that it's become almost a family tradition—my father's golden flight wings were lost, old letters with descriptions of Great War military combat— lost, heirloom jewelry—lost. And on and on. Not me though. I grip things tight and keep them bound to me.

Anyway, enough of this. I've got other things to worry about. With a slightly too hard caramel I pulled a filling from one of my very back molars and now a big chunk of the actual tooth has fallen out. And it's released—I don't know what, but some greyish clumps keep pushing their way out of that cavity. It's a problem at meetings—I have a choice of raising a hanky to my lips and spitting out the disgusting stuff or else I have to swallow it back down. There's no pain and of course I won't go to the dentist. But it's making my face cave in on that side, it's making my visage look out of alignment. Dammit. My face is important. But I won't go to the dentist, no, I won't see anyone with any sort of narrow medical background. They're the ones who apply the kiss of death, them in their white coats and antiseptic stink and putrefaction throughout the office. Especially if your complaint is sugar-ingestion related, look at what happened years back, we just let that kid eat too much candy, and candy then was shot through with chemicals, and we were both too young and foolish to know that or to know anything, least of all keep candy away from babies. But that's all dead and past now and actually never really happened, I'm proof it never happened, I'm proof, I've lived all these years and never been healthier, never stronger or more virile or potent. In fact the new breed of bio-techs tell me the dormant intestinal infestation I suffer is actually protection, armor. Sugar helps me. And my teeth, no problem. Bashingfrome's were mahogany, state of the art then I assume. Mine are porcelain, the best of this particular age. And so I follow in a great tradition.

But I've got to get control of my mental state, I've got to get all this bleak venom in my heart under absolutely rigorous control so that I can direct it efficiently, so that I can do what I'm famous for: spew omnicides at evil in my trademark laser-like smart-bomb sort of way. I'm good at it and so of course I'll do it. Otherwise what point is there to life. What was I put on this pathway for and made to run through the narrow dogtrack of being one of the eminent, the movers and shakers, the moneyed. God only knows. But there it is and here am I and who am I to try to divert things from the well-trod road, who am I to arrogantly try to digress. I know about Robert Frost, I went to school, cranky old guy, beat his wife, took one path, fine, I took the other. The important thing for me and my kind, the lesson learned, is to keep hurtling along down the well-beaten path, to pound down hard on it, to emulate those Olympic bobsled guys — throttling full speed ahead, thrusting blindly forward on that rigid pre-packed trail. Tough work. Not without its rewards. Somebody's got to do it."

Arabesque

Saqqez

Every night I've heard the bombing come closer and I'm certain I'll be killed at last. The people in this godforsaken town seem only slightly perturbed by the war, and they continue to watch their honored lord-on-earth as he orates against America and for Allah. America is behind the attacks, he says, and I guess it might be true. I'm not into any sort of nationalism myself although for psychic protection here I sometimes replay in my mind the Jimi Hendrix rendition of "The Star Spangled Banner." That shrieking and caterwauling comforts me. I got my butt kicked once at Boy Scout camp because I hoisted the flag upside down. They acted as if I'd pissed on the president's grandmother. Big hot dogging deal, I thought to myself. I quit the Boy Scouts and started listening to Iron Butterfly for hours on end. Nationalism—I had its number.

I have to write this so I can keep up on my English and so I maintain my mental distance from this situation. I suppose I am a hostage in a sense, but my real feeling is that the outside world has forgotten my existence. This doesn't bother me unduly. I have found some comfort in my present daily life. I have forgotten the confines of western garb and have grown to enjoy the native dress, the cool cotton shirt that drops to the ground. My ear has grown accustomed to the loudly piped call to prayer; I listen for my favorite muezzin. The desert surrounding us holds no terrors for me. I've plucked melons there that are inedibly bitter but smell heavenly. I'm in a small town called Saqqez about a hundred miles from the Persian Gulf. In other words, nowhere. The last American I saw was Ridley, but they took him somewhere else months ago. They let me watch TV (hah!), read newspapers (hah!), even make phone calls though there's no one to call. The lines don't carry beyond the town. I can come and go as I please. The only thing they insist on is that I show up for work every day. And that's easy since I live and work in the same building.

I work for a baker named Eza, and I live in an apartment above the bakery. Eza's brother is the minister or intelligence officer who arranged that I come here. Eza and his wife Shabvar treat me very kindly and sometimes even I am convinced that I must be a CIA plant. Eza pays me for my bakery work, and every month Shabvar shows me deposit slips from the local bank. In two years I've earned four hundred bucks or so, though I'm not certain if the exchange rate I'm using is in any real ballpark. Now I know how people in mental wards and minimum security prisons must feel: mired in mud but not completely uncomfortable.

But they try to keep me happy and they even bring me women. One was a fat widow, about forty-five. I couldn't do anything with her, and she laughed and sat and shook like jello, and patted my head as she left. But then they brought me a pretty girl named Homa who had a very tiny baby with her. She told me he was seven months old and big for his age. She's I figure about thirty, about my age, so not really a girl, I guess. She's dark and tiny. Anyway, when Homa and I went up to my room, Shabvar was happy to take care of the baby down in the bakery.

Eza is about fifty-five, and from the beginning he seemed resigned to having me here. But we get along fine, mostly because he knows I enjoy the bakery work. And he's enjoyed teaching me. He's an important and well-respected person in this town, even though he spends almost the whole day in his hot kitchen. Government people such as postmen and tax collectors are always coming in and out, exchanging double and triple hearsay. They greet me with respect, and I listen to what they say to Eza. It takes them a while to catch on that I know the language so well; it always surprises them. But even then there's never any secrecy. There might be if I'd ever tried to escape. I haven't.

I've gained thirty or forty pounds from working in the bakery. The steaming-fresh bread is too tantalizing to resist. The ovens are hot and you'd think I'd sweat if off, but it doesn't work that way. I explained to Eza about bagels and he was intrigued, so we tried to make them but they didn't turn out. I really haven't a clue about how to make them. But I've learned how hundreds of dark and aromatic loaves are produced daily in what seems like a tiny bakery. The locals come with sheets of newspaper and I use tongs to throw the hot loaves onto them. It's good bread, a given here. it still kind of amazes me.

I don't even think about Carol or my parents and brothers any more. They just seem distant, like my work consulting on pipe engineering. And maybe all this Allah stuff has rubbed off and I've become religious, because I know they're all right. They're just way over there and I'm here.

Anyway, before the war heated up, an odd thing happened involving Eza and Shabvar and Homa, the girl with the baby. Homa didn't live with a man when I first met her, and no one really knew who fathered her baby or at least that's what Eza and

Shabvar told me. Homa was somehow related to Eza and that's how they knew each other. Homa's reputation in Saqqez wasn't very good; she was known for all the men she allowed into her room, and that's how Eza knew to bring her to me. The sexual side of these people isn't as black veiled as westerners like to think. Which is not to say they were going to present me with a quivering fifteen-year-old virgin. Anyway, Eza brought me Homa and I was grateful but I wanted to ask him, hey, what's the schtick. Not to look a gift horse in the mouth, however, so I said nothing.

Both Eza and Shabvar always treat Homa with a sardonic kind of disdain, a behavioral response that I've noticed Muslims have truly mastered. But because of the family connection they watch out for her. When she's broke they give her money. She has no regular job and I'm not in the position to ask if men pay for her services. She's always neat and clean and so is her baby; I've noticed that Eza's and Shabvar's disdain doesn't extend to the baby. They give Homa food and clothing for him, and Homa drops him off with Shabvar when she's got errands to do. It didn't take me long to realize that the tiny boy was a substitute child for Shabvar and Eza, who have no children. I mentioned this one day to Eza. He shrugged it off with a wave of his hand.

"It is the only real tragedy in my life," he said as I weighed flour. "And for me it's nothing compared to how Shabvar has taken it. It's made her a sorrowful woman. She thinks life has disregarded her. For ten, twelve, fifteen years we waited patiently. Finally we realized it would never happen."

"Couldn't you have adopted a child?" I asked.

"Perhaps yes, but after waiting all those years our energy was spent. So now it just seems too difficult a thing to do. We're not young anymore. We could only play the role of grandparents now."

"You're not old," I told him. "You and Shabvar have many

strong years ahead of you."

He shook his head and laughed. "No, no. My life is like a block now." He bent to test the oven heat and I began working the dough.

A few days later I went over to Homa's apartment for the first time. It is a cramped room in the large house of a retired lawyer. I discovered that Homa earns her room and board by cooking for the old man. She makes hot meals for him in the kitchen and serves him there, and then eats her own portion up in her quarters. We sat up there together on piles of bedding.

"You eat this," she said to me, handing me a plate of rice and meat. "I'm full from watching it cook." She is slim and tiny, serpentine. I accepted the food and ate it while she breastfed the baby. I realized she didn't want to make love; she'd given me her food as a substitute.

"I'm very poor," she said. "The baby makes me poorer. Perhaps you could do me a favor."

I'd never given her money. She'd never asked and it had never occurred to me to offer. Now I realized I should have. "I have a little money," I said.

"No," she said. "The favor is more than that. The baby keeps me poor." He'd started crying so she switched him from one breast to the other and then she looked at me closely. "I had another baby which I gave to my sister. Years ago, eight years. Eza and Shabvar know this. I was younger but really no different than I am now. I can't keep a baby and watch it grow. Even now sometimes I leave the baby for hours and Ali, the lawyer, must come and stop his crying." She looked at me, examining my reaction to her story.

"Do you want me to babysit for you?" I was afraid she was going to ask me to marry her.

"No, no. What I would like is for you to ask Eza and Shabvar to take the baby. They have money and they love him already."

"You want to give up your baby?"

"They would be better parents. They care more for him than I do. They would give me some money."

"Why don't you ask them yourself? Don't you think they'll say yes? What influence do I have?" I asked.

"You can tell them I'm a bad mother. Tell them I don't eat right and the baby's milk is thin. They would never agree if I asked them to take the child. Shabvar would suspect. They would feel it was a crime, unnatural for me to give him up."

I didn't understand at all. "Why don't you want the baby?"

"But you see," she said, ignoring my question, "if you convinced them I didn't care for the baby then they would worry and would take him from me. Legally they could do it, their brother would help. And they would give me money. I could pretend to object, to go to court, and they would give me money to be quiet."

"Why don't you want the baby?" I repeated. She breastfed him, I'd never seen him more than three feet from her except when Shabvar tended him; it was impossible to separate the lives of mother and baby.

"I like small babies," she said. The child was asleep now in her arms. "I like to nurse them. I liked the two births I've had. But then I stop caring. My mother had too many children, twelve. There's no reason why I can't keep the baby. I just don't want to." She spoke without looking at me. I had a sense that the note of desperation was partially feigned. Or perhaps my language ability was failing me.

"Your first baby. Do you ever visit him?"

"No, no." She waved a thin arm, jangling her cheap bracelets. "My sister lives in Rey, near the capital. It's too far to travel. I hear the child is well. Very beautiful. And my sister is rich, married to a car dealer." A smile came into Homa's eyes. "They gave me a car for that little boy."

I was shocked and couldn't say anything for a few minutes. "What happened to the car?" I asked. I hadn't seen any women driving cars in this dusty little village; it seemed unlikely that Homa could have ever actually owned one.

"The baby would have a better home, you see. Shabvar loves the baby when I visit. You must have noticed."

"But why don't you pretend you're a bad mother so they think of it themselves?"

"They never would. Unless someone else spoke to them first. They would consider it as a terrible breach of etiquette and morals. You see, we're not closely enough related." She stopped and thought for a moment, and I couldn't tell if she was fabricating a story line or considering which bits of the tale to censor. "I'm only a little related to a distant cousin of Shabvar's. And I can't pretend well enough to convince them. I couldn't really hurt the baby. But it's true that I don't care. Ask the lawyer."

"Why do think they'd believe me?"

"You're bright, you know special things about medicine and children, all Americans do. They would believe you."

"Is it really just some money you're after?"

"No. I love the baby, too, so I want him to have a better home. But yes, I want the money. Think of it that way. That will help me more."

"I don't believe you," I said.

She shook her head and half smiled. "That is not important. Will you help me?" she asked.

I guess I must have been getting bored with the bakery, because I decided to help Homa with her crazy scheme. I was afraid she would cut me off sexually if I didn't play along. And she was right about Eza and Shabvar probably being better parents.

"Do you think Homa will have troubles raising her boy all by herself?" I asked Shabvar one morning as she and I ate breakfast together.

"Troubles? Of course she will. Homa is a grown woman but has a child's mind. She is selfish. She was the youngest of many children and she still thinks she's the only baby in the world. The boy will not turn out well. See? Even you expect trouble."

"Why did she keep the baby?" I asked.

"Why did she keep the baby? Of course she kept it. She's a mother. The boy needs his mother. It might have been worse if she'd given it away. She may be selfish but she's not bad or lazy. One cannot give one's child away."

"That's what I think, too," I said. And I did think so. But it seemed I'd steered into a dead end. I'd have to try harder.

"Do you think she treats the baby well now?" I asked, hoping the ice wasn't too thin.

"Why do you ask?" Shabvar asked. She peered into my eyes. "What has she done wrong with him?"

"Oh nothing. It's just that she seems…."

"Seems?"

"Seems like she'd be happier without it. Him. I mean, does she feed him right?"

"Feed him right? The boy is fat and happy," said Shabvar. "Of course she feeds him right. What do YOU know about babies?"

"Nothing really. I just wondered. Sometimes he looks a little pale to me."

Shabvar let out a loud laugh, the first I'd ever heard from her. "He's very healthy, don't worry."

Then she looked at me more closely. "I can see you're like me. He's stolen your heart, too."

I reported to Homa that I was getting nowhere. She told me to try harder, lie more. When I asked her exactly how much money she wanted to extort from Eza and Shabvar, her figure was in the range of two thousand dollars. The quantification of the whole thing made it seem like a more viable project. I kind of got swept up in it, and I began seeing myself in some cockeyed romantic light—a baby provider for the sweet older couple. And Homa hadn't touched me since she'd brought up her idea. I'd developed a craving for her, so I tried to please her.

"Well, what lies should I tell?" I asked her.

"I've thought it out. But you'll have to change things depending on how they react. I don't know what they'll think is bad enough. But try this. Tell them you came here and found the baby alone and you had to feed him and change the diaper. And then tell them the next time you came you found me gone and Ali very upset and changing the boy's diaper. That will be very shocking. And tell them Ali was so upset he complained to you about me."

"But won't they ask Ali about it?"

"No, no. And if they did, he would never admit that such a scandal went on in his own home. But it's quite believable that he would complain to you in the heat of the moment, and you come so often he sees us as close relations."

"Oh," I said. "But what if Eza and Shabvar decide to visit, to see for themselves?"

"No, they never come here. I always go to them."

"OK, I said. "But this may take quite a while. They really don't seem to think you're too bad."

"Frighten them," she said. "Frighten them."

I told the diaper story to Eza while we threw hot loaves from the ovens.

"Well?" he said. "She is not very clean." He paused and looked at me. "I'd be careful if I were you. Wash carefully. If you think you need a doctor, let me know." Then he moved to another part of the bakery and I realized he was evading any continuation of the discussion.

I took my tales to Shabvar. This time I made it sound like the baby stewed in his own filth for days on end.

"And just yesterday," I said, "she was off buying stockings and I found the baby asleep on the floor in the hall. He could have fallen down the steps."

Shabvar's reaction was much more encouraging. She made a sort of cluck and then flew off to find Eza.

I felt well on the road to success. When I told Homa how things were going she smiled and patted my head. She stared into space, smiling and gazing at the pictures in her own mind. Then she remembered me and put her hands on either side of my neck and gently stroked. We spent a pleasant evening together—the first in a long time. But after she left and I went to bed, I was awakened by nightmares of me and Homa going from one car dealer to the next, bartering for the fanciest car possible in exchange for the fat little boy in the basket under my arm. And all the car dealers were Eza.

The next day after lunch Eza brought me a cup of tea and told me to talk with him for a few minutes. I sat on a barrel of flour.

"Please don't tell those stories about Homa to Shabvar anymore," he said. "She knows they're not true, but still they upset her."

I nodded and said nothing.

"Don't feel bad," he said. "Homa is kind of a bad girl. She's put you up to this, Shabvar and I can tell. Let me tell you a little story about Homa. A month or so before you came here she came to see me. A "business call." She said she'd give me the boy if I gave her a certain sum of money. Well, I'll be honest with you, I thought about it. Shabvar and I talked it over. She'd always wanted a child so badly. Our first impulse was to give Homa the money and take the child. But very soon we both realized it was wrong—not that we'd be bad parents, but what would this baby do when he's not a baby anymore? How could this boy cope with life knowing he was traded for a sum of money, treated like a bag of rice?"

Eza shook his head and looked at his hands. He was talking more to himself than to me. I was a little surprised by the story, but it made sense.

"So Homa's just plain crazy," I said.

"Well, she's a mixed-up girl. She doesn't know what she wants." He patted me on the shoulder. "She's very fond of you."

I snorted. I'd like to have told her off, rubbed flour in her face.

"No, you must be understanding," Eza said. "She's not all crazy. She doesn't really hurt the little boy at all." He paused. "And she treats grown men very well."

"I guess so," I said. I felt disgusted.

"Oh yes she does. She treats men well," he repeated for some odd reason, and I began to feel the burgeoning of some unwanted knowledge. "It was hard for *me* not to take the child. I didn't have to tell Shabvar about the money, you see. But I did."

"I see. I see," I said, resisting awareness and suddenly feeling myself emotionally aligned with Homa again, groping to side with another underdog. I decided for safety's sake not to try to examine all this too closely. It's not my culture. I'm a prisoner here, a pawn in a lot of what goes on.

All this business ended before the war got so very near and terrifying; I think I already mentioned that. Homa and I are on good terms again even though I had to tell her I'd blown her little scheme and wasn't going to try it again. She shrugged and gave in gracefully. Just like the queen of Sheba. Just as if she had a lot of real options.

To be honest, we enjoy each other very much. Her baby doesn't really have a formal name yet and as a joke I've been trying to get her to call him Jimi or Elvis. She laughs. He walks a little now. We sit out in the lawyer's garden; I water the oleander and fuchsia which somehow spring so brightly out of the parched clay. If I live through this war I'd like to move in with her, or get a bigger place together. The lawyer has noticed some of my work around his old pile of a house, and he's started making inquiries regarding my availability for employment. The novelty of the bakery has worn off. I wouldn't mind cajoling more blossoms out of this cracked earth.

Bashfulness Is Required in the Kingdom

"Saudi Arabia has a desert in the sad heart of it," writes one of my English composition students. After a bit more scrutiny I realize she may mean southeast; her writing is close to illegible. Teaching English to young Arab ladies in Riyadh is pleasant and undemanding, and on the whole I am enjoying my time here as a young married woman, off on an adventure in a foreign land and even earning a respectable salary. My students, all Muslim, are mainly Saudi or Palestinian, though there are sprinklings of Syrians, Bahrainis, Yemenis and Egyptians. They're university students of eighteen to twenty-two years old, and they're eager and attentive; they fight for the teacher's attention: "Missus, Missus, Missus," they call out as they lean forward, arms flailing toward me. They are generous in their affection; it's not unusual for them to take my arm as they accompany me down the college corridor. But they quickly determine the religious status of all their teachers: "You are Christian?" they ask with disgust and incredulity. I can't explain that I'm nothing really, for atheism and agnosticism are blasphemous stances here. However, the non-Muslim and thus infidel status of me and most of my fellow western teachers is generally ignored; the students accept us graciously, kindly, with open arms.

The mores in this land are intricate and inscrutable. I come to the country with a simple Panama hat: excellent sun protection, I think, and quietly elegant, to boot. But when I wear it I find locals doing double takes and generally staring at me in a perturbed way. A fellow teacher named Mary, a stalwart widow from Minnesota whose children are grown, informs me that that type of hat is slightly taboo—the broad brim is seen as flirtatious.

"But I'm covering my head," I say. "I thought that's what they liked."

"Nope," Mary tells me. "Hats are not the thing here."

I learn that it's perfectly acceptable for non-Muslim women to appear in public bare-headed, but their hair must not be loose and flowing. Mary takes me to the souq, the ancient labyrinth of shops in the center of the city, so I can buy the ankle length skirts and dresses that are *de rigueur* here.

We think of our students as girls though perhaps half of them are married and have children. Child care is not a problem for almost everyone lives within an extended family. There is a pervasive girlishness at the college, and the typical student dress throws a western woman off a bit. Below their floor-length skirts they wear candy-colored high heels. The skirts are usually cut very narrow, so the girls mince around, knees close together. The university dictates that all students enter and exit the college completely veiled in black. The trip between Mercedes or Nissan Laurel and the college entry gate is made as Hugh Hefner fantasy material: slim, veiled virgins in spiked heels, knees somewhat bound.

Once inside the college, the girls roll their black silk capes into tiny bundles and stow them away in their purses or book bags. The college consists of four two-story oblong buildings, and there are small garden areas here and there. Between classes the girls sit strewn among the oleander and fuchsia, laughing, chattering, eating ices or tabhouli salad. They are in the loveliness of full bloom, but one notices a surprising number of crossed eyes and unchecked acne problems. Clothing is generally polyester and mismatched, though certain students have startlingly lovely collections of silk blouses. The university suggests the girls wear green skirts, so one sees every shade of green. Among the students there is an evident weakness for T-shirts covered with Mickey Mouse or P.L.O. symbols and slogans. T-shirts with English expressions are also popular, but the language barrier creates oddities: one student occasionally wears a shirt that announces "Piss Artist." Another girl sports "I'm like wine. I improve with age." We western teachers goggle at that one, for alcohol is verboten in this land. And a third girl sometimes walks around with I-like-to-screw in pictogram across her chest: an eye, the word like, the number two, and then a drawing of the metal bit.

Most of the girls wear gold chains and bracelets. It is the soft, dully gleaming 21 karat gold that is prevalent here. No silver is seen; it's inexpensive and looked down upon. No traditional heavy Bedouin crude beads or tarnished metal adornments are worn; that's the style of their grandmothers and the girls love what they consider modern, up-to-date. And yet traditional henna use is quite common. The reddish rust tone is in their hair, on their fingernails, and even on the palms of their hands and the bottoms of their feet. "Beautiful. It's beautiful, Missus," they say when I ask them why they do it. They explain to me that a bride might henna her legs from toe to knee so that her groom finds her especially enticing. "Very beautiful, Missus."

These delicate and amiable creatures are the sheltered nucleus of this exotic Islamic world, and so the women's college is a very cloistered affair. No males except repairmen may set foot inside, and only well after college hours. There are a number of male teachers but their presence is strictly via video.

The Saudi girls seem happy with their lot; I try to scratch through to any interior discontent, but I only seem to find more layers of a very simple-seeming happiness. They are cheerful, smiling, giggly, pliable. But then perhaps they have no reason not to be; they are the pampered children of a people who were used to eking out a minimal survival until oil brought them every imaginable material comfort. The girls live amidst parents and grandparents who tell them tales of an arid and dusty past; it seems they realize how charmed their lives are.

The Palestinian girls possess a more western complexity; they haven't known insulated, trauma-free lives. They carry passports that label them refugees, and I've heard a Saudi girl remind them of it. "I'm not one of these refugees," she said haughtily, throwing her head back toward some of the other students, when I asked her where she was born. Palestinians in Saudi Arabia are second class citizens who can't own houses or control businesses.

Arab students are accustomed to learning by rote, the way they learned the Koran. Some sit through months and months of daily English classes and still say "me" for "you." "What is your name?" my workmate Mary asked a particularly obtuse girl every morning for nine months, and every morning that girl turned to a classmate for a translation of the question. "You develop a lot of patience here," Mary says, and she's right. The prevailing atmosphere is gentle and relaxed nurturing; after all, we students and teachers are together in the complex five days of the week. There are no Saudi instructors who teach English, but it is clear that Saudi teachers on campus have authority over us infidel westerners. We give them a wide berth and they mostly ignore us, but in a pleasant enough way: there's a tacit agreement that we don't share a language of any sort.

The students too are not overly curious about western teachers' lives nor about Britain or America. Their knowledge of the U.S. seems limited to Disneyland and Michael Jackson. They are puzzled when they come across the term "hot-dog" in a grammar exercise: "You eat dog in America?" one Saudi student quietly asks me, her face pale with disgust. I learn at some point Mohammed didn't care for dogs; the Koran instructs the faithful to wash their hand seven times after touching a dog. "Oh, no, it's not really dog," I tell them, and then I hesitate for I can't go too far in explicating hot dogs for aren't they usually made of pork? And of course pork is not a topic for polite conversation here.

As an exercise I instruct the students to ask each other what countries they'd like to visit.

"Bahrain," says a little Bahraini named Huda.

"America," says a Palestinian named Awatif.

"Qatar," says Jamila, a Saudi. "Men from Qatar very handsome, beautiful."

"Are they?" I ask, impressed with her ability to make fine distinctions, for to me all Gulf Arabs are equally lovely—the most breathtaking people in the world with their piercing dark eyes and their flashing white teeth.

"No. Bahrainis are the most handsome," says tiny Huda.

Flurries of discussion in Arabic.

"Kuwaitis are handsome, aren't they?" I say, trying to steer the conversation back into English.

They register my remark, but they continue to twitter in their own language. Amid the hubbub Jamila says to me, "Missus, I can only marry from my family. I can only marry a man from my family." She belongs to one of the four tribes that ruled this part of Arabia previous to the reign of the Al Saud, the current ruling family.

"Why?" I ask.

"Because we only marry our family. Our family old, old. Powerful before...." She hesitates, glances about. "Powerful before Abdulaziz." She pronounces the name of the first Saudi king with slight disgust. "Our family from before that. Our family thousands, thousands years old."

"I see. So your family wants to stay together to stay strong."

"Yes. But I don't want to marry from my family. But I must. I can't choose. Before wedding I see pictures only. If I don't like pictures, I say no to man."

Huda, the Bahraini, has been listening, and now she jumps in. "She can't have love first. She can't marry the man she love."

"So you can't choose at all?" I ask Jamila.

Jamila shakes her head, and Huda draws a finger in a quick line across her throat. "If she fall in love...." she says, laughing.

I teach three different groups. The group with Huda, Awatif, and Jamila includes twelve students—six Saudi, five Palestinian, and one Bahraini. This is the usual mix.

Western teachers receive only one instruction when they sign their contract: not to speak to students about sex, religion, or politics. Everyone understands that controversial classroom discussions will be the basis for dismissal, for non-renewal of contract, perhaps even for quick escort to the airport with immediate exit/no re-entry visa stamped firmly into one's passport. However, all three topics come up frequently, of course. One day my students ask me what my name means. "Christine, Christine, Christine," I hear them whispering to each other.

"It's a Christian name," I say, feeling a bit tentative. "But it's just a name. Jewish people probably don't give it to their children. But Christian people probably aren't thinking of religion too much when they give it to their child."

There's a pause, and the girls look at me skeptically. But all of a sudden they come to life. "When you learn Arabic, you be excellent, Missus," says Awatif.

"You have a son, you give him Muslim name," says Jamila. "You name him Hussam."

"Hussam? What does that mean?"

"Hussam mean knife. Knife for war."

"Knife! But that's so cruel, so hard," I say.

"Yes, Missus, power, strong. Good name," they say. A number of the girls are named Hend, and later I learn this means scabbard.

"I bring you Koran, Missus," says Manal, a Palestinian. Then the girls quickly confer among themselves in Arabic.

"What are you saying? Say it in English," I order. It's my mantra with them.

They look at me, reluctant to speak. "Missus," Jamila finally says, "you must wash before reading the Koran. You must wash all body."

"And the eight days, Missus, the eight days that fall down on a woman," says Huda, "you must not read Koran then."

"I see, I see. But why? Who told you this?"

"That's what it says," they all say. "That's what we're told."

"Missus, sometimes when I read Koran, I cry. It's so beautiful," says Manal. All nod in agreement. "Beautiful, beautiful, Missus," they murmur. It is a widely held Arab belief that Arabic is the most beautiful-sounding language in the world, and I too come to believe this, especially as I listen to the daily calls to prayer that are broadcast aloud throughout the city. The sound is lush and melancholy and resonant. I feel charmed to live in this special aura, for the people's devotion is touching, deep, genuine. Even the most flighty-seeming girls are devout in word and in practice. Every college toilet stall is material evidence; all are equipped with spray hoses so that the faithful may wash private parts and feet before prayer. And every day the restroom floors are flooded. We western teachers, still unaccustomed to our long skirts, curse to each other as we slosh through the wet restrooms.

The students lean over the banister on an upper landing and watch for the approach of the teachers. When the teachers are sighted, the students giggle and rush off toward the classrooms, hand in hand. To me they seem innocents without enough objects for their affections but I realize it's partly that I'm more used to western taciturnity. One of the Palestinian girls comes up to me one day and asks if she can talk to me for a few minutes. She is obviously upset and on the verge of tears.

"What's wrong, Awatif?"

She blushes and shakes her head and looks away. I put an arm around her.

"Oh, what is it? You can tell me."

"I love you, Missus," she finally blurts out. She covers her mouth with her hands. "I love you all my heart."

"Oh," I say. It is the first declaration of love I've ever had from a nineteen-year-old girl. "You live at the hostel, don't you, Awatif?" The hostel is a student dormitory and is considered a pathetic place to reside; the great majority of the students live at home or with local families.

"Yes."

"And do you have sisters at home?" I find I'm automatically scrambling to change the subject, to twist the matter into some recognizable formula.

"Yes. In Al Jouf."

"Oh. So you must miss your sisters. You must want to have a sister here. Well, you and I can be friends." I say.

"I love you, Missus," repeats Awatif. "I love you like my sister."

"That's nice, Awatif. It's nice to love people," I say, sounding as lame as I feel. "We should get to class now."

She gives me puppy dog eyes for a few weeks. I usually don't have to deal with problems any more difficult than this one. We teachers are lucky here. These students are as eager to please as small children, but they're quieter and less restless. Teaching in the west is more of a challenge because the students there test the teacher constantly; they don't accept your authority until you've proven yourself. Here there's very little battle of wits with the students. That's why Manal, one of my Palestinian students, irritated me so very much at first. She stuck out; she was the nearest thing here to a class mischief maker. She'd stroll in to the class late and hiss "sssssalaam alaykum" to everyone, and she'd draw out that initial "s" needlessly, annoyingly. Then she'd joke in Arabic throughout the class and distract the other students. I could feel my antipathy toward her growing until I realized that she was the only one who had a healthy disregard for teacherly authority. Generally the girls are the meekest of lambs: one day I sat atop my desk cleaning out a folder as the girls worked on compositions. I took a pile of old memos and ripped them in half. All the girls' heads jerked up at me; I read fear in all their eyes. They thought I was ripping up unsatisfactory student work, or some such thing. "It's nothing," I said sheepishly. "It's just trash, old things." Manal wasn't there that time, but if she had been she would have laughed at the other girls. It's a blessing that she's here; perhaps she'll teach the other girls something about assertiveness, about individuality.

I bought myself a traditional Bedouin dancing dress but I found I couldn't get my head through the opening. It was tunic-length; I thought it might look great with black pants, if I could only get my head through. Finally I took it to the college and asked the girls. They immediately started to laugh. "For little girl, Missus!"

"Oh, of course, " I said. Tunic-length. Stupid me.

Anyway, a week or so later, Huda, the tiny Bahraini, brought me an adult-length dancing dress. It's a traditional Gulf Arab garment; this one is red chiffon-ish stuff, heavily trimmed in gold sequins and brocade. It's lovely and the perfect thing for costume parties back home.

Huda weighs thirty-five kilos and her feet dangle a few inches off the floor as she sits at her desk. If she and I stand together in conversation, I have to fight the urge to squat down like you might for a six year old. Her figure is a perfectly formed woman's figure; it's just minuscule in scale. She's been banished to Saudi Arabia by her strict parents who feared the more westernized social milieu of Bahrain. "I play too much with boys there," Huda tells me. "My parents very angry." She's clearly homesick for Bahrain. Every time I ask her to use a verb or invent a sentence, she brings up Bahrain: "I would like to go to Bahrain." "Bahrain is a beautiful country." One day she tries the patience of Jamila, the Saudi. "If you marry Saudi boy, you stay in Saudi Arabia," Jamila tells her, an edge of malice in her voice. "You never go back."

"I not marry Saudi. Never," Huda laughs. "I marry Bahraini, Kuwaiti. Not Saudi."

I nod and smile and move back to a grammar issue, but I'm storing this little exchange in my memory as a bit of evidence that there is general recognition among these students that this country is a cage for women, gilded though it might be.

Huda tells me she loves to write and keeps a diary. "I write songs in it," she says. I'm very impressed and ask to see some of them. She brings her diary in and lets me examine it, but I'm disappointed to see that it contains only lyrics of western pop hits: oooooh, love to love you, baby—and other stuff of that ilk. But then I realize she is practicing writing English and on top of that I am touched by her romantic streak.

The students are fine makeup artists; all highlight their dark good looks with eye makeup and lipstick, and many use elaborate foundation lotions despite their youth. They look like China dolls, and it's all for each other. If they don't have time to apply their morning makeup, they tend to sit in the back of the room and huddle behind a book or to make some excuse to run off to one of the restrooms.

One of the students brings a friend into the class. They sit together in the back of the room. "Where do you come from?" I ask the visitor.

"From Yemen."

"Ooooooooooh," cry out many of the girls in disgust, as if they've come upon a squashed lizard. They turn and look at the Yemeni. She blushes and shrugs. I stand in front of the class, shocked and at a loss.

"Oh, no," I say to them. "You can't …. you can't say things like that. It's not right."

"Yes, Missus, Yemen very bad," says Jamila. "Very poor and dirty."

I see that the visitor is struggling to maintain a brave face, and I change the subject. Later I feel guilty about not lecturing the girls on prejudice, but then I realize it would be swimming through mud.

Mary and I discuss how much we miss the exuberance and energy of American students. The girls here are attentive but tentative, bird-like, and easily scared. They very rarely ask questions about anything; analysis and curiosity are not parts of the educational fabric in this part of the world. I never yell at the students or display the slightest annoyance—I've taken the cue from them, for they always seem completely pleased and delighted with me.

One day the girls invite various teachers to a college activities evening. Mary and I decide to go together. It turns out to be a sort of amateur-hour variety show. Two sisters roller skate, a group of eight does very simple acrobatics, another group in pink leotards performs a very childish and inexpert ballet. All legs are covered in baggy warm-up pants; "Bashfulness is Required in the Kingdom" proclaims a bulletin at the entry to the gym. The bulletin goes on to specify that lady swimmers must cover their legs. These rules are enforced even though all sports activities are strictly sexually segregated: women may not even bare their bodies among one another. Mary and I whisper to each other and plan to remove the notice to keep as a souvenir, but there are too many young Arab women wandering about and we as teachers certainly can't be caught stealing. "Be sure to jot down the main points when we sit down," Mary says to me in an undertone.

The audience at the show is all-female, of course. Some spectators are dressed in trousers, but most wear elaborate full-length party dresses, frothy concoctions of lace and gold lamé and fluorescent polyester. Girls walk around distributing chocolates, hard candy, and bottles of water. The show makes my blood run cold after a while; here are twenty-year-old girls performing at a level of six-year-olds at a dance recital. There's a booth of judges, all princesses of the Al Saud. In front of them are stacked piles of gold medallions, elaborate china tea sets, and other prizes. Mary and I gaze at their splendid clothes and royal visages. Every performer wins a prize, and all prizes are first prize. It's all very pleasant, but I feel stifled, hemmed in by what I perceive as excessive treacle. I am comforted that Mary sits at my elbow and we can exchange glances. There is one piece that has a zestful panache—a wedding dance in which a Jordanian student takes the part of the man. She dances with verve and imagination, and the audience howls at her imitation of a male. The other acts pale in comparison.

Throughout the show our students run up to us in their fancy dresses; they show us their prizes. We nod and smile and give compliments, but I feel hypocritical, unethical, and I notice Mary shifting around in her seat. I'm thinking I have to help these young women realize how thwarted, how aborted their lives are. I can't pass my horror off as simple cultural chauvinism. Mary and I go home bored and depressed and slightly nauseated—the evening lasted seven hours and only that candy and water were available.

One day I walk into the classroom and all the girls are in heated discussion. It's something quite unusual.

"What are you saying?" I ask.

"Oh, Missus," says Jamila. "Jews very handsome. Jews most handsome men in world. Do you think?"

"Jews?" I repeat, not thinking I'd heard correctly.

"Yes, Missus."

"Yes, some of them are very handsome," I say, opting for neutrality. "Just like people everywhere, some are very handsome, some not."

The Palestinian girls murmur indistinctly. "No, no," says Manal. She shakes her head at Jamila.

"I wish I marry Jew," bursts out Jamila.

"No, no, Jews terrible," says Manal. She flings her hand forward, dismissing the subject.

"There are handsome people everywhere," I say lamely, trying to steer the conversation into safer territory. "What about Italians?"

"Oh, Italians!" say the girls. "Yes, Italians!"

I can't decide whether the discussion of Jews was meant to tease the Palestinians or was conceived from the exotic and untouchable picture these girls seem to have of Jews.

One of the students comes up to me and says she saw me in the gold souq—the multiple small shops of the gold market. Everyone living in the Gulf always has a moderate gold fever. Westerners frequent the gold souq as one of the few legal leisure activities here; in addition, they convince themselves the gold is a good investment akin to stocks, bonds. And the locals too are regular purchasers of gold; brides traditionally are given much gold jewelry, and it is considered their bank account.

"I followed you around," this student is telling me. "I watched you shop in the gold souq. Me and my mother," she says, giggling.

"Why didn't you come up and say hello to me?" I ask, slightly horrified at being spied upon.

"Our faces covered. You not see us." She giggles again. "We follow you around, we watch you."

I nod and quickly start speaking of something else for I feel bemused and a tad violated. But perhaps it's fine that I served as entertainment for the girl and her mother.

I ask the girls to make some comparisons between Riyadh and Jeddah.

"Jeddah very nice," says Manal. "In Jeddah women don't …." She makes the sharp gesture downward across her face that the students use as shorthand for the word veil.

"Oh, I see. They don't veil." I write the word on the board for the umpteenth time. "They don't cover their faces."

"Yes, very nice, Jeddah," says Manal.

A pregnant Saudi student turns to her. "Good Muslim women do…." She finishes the sentence with the same downward hand sweep. "In Jeddah, yes."

"I see. Good Muslim women veil even in Jeddah," I say.

The pregnant girl nods vigorously. Manal, seated behind her, shakes her head and shrugs.

"Scuse me, Missus," Jamila says in class in the middle of a lesson. "Was this book written by a man?" I pause, wondering what she has in mind. "Because you see it says women talk, men listen,'" she explains, smiling and pointing to one of the exercises. The students laugh. I'm pleased; it's a novelty for a student to make a joke in English, and a joke with a hint of feminism.

Faten, a married Saudi student, always wears a large, crudely worked but valuable gold necklace. "See what her husband give her?" says Jamila, touching Faten's necklace. Another student says something in Arabic and everyone laughs.

"Tell me in English," I say.

"She say we all too old to marry, Missus," says Jamila.

"We very old. We too old to marry. Get marry here at fifteen. We nineteen, too old," says Manal.

"My mother marry when she twelve years, Missus," calls out Jamila.

"Here twenty old woman. Twenty-three very very very old. Twenty-three only marry old man—forty, fifty."

"My aunt and uncle tell my father get husband for her, get husband—she too old.' I nineteen," says Jamila.

"What do your parents say?" I ask.

"They say no, I too young to marry. I only girl in family, I young one in family, they want to keep me at home. They love me too much, they say," says Jamila.

"I see, I see," I say. Now that the opportunity has arisen, I think over other marriage-related questions I'd like answered.

"Do many men have more than one wife?" I ask.

Responses burst out.

"If I marry and husband take a second wife, I kill him," says Jamila immediately. She is smiling but definite.

"If he take a second wife, I leave him," says Manal.

A Saudi girl rubs her thumb across her fingers and laughs and shakes her head. I can guess that she's saying it's not that easy.

"What are you saying, Kadija?" I ask her.

She chatters in Arabic to the other girls. They laugh. "She says, Missus, that if husband give her twenty-five thousand riyals before marriage, if she leave him she must give it back."

"If he take another wife, I kill him and her. I kill them both," says Jamila.

"Does it happen very often?" I ask her.

"Yes, Missus, my brother, my biggest brother have two wives. He marry one and she have one baby, but her mother not good. Wife's mother not good. So he leave first wife and marry a second wife. She have five children with him. Then he go back to the first wife and want to keep second wife, too," says Jamila.

"So how does the second wife feel?" I ask.

"She angry, she cry, she very sad. But now she say yes, now she used to it."

Occasionally there is a chink of light. "Missus, I move to Milwaukee," Manal tells me one day out of the blue. She still comes to class late; she still hisses "ssssssalaam."

"You're moving to Milwaukee?! I ask. She might as well have said the moon. "Milwaukee, Wisconsin? Milwaukee in America?"

"Yes, Missus. Milwaukee America. I study English there. My sister there now studying engineering."

"How wonderful!" I say. I'm thrilled for her. It seems crystal clear to me that a young Palestinian girl would be much better off in the midwest of America than here, here in the sad-hearted desert. "It's very cold in winter there!" I say to her. "You'll need very warm clothes!"

Manal brings in her sister, who's in Riyadh on semester break from the University of Wisconsin in Milwaukee. "Milwaukee is very nice city," she tells me. "People in Milwaukee very nice, very friendly. People in Milwaukee like the P.L.O. I love Milwaukee. Chicago very bad, very dirty, but Milwaukee nice."

"Oh yes, Milwaukee's a wonderful place," I tell her. The words echo in my mind for a split second and I realize I'm just blustering. I know Riyadh better than I know Milwaukee. But still, Manal's imminent escape from the Kingdom makes me very happy for her. The two sisters invite me to their home for a farewell party. I notice their passports lying on a tabletop, and I ask if I may take a look. Manal flips hers open to the page with the entry visa for the United States. I look at it and then look at it again. It's a three-month tourist visa. It specifies non-student, non-worker status. Manal's sister notices the expression on my face when I look up. "No problem," she says. "We change it there. No problem."

I hope she's right. I don't worry about it too much; the important thing for Manal is to get out of the Gulf and marry a nice Milwaukee college boy. A month later I hear that she's very homesick and cold in Milwaukee. I don't worry a single speck. She'll survive, I feel.

The mid-semester exam reduces the students to tears. A crowd of seventy takes it in one room. One starts to cry and then another and suddenly it seems that dozens of them are weeping. We western teachers stand with hands on hips, looking at one another, wondering what to do.

Awatif, the Palestinian who told me she loved me, worries me more than the other students. She's a sweet but bumbling eighteen-year-old who follows western teachers around like a puppy, pleased with the slightest show of attention. She possesses a lopsided smile and a propensity to grab and hug one when no other students are around. She's short and femininely rounded, and she wears her hair loosely on top of her head in a Victorian bun. Sometimes she looks slightly dirty, so I've asked her about her home life. She no longer lives in the hostel; her brother has moved to town and she lives with him. She does all the cooking and cleaning. They fight a lot about the television and the stereo, she says, and who gets to use what when.

During class I've sometimes noticed her smiling at me in a pleased cat sort of way; she's clearly paying no attention to the lesson at hand.

"You happy, Missus?" she asks me one day after class.

"Yes, Awatif. I'm happy. Are you happy?"

"You happy, Missus, I happy," says Awatif.

Awatif's native intelligence has not been cultivated carefully; many western teachers smile grimly when her name comes up. Whatever the case, she never scores high enough to pass any of the English proficiency tests although she returns semester after semester. The only time I've seen her unhappy was at the end of a final exam session. She performed miserably and she knew it, so she refused to give up her exam paper. She seemed to think that if she stewed over it long enough, she would come up with some correct answers. We western teachers were anxious to escape from the exam room, so three of us ganged up on Awatif and took the paper. I'm ashamed I didn't do more to comfort her at that moment; I still remember her captured-doe look as she held on to the exam booklet while we three infidel bullies tried to take it from her.

But the truth is, Awatif doesn't work very hard. I don't think she knows how to, and I haven't had much success in helping her improve. Everything she hands in is done in a hasty, slapdash way. At first I'd administer bromides like YOU'RE IMPROVING! or KEEP WORKING! written in block letters across her papers. But Awatif got in the habit of coming up to me and demanding a more judgmental response. "Good, Missus?" she'd ask, holding up a miserable piece of work. "Well, not really, Awatif," I'd say. So I began writing harsher comments: POOR WORK! YOUR HANDWRITING IS TERRIBLE! CORRECT ALL THESE VERBS! I CAN'T READ THIS! But even this wasn't clear enough for Awatif.

"Good, Missus?" she asked me one day, holding up a paper upon which I'd written ALL WRONG!! DO THIS AGAIN!

"No, Awatif. This is not good. Do you see what I wrote?"

"Not good, Missus?" Awatif asked, and I noticed a twinkle in her eye; she was flirting with me.

"No, Awatif," I said, smiling at her. "It's not good. Please write more carefully, work more slowly."

She never has, of course. Everything is always done devoid of capitals, verb endings, punctuation. One day I sit correcting papers and find that Awatif has handed in a particularly atrocious piece of work on a filthy sheet of paper torn from a notebook. I am short-tempered this day, so I block in BAD! across the top in huge red letters. The next day I return the papers. When I happen to look over at Awatif, I see her huddled over her desk, crying. She has crumpled the paper and thrown it under her seat. She mopes and weeps quietly through the rest of the class. I feel a little annoyed with both of us; she is acting like a baby, and I'd been mistaken in giving such a negative response.

The next day Awatif comes up to me after class and hands me a tape cassette. She's given me tapes before—third-rate pop groups such as Boney M and Bananarama—the same stuff all the girls listen to. This time, however, the tape is a peace offering.

"For you, Missus. Michael Jackson."

"Oh! Michael Jackson. Thank you, Awatif."

"You angry by me, Missus?"

"No. Why?"

"Because yesterday I throw paper under chair. I sorry, Missus."

"Oh, that's all right, Awatif."

"Tape very beautiful," says a beaming Awatif. "Michael Jackson very beautiful. He American, like you."

The tape is a copy she's made herself, and it reeks of perfume. And she's inked carefully on it: To Mrs Cress, my fraind and sester—remember me. She's even made a delicate tiny drawing of an arrow-pierced heart.

One day in class I notice that something is wrong with Awatif's nose; there is a perfectly round, nearly dime-sized burn on it, just slightly off dead center. I can't imagine how she'd gotten it; I glance at her frequently trying to figure out possible origins. It looks like a burn from a car's cigarette lighter. The more I look at it, the surer I am that that's what it is. Oh god, I think, what chasms of mystery.

"What happened to your nose?" I ask Awatif after class.

She looks slightly upset. "My brother. He mad at me because I forget to wake him up."

I feel suddenly frozen. I have to force myself to speak. "Tell him not to do that again," I say slowly and clearly.

"He good man, he make mistake," says Awatif. She gives a little wave of her hand. "He not bad."

That day when I get home I send a friend in the States twenty dollars to send me a Michael Jackson T-shirt; it will be a gift for Awatif.

Awatif strikes us as innocent and mildly retarded, but she's got a devilish streak. Lately she's begun querying us about sex.

"What meaning orgy, Missus?" she asks in the middle of class, pronouncing the word with a hard "g."

"Pardon me?"

"Orgy, Missus. What meaning orgy? O - R - G - Y."

"Oh." I pause. "Well, it's a party, it's a kind of party." I keep my face bland. "Where you have too much of something. For example, if two people eat a lot of chocolate, an entire cake. That's an orgy of chocolate."

"Party, Missus?" asks Awatif, scrutinizing my face closely.

"Yes, like a party." I immediately realize this definition might be a mistake; parties are among the few highlights of these girls' lives, and they write about them often in compositions. Now they might refer to them as orgies.

The next day Awatif comes up with another request, but this time I am on guard.

"Missus, what meaning planzation?" she asks, again in the middle of the lesson. The other girls perk up their ears; they see the little smile on Awatif's lips.

"Planzation?"

"Yes. Planzation."

"Hmm. Planzation. Do you mean plantation?" I sort through possible sexual aspects of the word.

"Planzation," she repeats.

"There's no such word as planzation, Awatif. You must mean plantation. It's a large farm."

"Large farm, Missus?" Repeats Awatif, giving me a skeptical look.

"Yes, a large farm." The other students lose interest and their faces relax back into incuriosity. I realize Awatif must mean implantation. She's perhaps gotten hold of some sort of sex and reproduction manual.

Sure enough, the next day Awatif has another query, but this time she asks a different teacher, a Scottish woman named Jane.

"Hingman, what or who's a hingman?" asks Jane as she strides into the teachers' office and heads for a dictionary.

"Who wants to know?" I ask.

"Awatif from your class."

"Hingman?" asks Mary. "How is she spelling it?"

"Hingman," I say. "Oh. Hymen. She must mean hymen. She's into sex lately."

We teachers enjoy a brief laugh about this, but I feel a passing stab of regret that I can't rescue Awatif, that I can't do more to improve her lot.

Not much later than this Awatif gives me another tape. "To my fraind Mr crass" this one says across the label. I'd devolved slightly from Mrs Cress. "I remember you every day" is scrawled across the tape. "You my dear and my fraind (forever). Love, love, Awatif. I listen to the tape at home; it is Arabic music but too garbled and badly recorded to enjoy. But I keep the tape because of Awatif's written messages.

"You have brothers?" Awatif asks me one day. "Brothers in America?"

"Yes, I do. Three brothers."

"You have pictures, Missus?"

"No. I didn't bring any, Awatif. Oh wait a minute, I've got a picture of my husband here in my purse. Would you like to see that?"

Awatif gives me a blank look. "No pictures of brothers?" she persists.

I shake my head. She's looking into my eyes. We gaze at each other and say nothing, paying a kind of fleeting respect to this escape fantasy of hers.

The failing students who retain little English come back semester after semester even though Mary and Jane and I and all the western teachers try our best to dissuade them. But our powers are limited; flunking out rarely occurs in Saudi universities no matter how richly the student deserves it. Awatif is a classic example, a student who stays in the beginning English courses term after term. And yet we don't especially mind; it makes for a bridge between semesters.

And so back to the college for a new semester after vacation escape to westernized lands where I can wear jeans and drink wine in sun-splashed cafes. Awatif, the sweet, the crafty, the nebulous, grabs me and kisses me twice on each cheek.

"Welcome, Missus. Welcome."

"Hello, Awatif. What are you going to study this time?"

"Of course English, Missus. I like it too much. I want to read Shakespeare."

"OK, Awatif. That's fine," I say. The vacation has put me

back in the grip of western efficiency, of perceived practicality, so I become didactic: "But I want you to know that you'll never succeed. You'll never be able to take courses beyond the beginner's level." This is sad, but true. Awatif's English is not good enough to meet even the very low standard of the English literature department.

"It is hopeless, Awatif. You won't be able to go on to advanced English. It is hopeless." I feel like I am doing Awatif a service by ladling out this bitter medicine.

"Hopeless, Missus?" Awatif says. She has been watching me carefully and is on the verge of tears.

"I'm sorry, Awatif. Yes, it's hopeless."

The next day Awatif comes up to me, beaming happily. "Not hopeless, Missus," she scolds me. "You say hopeless. Not hopeless. Nothing hopeless."

I feel reproved and I conjecture that she's spoken to someone who's bolstered her confidence, someone Muslim. Or maybe she's prayed about it. Good Muslims would never call anything hopeless; all is in Allah's hands. So Awatif, Muslim that she is, continues studying English, confidence unabated.

As the academic year draws to a close, the students finish the English workbooks. As I leaf through the last lessons I notice Awatif's scrawl to me on the final page of her book: "Don't forget me my dear and my fraind for ever for to ever. Awatif."

She still never bothers to concentrate during class. She seems to feel she'll absorb lots of English by osmosis; she isn't wrong, of course. "You give me the hope, Missus," she says to me. "You give me the hope." I decide to quit giving her advice; it's a breach of good Islam for me to be so arrogant as to feel I can predict the exam results. I warn her to study hard, however. She just laughs. "But Awatif," I say, and I break off, frustrated.

"But Missus," says Awatif, starting to giggle.

"But Awatif," I say, looking into her smiling, child-like face.

"But Missus," says Awatif. "But Missus." We are both giggling now.

"I'll see you tomorrow, Awatif," I say.

"Goodbye, Missus," she says. "Good afternoon."

At first it didn't bother me that western men, especially the sexually-deprived single men, salivated over the veiled Arab virgins. I was blinded by the novelty of the land. But after a while I become more and more angry at the confines, the enslavement, the subjugation of these young women. Seeing them draped in black makes me turn away in horror and disgust and sympathy. I hate seeing them mincing along in their ridiculous high heels. It reminds me of Chinese ladies of a past era, Chinese ladies with tightly bound feet.

I don't really teach anymore. The semester has drawn to a close, the exams are soon to be given. Everyone has cabin fever although the campus is still lovely and there are new plantings of flowers. It's impossible to teach. I just sit in front of the class and giggle and all the girls giggle, too. Sometimes for variety we have hysterics. The girls lose patience toward the very end and begin racing up and down the corridors, slamming doors, turning off lights, crowding into restrooms to re-do makeup. Teachers too feel the freedom of summer beckoning, and we let the students enjoy their energy, the energy of that cusp between childhood and adulthood.

It's time to leave Saudi Arabia for the summer, and maybe

forever.

Tiny Huda invites me to visit her in Bahrain and to stay with her family for as long as I wish.

Awatif asks for my New York address.

Jamila gives me a gold ring with a sapphire.

I fly out of the Kingdom on Air France, and I find that I can breathe deeply.

(Afternote: The author admits that this piece is more in the realm of the actual than the realm of fiction.)

The Past

Escape

I don't want to live in this world, Frances thought. The idea was diamond hard and complete and Frances realized it had been creeping toward her for weeks. The fatigue, the blackness, the dearth of blood running through her body. She couldn't stand it any longer. Her mother had come up again and entered without knocking, she needed birthday candles for Tad's cake, she needed eleven of them. But really she'd come to help with the newborn. Frances knew this. I want to escape, she thought. I want to exist quietly on a vast ship, peering out at horrific choppy waters. It was easy to think these very clear thoughts now that the child was asleep, child, yes, just barely, just a few weeks beyond the fish stage but yes, it was a child, and yet its voraciousness had torn at her nipples and she'd felt as if ground glass were lodged somewhere inside her skin there and she knew she'd been screaming when the doctor had given her the injection of antibiotic and now of course the baby was being bottle fed.

Antonia, her mother, was back again and the nurse was there also. Frances cocked her head slightly to hear if they were whispering but of course she heard nothing because the house, her father's house, was capacious enough to comfortably contain herself and her husband upstairs while her parents lived downstairs with soon-to-be-eleven Tad, her brother, her little brother who'd been so thrilled with a new pair of roller skates; she'd gone along with him to the shop to watch that he got fitted properly with those skates of buttery brown leather, she'd laughed in glee at his pride in ownership. What a piker he was, he'd saved all the money himself. Tad was the real child in her life but now there was this small squalling thing and the books didn't work, all those books of advice on baby care, crammed full of schedules and measurements and endless admonishments. Why had everything changed so radically so suddenly so overwhelmingly?

I can't do all it says to do, she'd screamed at her mother.

Don't bother with those books, Antonia had replied sharply, *I can tell you exactly how to care for a baby.*

But it's 1938 now and things have changed, Frances screamed at her, she'd screamed this days ago, four, five? And now she saw that that had been the end of her attempt, the last gasp of her real effort at being a mother.

Her mother and the nurse, were they whispering? But then Frances laughed to herself for she knew it was merely a dream of hers that the two more capable women would whisper to each other and then bundle up the baby and take it off somewhere. But it was true that her mother Antonia had been darting clouded brows at her, the dark looks had started back in the hospital when Frances couldn't resist turning her head and feigning sleep rather than reaching out and holding her newborn. She'd recalled Edward, her husband, out in the hall and jubilant at the news of a son, and she'd felt herself softly starting to shake. Her mother, why must she persist in wearing that exhausted and wary look?

The books, she'd noticed her mother covertly gather them up and disappear downstairs with them, she'd overheard her mother talking to Edward on the steps. I'm locking them up,

Antonia had said, and Frances smiled a little bit for she knew she was now beyond those once nightmarish books, and then she tried to imagine where her mother might hide them. Up in the attic perhaps, next to the copper brewing tins. Oh, how relaxing it would be to slip up there and lie between those tins where no one could find her. She'd be able to rest and dream.

And then one day Frances thought she'd heard Antonia on the phone describing to some female relative the blackness and odd skin texture of her, Frances' breasts. Was it the birth or was it bad breast feeding, she'd thought she'd heard her mother asking. Yes, her nipples had turned blackish. She refused to show the nurse and of course the doctor kept his dignity and didn't ask. She'd take care of her own breasts, she'd keep them tightly shrouded and inactive, she wouldn't glance down at them when she bathed or dressed. And of course she'd have no more children, this one had surely been a mistake. She was thirty, too used to her own world, her body adult and stable, her hours regular, her job secure and rocklike in its changelessness, secretary to the U.S. Marine Hospital, she'd been there over ten years, the sea, yes, she was connected. It was a calm job, it was an ocean of tranquility.

But now she was the mother of a son, a tiny creature she couldn't tend properly. The creature was quiet now, thank god. It was in the hands of the nurse and her mother, and Frances had been ordered to lounge on the sofa and rest. Yes, I dreamt I'd gone whaling with Ishmael. I stood on the deck of the Pequod and I too was lashed about by the winds. The sea, well, here it was a great lake and the shore lapped instead of roared and yet she clearly pictured herself running to it, she heard the waters murmuring to her in a clear promise of soothingness. And suddenly she wasn't on the sofa, she was standing balanced on the tips of her toes. The door, she'd just run out quickly and fly down the road and toward the lake. She'd rush down there and weigh the possibilities. And so she grabbed a scarf and ran from the house, taking care to click the door latch softly so as not to alert the baby tenders, and she felt her face stretch into a wide smile as the air hit her and she headed toward that unsalty sea. She ran, she ran past all the familiar shopfronts. A glossy unfamiliar magazine caught her eye in the window of the news agent and it flashed through her mind to run in and snap it up, to hurry down the road with that magazine under her arm, a woman on a mission, a different woman, but then she remembered that she hadn't brought her bag, she hadn't a cent with her, she wasn't wearing a hat, the scarf was loosely around her neck and threatening to flicker off somewhere and it was her mother's scarf but what did that matter now? She was like an animal on the loose and so she hurried on; she turned toward the downhill route away from the house.

But how strange for suddenly there was Edward and her entire plan crumpled up; she felt a claw in her throat, she felt snagged. He'd caught sight of her as he stepped out of a greengrocer. What with all the chaos in the house it had fallen to him to bring home fresh vegetables. "Frances," he'd called out in a deep but puzzled voice, and she knew she was walking in probably such a strange but steadfast way and yet not toward anything that he would recognize and so of course he followed her, ran after her and took her by the elbow, she'd seen him out of the corner of her eye and had resolved to ignore him but then his touch on her elbow and his confused face blasted her warm dream.

Why are you out without a sweater he was asking her, and yes, she noticed now that everyone was wearing an overcoat; it was April but still chilly and there were harsh winds off the lake. Her hat, she waited for him to comment on that being missing, too. But no, and her mother's scarf didn't seem to register with him. She noticed his grip on her elbow was more than just a gentle steering but it quickly dawned on her to play along, not to shake him off, not to let on that, yes, something was amiss. Oh I just ran out for a breath of air and then I wanted to buy some fruit. But there was no point in her continuing for she could tell that he wasn't really listening, and she could also see that he was darting tiny covert glances at her. And so she returned to the house with him and at the back of her mind she could hear him repeating but where were you going, where were you off to, and the slight note of hysteria registered somewhere in her consciousness and she resolved to try again, a drop of steel resolve, she'd try again and next try she'd be cleverer, more furtive, furtive, yes, it seemed a delicious plan, furtive, she hadn't had much practice, but now when it was needed so very badly it'd come to her, she'd excel at being sly and she'd get down to the water. Her plan was set now and she turned to him clear-eyed, he was opening the front door for her, *I must see to the baby*, she said to him in as orderly and sing-songy a housewife's voice as she could muster, and she made off for the baby's room, trying to keep down the bile that seemed to lodge up and push at her lungs. And yet she felt a slight trill in her heart, here was a project to throw herself into. Briefly of course, for she wasn't an actress, she wasn't a professional performer. That much she knew. But it wouldn't take long, she'd merely have to play the role for a day at most and then, why then she'd be released.

And after actually having mounted the steps and entered the baby's room, well, the baby was not quite visible, the baby was snuggled in the folds of its bed, and the nurse was there, and all was momentarily fine, and yet her rush into the room had made her mother stand up and cast those fearful eyes on her and so Frances smiled calmly, forced herself, no, she couldn't look at the baby, she couldn't let its tiny crumpled beauty deflect her from her essential plan. It was a lovely secret plan but to carry it through she'd have to paint it over in tones of rose and gold and lusciousness, and so she didn't look at her tiny boy, she couldn't, she was to blame for releasing him into all this, all this, I've got to get it away from here, from the baby, I've got to get rid of it, but the puzzle was that the thing to be gotten rid of was inextricable from herself, that was it, it was just she, Frances. There, she'd solved it. And so she turned away from the tiny creature and looked instead into the face of her mother. And then there was Edward, too, having loped up the steps after her, and now these two were both watching her in the cold and frozen way that she would no longer try to analyze. Greens, her husband still held them clutched to his chest. Frances went up to him and took the vegetables and headed for the kitchen. She'd cook.

But on entering the kitchen and placing the packet on a counter she saw why her mother had come up, candles, tiny candles for the birthday, oh, Tad's a little uncle, she realized for the first time, he's another one who can love the tiny creature, the two of them can be pals, yes, I'm not needed for of course there's also Antonia and Edward and my father—they can hover about, oh yes, the house contains a surplus of people to tend this infant, thought Frances. Tad, he hadn't yet crashed through the front door back from the roller rink. His birthday. That was a tiny crimp in her plan after all. Should she wait until that was done, cake eaten? Three, four more days of holding her plan in abeyance? No. The crimp, she'd ignore it. She had to be strong. She picked up the candles and dropped them into the trash. And then Edward was in the kitchen, just behind her, and she looked for the proper pot to cook the vegetables in, and she vaguely wondered if he'd seen her throw away the candles but then the wonder fell out of her mind for she had other things to ponder. Cook dinner. Have a pleasant enough night. Act as if orderly normality were seeping back into her. Don't look at the tiny creature, no, not once.

Bloop, Bleep:
We Posted It Everywhere

Bloop bleep, I remember with a sinking heart. Why does it depress me so? Children are thoughtlessly cruel, children are unscrupulous, amoral. I was. I am I sometimes imagine a good person now, gratefully immersed in the sobriety of adulthood. Clockwork precision, that sustains me now. My heart, however, remains encrusted with shame and chagrin. Can I ever be forgiven? Can the blackness ever be expunged? No. That was me and still I am that person. *Pace* contemporary pop psychologists, priests, and other dispensers of comfort.

Quite simply it was this: In junior high school Katie Bloom and I were best friends for a long time but then we grew to hate each other and I arranged it so that a lot of other people hated her, too. Katie Bloom, I ruined her. I ruined the girl who laughed at everything, the girl who came to school clad in a new outfit for a record-shattering forty-seven straight days, the girl who began menstruating before many of us fully understood the function of tampons. Katie possessed a cool that none of us could touch. She could set off laughter—my laughter, specifically. I wasn't able to laugh silently then; no, I was eleven or twelve and given to shoulder-shaking explosions of mirth, uncontrollable eruptions at the worst possible moments such as funeral Masses for elderly parishioners, sad extinguished creatures with little family and few friends. We parish school children were ushered in to fill up pews and sing hymns, an angels' chorus. The casket would roll up the aisle and Katie Bloom would cast an upraised eyebrow my way and wrinkle her nose slightly and my feverish giggling would be unleashed. Our homeroom teacher Mrs. Powell once had to come and slap me briskly on the shoulder. But a day or so before it had been announced that I'd again scored highest on the Iowa tests, so the shoulder slap had little reverberation for me. I held my breath and tried not to shake for a moment or two; I tried to convince myself that my continued giggling might be read as sobbing. But when we left the chapel I heard the principal yell Mrs. Powell, Mrs. Powell, you've got to get your seventh-grade girls under control, they're a disgrace. Katie controlled her own laughter admirably; she never heaped dishonor on herself the way I did. The two of us were great friends for quite a while but then we came to odds. I didn't kill her, no. I didn't fantasize scenes of tossing venomous snakes her way, snakes that she could have batted away. Would that I had, rather than what I did do. Would that I had known the strength of my own psyche, the caliber of my willfulness.

Certain scenes I remember vividly. We were in the playground and Katie Bloom was taunting me for being in love with Robert Tomovich: she was making a big production out of it so everyone would hear, and I half-wanted to kill her but at the same time I was thrilled and hoping Robert Tomovich was taking note. The usual gaggle of girls—Angie, Gail Schmitz, Sue, Dana— crowded around us while Katie loudly detailed how I'd searched out the name Tomovich in the phone book and made various anonymous calls. But she herself had been the one who'd egged me on to look up the number. I hated her a lot of the time even though we were truly best friends. We were thick as thieves at school and after three o'clock we'd hide up in my parents' bedroom and make crank calls to strangers. Tell me, we'd say, what do you think of the Twiggy look? When my mother hollered up the stairs at us we'd shout that we were doing market research, a requirement for Current Affairs class. Katie spent a lot of afternoons over at my house because her mother didn't get home from work till almost six, and even when she went home she'd call me and we'd talk on the phone for an hour or more. My mother gave me a little egg timer and shouted at me to use it—three minutes, Jenny, she'd yell, only three minutes! That was the extent of my communication with my mother at the time—fencing about phone use.

Katie's mother didn't allow us to play in her house unsupervised, but I managed to sleep overnight there relatively often. Katie was an only child and her mom had been divorced for years; in sixties suburbia such truncated domesticity was still something of a novelty. Their house was tiny and warm and the kitchen was always stocked with potato chips and Oreos and Coke, items my own mother eschewed. Katie showed me the built-in ironing board that pulled from the kitchen wall. My father made this house before he left, he built it himself, she told me. I couldn't reply, I tried to hide my deep embarrassment for Katie. Parents weren't meant to build houses, not with their own hands. In that one-storey wooden cottage Katie would gaze at copies of *Seventeen* and *Glamour* while I tried on her latest poor-boy sweater or fisherman knit or hip-hugger jeans. My theory was that Katie's mother made up to her for the missing father by giving Katie *carte blanche* at the local department store, a theory only partly torpedoed when Katie airily informed me that her father sent her a monthly clothing allowance. Clothes were not real wealth—I knew that. And I had a vague notion that a house with two floors was an essential, a bare minimum. To my mind then, people who lived in small houses were poor, bordering on pathetic.

I never invited Katie to spend the night with me. I never dreamed of suggesting it to my mother. Of course I knew it was impossible because although Dad officially lived with us, we never really knew when he would be home, and I knew that if he *were* home there was a good chance they'd be fighting. Katie used to bug me about this a little. When can I stay overnight at your house, huuuhhh?? she would ask in a teasing snotty sort of voice, half-suggesting that she knew the reason. Which she didn't. I was too clever to talk about family stuff to any possible big mouths or to anyone at all for that matter. And even though Katie was my best friend, still I didn't consider for a second discussing my family's chief problem—the screaming matches between my parents, the threats, the tears, the midnight noise that drove me into my little brother Matt's room. I'd get into bed with him and snuggle up; I'd pretend to be comforting him, but really I'd be listening—his room was slightly closer to the stairs. Mother always closed his door firmly after putting him to bed, but after sneaking in I'd leave it open. I was trying to piece together the cause of conflict but I kept missing the truly pivotal bits no matter how I strained. Occasionally the shouting would wake up Matt, and he would lie next to me, his open eyes bottomless pools of black. He rested there like marble, staring nowhere. Sometimes I would close my eyes tight and shiver, horrified at my part in exposing him more closely to the chaotic and appalling shouting. He was such a tiny boy still, six, seven. But my need to know overrode those jabs of guilt.

Matt wasn't outgoing like I was, and he had few friends. He hated school and begged my mother to allow him to stay home, which of course she never did. I never told Matt that school could be a good thing. I thought he'd catch on soon enough. To my mind then my happy school life more than made up for my painfully jagged nights, and so early on I'd decided to keep them absolutely separate; at all costs I wouldn't sully the joy of school with the nightmare of my parents.

Katie and I publicly declared ourselves blood sisters and nurtured our classmates' tales of needles and *Exacto* knives and basement transfusions. We spent a lot of time outdoors, too, wandering around the suburb together, our sterile circumscribed locale that had until quite recently been farmland, cow pasture. Silos still existed here and there and red barns stood deserted, awaiting their next incarnation as homes or retail outlets. Katie and I ambled around in the waning afternoon light, trespassing onto building sites—skeletons of future houses, those big four bedroom split level bastardizations of Frank Lloyd Wright that sprang up everywhere then. She stole her mom's cigarettes; we experimented with them while half-hidden behind plywood and two by fours.

The cigarettes inspired us. One cold winter afternoon in one of those future houses Katie said bloop. She'd just gotten over a cigarette-induced coughing fit. She tossed the butt down into the bowels of the house. Bloop, she shouted again, and after a brief pause I answered bleep. Bloop, she said again. Bleep, I returned. We were on the same wavelength. Bloop bleep. We laughed and kept repeating it, mimicking underwater explorers, midnight bathroom drips. It stayed with us. Bloop bleep. We began secretly scribbling it all over the school in our ongoing attempt to drive all authority crazy. At first we never said it out loud, we only whispered it to each other. Then I came up with the brilliant notion of having it printed on those tiny little return address stickers that could be ordered through the mail for less than two dollars. So we did that. They came back perfectly, bloop bleep three thousand times. What is that? my mother asked in her querulous way when the small packet arrived, but I quickly whisked it into my school bag and she lost interest. Katie and I began sticking them up everywhere, even sneaking into the boy's restroom to post them so that teachers wouldn't narrow the hunt down to females. We were only in seventh grade but we were more creatively rambunctious than the eighth graders, and soon the whole school was swaying to the chant of bloop bleep and the teachers were impelled to accelerate their perpetual eye rolling. Bloop bleep. The janitor cursed as he tried to remove the little stickers, and I recall the two of us shrieking and careening down the hallways.

Get a bra—Katie started that. She was so suave and grown up; she taunted girls who still wore undershirts. She'd catch their eye during a really dull history or geography class and mouth GET A BRA at them. They'd crimson quickly and turn away, pretending it hadn't happened. She did it to her friends, too; she did it to me. But I was cool and knew enough to laugh when being teased. Usually, however, I was the fall guy to her straight man. She was Moe and I was Curley. On the surface, anyway. Actually I was smarter than she was. Hadn't the Iowa tests proven that? Or perhaps I was just more diabolical, more sneaky. Anyway, when she broadcast it everywhere that I had a thing for Robert Tomovich, it didn't bother me unduly. I mean, I was smart enough to realize that embarrassment would be a dumb nonploy reaction. I thought to myself maybe this will work out all right, maybe he will get the message that I like him and he'll start paying attention to me. Such are the pubescent person's thought patterns. Patterns? No, miasma. Murk. Total chaos.

Then there was Father Fagan: he too inspired our lunatic shenanigans. When he came into our classroom to give his weekly talk, Katie and I both covertly laughed our heads off. He was a poor speaker; every second sound was *uuuh, uuuuh*. I was the first one to suggest an *uh*-counting contest. It will give us something constructive to do while he's in our class, I informed Katie and Sue and Dana and Dick Hurley, keeping my face serious, my voice solemn. So we started doing it. But Katie would wiggle her eyeballs to make me laugh, to unleash my volcanic and unstoppable giggling and then I'd be in trouble once again. Anyway, the *uuh* counting contest was my idea, but then Katie began trying to take it over, to pretend she'd thought of it. We soon got Gail Schmitz and Angie in on it, too. I'd thought of it, I was slightly miffed that no one remembered that. No one consulted me on the niceties of the game. Katie hogged the whole show.

I too was the one that began the pea shot game—writing a little note and crumpling it into a pea and then throwing it to someone while Fagan's back was turned. The point was to keep staring forward with a straight face. But finally that idiot Dick Hurley caught one and he threw it right at Fagan's head when he was turned toward the blackboard and then there was hell to pay. Fagan stormed out of the room and Mrs. Powell lumbered back in and glared right at me and said were you one of the instigators? I couldn't say yes or no, I was just shaking so hard with my damn convulsive mirth. Katie Bloom spoke right up in a really offended but fakey tone and said no, it wasn't Jenny, it was Dick Hurley. No, it's not Jenny, it's never Jenny, Mrs. Powell yelled at her—sit down Miss Bloom, she said. She glowered for a while and then hollered get out your geography books and start copying from page a-hundred-and-seventy-two, and she meant the entire class, so everyone gave me and Katie and Dick Hurley real death glares, and then Mrs. Powell left the room for a moment and Katie piped up that this was better than listening to Fagan, and then Powell dragged back in with her bad leg that got shot up in World War II when they mistook her for a man and sent her to the front, or so our legend went. She plopped down into her chair and gave us mud gloom doom stares while we all scribbled for the half hour or so before lunch. I was slightly surprised she didn't make me and Katie and Dick and the usual suspects go out in the hall and do duck walks. I guess she'd finally caught on that we kind of liked it; it wasn't really an effective punishment anymore. It was that idiot Tommy Dorlock's fault, he was the one that told Powell it had strengthened our legs and improved our soccer game. But against me, personally, Mrs. Powell had a mega-grudge. She hated me because I shook and laughed and spluttered and giggled at Mass every single morning, even at the communion rail. I still don't understand why they didn't just excommunicate me and be done with it. But it wasn't really my fault, it was Katie Bloom. Katie Bloom made me do it with her whispered jokes and her wiggling eyeball act and the yellow tissue she stuffed into her bra cups so that the boys would stare at her. I just couldn't stand it, especially up there at the communion rail. So Mrs. Powell really hated my guts and I could very clearly understand why. If I had been the teacher I would've hated my guts, too. On the other hand, Mrs. Powell had to remember that I'd won the diocese science fair. I'd collected a lot of chicken hearts and sliced them in a variety of ways, and I'd come home with a blue ribbon. Mrs. Powell had gotten a lot of the glory since she was the science teacher. So I had some leverage there.

All in all Katie and I were the worst girls in the entire school. I'm proud of this, I'm proud even today that for a while in seventh grade Mrs. Powell made me sit in isolation at one side of the room. I'm proud that we talked practically the entire class into saving banana peels, letting them dry, and trying to smoke them. On the edge of our awareness was knowledge of glittery things like high school kids who dropped acid and died in motorcycle crashes. Everything stretched out endlessly in front of us, and we felt ourselves as such divine, complete little creatures.

But then one day the first heart-stopping thing happened. The first blot upon my schooltime happiness, my feeling so sublimely in control and rotten and at the same time always winning all the prizes for smartness. (My happiness then has never been matched!) Katie Bloom did something truly wrong; she did something to me that sparked my darker skills. It was this: I'd been off cleaning erasers, and on my return to recess I overheard Katie talking about Matt; she was telling Gail and Sue and Dana something about him. Something's wrong at their house, she told them, and that's why he's so quiet and shy. She was talking in a soft, fake-sad sounding voice. It's their parents, they fight all the time, Matt should be in a special school, she was telling them, a school for children who are always sad.

I couldn't believe Katie was saying this. I just stood there dead, an ice pick in my heart. But then they looked up and saw I was there, and so I yelled nothing's wrong with him, he's fine, it's just that Miss Kunitz is a new teacher and a lousy one, he's not sad, that's just his personality. But my heart hurt and I guessed that Katie was jealous maybe, maybe because I'd done best on the Iowa's and she'd only tied for third. Or she was screwed up from living in a small house. Matt—he was fine. It was just that he was nervous because he still wet his bed and Mother and Dad couldn't figure out what to do and Mother screamed at Dad that maybe if he were home more often Matt would be happier and not have to wet his bed to get attention. I didn't say this to anyone at school, needless to say. What Katie was telling people made me blackly angry, angry, insane, like Hitler felt at the Jews. That's exactly what I mean: I was taken over by dark forces. I was shocked to my toes. How could my friend betray me like this? I tried to control my face and show nothing and then I tried to wear a sad look. It worked—Gail and Sue and Dana walked over to me and made a circle and kind of shoved Katie aside, and she ran off somewhere. She's just jealous about the Iowa tests, I said quietly and everyone nodded. I didn't have to say a word more, but I kept a certain look on my face, a frozen dead look. Gail and Sue understood immediately and so after school they made a point of all of us except Katie Bloom going off for french fries and Coke. Dana hadn't caught on and said shouldn't we get Katie? Sue gave her a disgusted look and said come on, Dana, shut up, we're punishing her.

That episode ended and my heart scarred over. After a while Katie was our friend again and I thought we'd taught her a lesson, but I still had that laugh-wiggle problem and Mrs. Powell was on my case and really pissed me off once because she called up my mother to complain about me. And my mother just looked gray, she wouldn't mention it to me, she wouldn't even look at me. She was always very nervous and upset about my dad and didn't have time to worry about me at school. I was annoyed with Mrs. Powell's crudeness, how could she not understand that my mother didn't want to talk to her? After all, my mother assiduously avoided PTA meetings of any type whatsoever, so how could Mrs. Powell so tactlessly try to force my mother into communication? Why couldn't people play by the rules?

One day it was time for lunch and Mrs. Powell disappeared and we couldn't go out for recess because it was raining buckets. Everyone as usual put their apples on Mrs. Powell's desk; everyday after lunch there was an average of nine apples lined up on her desk. She boxed them up and sent them to the Zulus in Africa, we knew that for a fact. Most of the kids went to the gym but Katie and I had to stay and wash the boards, that was our eternal punishment. Sue and Gail stayed there with us. Sue tried to juggle three of the apples on Mrs. Powell's desk. She dropped them all. Dana tried too, and began dropping them on purpose and letting them roll all over the classroom. Katie started showing off her long fingernails; she started poking holes in one of the apples. She poked about twelve holes in one apple and then held it up for us to admire. Look, she said, polka dots. We laughed like lunatics. Katie quickly picked up another apple and mutilated that one, too, and then we all joined in. Polka dots!

The bell rang and all the kids came back into the room, and

Katie reverently lined up the holey apples on Mrs. Powell's desk and sat down and assumed her buddha look of fake innocence. Mrs. Powell came in and we watched and waited. After we'd got started on pre-algebra problems Mrs. Powell suddenly jumped up; her chair fell behind her with a clatter. Between two fingers she held out one of the messed-up apples and screamed you are the limit, the absolute limit.

She slammed her book shut, picked up her chair and sat down. She'd really yelled loud and the fallen chair had made us nervous so we all worked quietly and carefully, not daring to look at each other, just glancing up now and then to see if Mrs. Powell had decided to focus in on one culprit or to let everyone share a generalized blame. I must say, life in that classroom was exciting.

And so for a while again I was happy with Katie; the strain between us had almost completely disappeared. We continued to ponder possibilities of horrible fun. But then inexplicably she again encroached into my most guarded territory. Gail and Sue ran up to me one day and said that Katie had been telling them and a whole big bunch of other people that Matt's problem was just that he was really really sad because our father was never at home and so Matt was always worried that our parents would get divorced. Really, Jenny, I can't believe she's saying things like that but we thought you should know, Gail told me. I felt like all my insides had been crushed, I couldn't believe it, I couldn't believe that Katie knew these things, I couldn't imagine where she got her information. And how could she imagine that Matt knew anything, anything at all about divorce. He was a baby in second grade. What a devil Katie was, what an evil being straight from hell. I felt like a truck had dumped rocks on me. We won't talk to her, Sue said to me, and Gail nodded. They'd summed up my motionless face, my eyes staring off nowhere. Dana had come up by then and was listening too. I won't invite her to my skating party, she said, I know my mother doesn't like her mother anyway. I just nodded and let them talk. Sue started giggling. She's such a jerk anyway with her big padded bras that she doesn't even need, she said. Why does she stuff yellow Kleenex in, asked Gail, why doesn't she use white? The boys hate her, Dana said, I'm sure the boys know they could get a disease from her. I kept a determinedly neutral look on my face and just listened, but I clearly remember making an effort to emit waves of yes, continue, heap a lot of poison on her. Then I suggested we go inside and do some practice cheers in hopes of making the glee squad. In my mind I tried furiously to sort out how Katie knew anything, anything at all about my family. How could she know? How dare she tread on my privacy like this, picking at wounds whose existence I barely even recognized? For some reason she'd been impelled to move into terrain that I couldn't approach. But from afar I could mine her entry into it, I could leave booby traps. I resolved to do so quietly, I resolved not to talk about her, not to mention her name. I left it to my friends to whisper about her jealousy, her communicable diseases. I trusted their malicious inventiveness.

Eventually we did things like going to Katie's house with a spray can of half-used deodorant and bars of soap. We'd leave them in the mailbox with short written messages such as: wash once in a while, brush your teeth at least twice a year, come on Katie! I stayed firmly on the periphery of these antics; abdication of any overt leadership seemed the wisest course. I noticed that Katie began having to sit alone at lunch. At recess she was reduced to jumping rope with sixth graders! That would make most kids commit suicide, but she just kept a plain straight face as if there were no problem. She stayed away from us. I didn't even have to do much to ensure she no longer received party invitations. A strange sort of spider web was working for me. I felt weirdly satisfied. The ultimate triumph was when we took the trip to Colonial Village and no one sat next to her on the bus ride out, and then Mrs. Powell sat next to her on the ride back! Gail and Sue and Dana laughed in glee. I let a slight smile play on my lips. I couldn't believe how powerful I felt, and yet I'd done nothing, nothing at all.

Katie Bloom never had any really good friends again at that school; she had no good friends through the entire eighth grade. Sometimes I had flashes of sadness about my part in this, but then my head would fill with black anger, black blinding bile because she hadn't minded her own business, she'd trampled on and exposed my family affairs, personal stuff, stuff she couldn't have known about or understood in a million, billion years. I'd protected myself, I'd done my bit to keep myself intact. I'd made her suffer, but that was excusable. She had asked for it. She had committed an unthinkable crime.

Years later I saw her waitressing in a pizza joint. We were attending different high schools and I'd almost forgotten about her. My table wasn't in her section. I half-hid behind my mug of soda, hoping she wouldn't glance over and recognize the profile of my face. Memories of our early goofy fun flit through my mind, and I even toyed with the idea of going up and greeting her: bloop bleep, I could say. But I didn't because I knew I had nurtured the construction of an ice mountain, a glacial obstruction clouded in mist. Now to her I could only be an object of horror, a destroyer.

I have tried to put Katie Bloom permanently out of my mind, but in a tiny locked corner of my heart a vivid remembrance of giggling at the communion rail remains, a remembrance of screamingly pure joy, glee, energy. But this is only half of it. The other half is the power I wielded so thoughtlessly, the ax I held so easily and let drop so heedlessly. Reckless disregard of life. Why did I do that? Is that who I am? In my own life, how do I eradicate these circles of black?

The author thanks the following people for encouraging her writing and/or teaching her about art and thought:
Robert R.Ammerman, Leonard Casper, Cynthia Cross, Jesse Dickson, Stanley Elkin, John Japely Faloon, Kelly Faloon, Mary Faloon, Donald Gertmenian, Susan Hand, Standish Henning, Frank Huss, Chuck Japely, Phil Japely, Sandy Japely, Alan Japely, Theela Huss Japely, Melanie Kershaw, Peter J. Kreeft, Susan Mayer, Charles McGrath, Mary Merlin, Manuel Puig, Ted Solotaroff, Scott Sommer, Diana Uhlman, Andrew VonHendy, and Cynthia Webb.

About the Author

Christine Japely has lived and worked in the U.S., Spain and Saudi Arabia, and currently teaches English at a community college in Connecticut. Her degrees are from Boston College and Columbia University, and she is the editor of *Curious Rooms*, a literary journal.